There's No Place Like Home

To Anastasia,
You're home!

Jasinda
Wilder

xo

JASINDA WILDER

There's No Place Like Home

Charleston, South Carolina; October 26, 2016

"**A**re you sure you're really ready for this?" Delta, my older sister, asks me, for the thousandth time.

I sigh. "Yes, Delta, I'm ready."

We are standing on a dock in a Charleston, South Carolina harbor. In the berth in front of us is *The Glory of Gloucester*, a deep-sea fishing trawler owned by a man named Dominic Bathory. In just a few minutes I'm going to get on board and depart for a transatlantic voyage, in search of my missing husband, Christian St. Pierre.

Three people have come to see me off: Delta, Jonny who is Delta's new love interest, and Alex, Delta's son, my adorable seven-year-old nephew. Delta holds my arms and searches my eyes—she's worried about me, for good reason.

Over eighteen months ago, Christian's and my baby son, Henry, died of an inoperable brain tumor; Henry never saw his second birthday. The loss of our son and the mountain of grief that followed…broke us. It shattered me, and it crushed Christian. Our perfect innocent little boy, all smiles and joy and warmth, was gone. How do you keep going? Chris and I couldn't. We didn't.

Chris ended up leaving me. He bought a sailboat and sailed away. In hindsight, I understand. Grief as sharp and unbearable as ours causes madness, and the sea was Christian's sanctuary. When his world collapsed, he went back to the one thing he knew: the Sea.

But the story doesn't end there. He and Jonny were caught in a rare, freakishly powerful, out-of-season hurricane which sank Christian's ship off the coast of Africa. Christian was lost at sea, and Jonny, his best friend and sailing partner, barely survived himself. Christian is still gone, still lost.

Jonny says it's *possible* he's still alive, but the odds are against it.

Odds be damned—I *feel* Christian out there. He's alive, and I have to find him. I have nothing to go on but the feeling, deep inside my soul, that my husband is alive.

I also have to find myself; I don't know who I am anymore. My husband is missing, my son is dead, and my home was destroyed by that same hurricane when it hit landfall in Florida. If Jonny hadn't come to deliver letters to me from Christian, and found me in the rubble, I would have died.

The only things I have left are my memories of Christian and Henry…and my determination to find my husband.

"You hate the ocean," Delta reminds me.

"Oh, I know."

"And you hate boats."

"I know that, too."

"You've never spent more than a few hours on one at a time," Delta says. "You'll be on this trawler for months, with no way off and nowhere else to go."

"Sweetie, I *know*," I say.

"You're the only woman on board."

"I have to find him." I brush her hair away from her face, smiling at her. "I know the odds of finding him are less than zero, but I *have* to try. I have to know. I have to do this for myself and for Henry. I just…I *have* to."

Delta looks at Jonny for support. "Honey, help me out here."

Jonny, tall and dark and quiet, just shrugs. "I can't talk her out of it, Delta. You can't either. It's her decision."

Delta groans. "I just…I'm worried, and I'm scared for you, Ava. I understand why you have to go look for him. It's just…you've been through so much already."

I hug her. "I'll be fine."

I try to project a confidence and a calm that I don't totally feel. "I'm looking at this as kind of a...a spirit journey, you know? A chance to think and reflect and maybe write a little bit."

"Just promise me you'll be safe."

"Dominic is a great captain," Jonny puts in. "You'll be as safe with him as you can possibly be. He's careful and competent. I trust him—I'd sail with him anytime. And, remember, he's the guy who saved me."

As Jonny has spent literally his entire life at sea, this is high praise indeed.

Delta lets out a long sigh, and then wraps me up in a tight hug, sniffling. "I'll miss you. I've enjoyed getting to spend this time together, even if the circumstances behind it were less than optimal."

For the past several months I've been living with Delta and Jonny and Alex on Delta's tour bus—she's a country music singer currently touring the US. Being able to spend so much time with my sister has been a gift.

I hug Jonny and Alex and tell them both, "Take care of her."

He nods and looks at Alex. "Don't worry, we will."

A pause, and then Jonny pulls something out of his pocket. "Here, one last thing. I found this when I was digging you out. I never gave it to you because Delta thought we should wait a little longer, for your mental and emotional stability. But...we feel like you should have it, now."

Into my hands he presses a tiny square taggy blanket, handmade by Delta when I was pregnant. Embroidered across one corner is a name: HENRY.

My eyes fill with tears. Henry loved this blanket. It was his "bah." He would shake it in both hands, grinning, shouting "Bah! Bah! Bah!" and then he would smother his face in the soft, bumpy material, hiding his eyes from me, playing hide and seek with his Bah.

My heart seizes as I bury my face in the little blanket.

"I'm sorry we didn't give it to you sooner," Delta says. "I was just worried—"

I cut her off. "No, you were right to wait. I'm not sure I could have handled seeing this along with everything else."

I'm still raw, but I don't say that, and I am a good bit more emotionally stable now than I have been. Thinking about Henry is still incredibly hard. But this blanket…it reminds me that there's joy to be remembered, too.

"Ava!" Dominic shouts from the cabin, leaning out the side door. "Time to go. We have to cast off."

I hug Delta, and then Jonny, and then Alex. "I love you. Thank you—for the blanket, and for everything. For saving my life, letting me spend time with you, just…everything. I'll be in touch, okay?"

"You *better* be in touch," Delta says, and then leans in to whisper, tearfully. "You'll find him. He's alive, he's out there, and you'll find him. I know it."

I nod. "I will. I will."

"Bye," Delta says, and then stands watching as I board *The Glory*, carrying my few pieces of luggage.

I wave to them as I stand at the rail. We cast off and I feel tears in my eyes as I think about what is to come.

I'm coming, Christian.

I know you're out there, and I'm coming. I'll find you, I swear.

On board The Glory of Gloucester; The Atlantic Ocean; November 2, 2016

Memory is a harsh mistress: she embellishes the beautiful and serene, yet she also sharpens the edges of pain.

All I have left of my husband, Christian, are memories. Everything else we shared is gone.

Our son, Henry, conceived and cherished and born and grown in the fertile soil of our love…is dead. He molders six feet under the black loam of a Florida cemetery. The home we created for ourselves in Ft. Lauderdale is a pile of rubble, demolished by a hurricane. That home, and everything in it, was completely destroyed. Even the rubble, by now, is likely cleared away. Family photographs, my laptop, my books. The thick brown leather guest book, embossed with our initials, containing the signatures of guests at our weddings, as well as the little photo booth photos of our friends in silly poses, wearing wild hats and oversized flowers and sunglasses, flashing peace signs and faux gang signs, couples hugging and kissing, Christian and me in our wedding finery, laughing as I playfully try to bite his neck.

My rings—even my wedding rings are gone—I'd taken them off to shower, or cook, or something, I don't remember; I took them off, and then the hurricane hit, and I lost them. I can still see them—they sat together in a small clay dish I made in high school, my wedding band resting on top of my engagement ring. I think Christian's ring was with them. Or was it? See, there's that bitch, Memory, messing with my head again: I can see his ring with mine, and then I doubt that memory, instead picturing a fleeting mental vision of him wearing it as he walked out the door the last time. Either way, the loss of them bites deep. I miss my rings. I want them back. I want the reminder of us, of him. Am I mad at him? Do I miss him? Both? Both, probably, but those rings…they symbolized everything we had, everything we were. Us, our family, our marriage, our future, our past. And now they're gone, and I want them back.

Just like Christian.

As I write this I've been on *The Glory of Gloucester* with Dominic and his crew for over a week now. It's been a week of hell, a week of seasickness, nausea, vomiting, and cursing the Sea, the waves, the wind, the rain, the sky, the sun, and everything to do with life on the open sea. Dominic's crew is all men—Bully, the mechanic and all-around handyman, Mack, an older man of about fifty or sixty, his teenaged great-nephew, Tom, and Shawn, a massive, sullen, hardworking black man whom I've not heard speak a single word. Then there's me. I'm not really part of the crew, but I am living on board the ship. I have to make myself useful; there's no room on board a deep-sea trawler for useless passengers. The crew has been using a rotation system for cooking meals—each person cooks meals for everyone for a week at a time. I'm no great shakes in the kitchen, but I can put together decent, edible, healthy meals, so I volunteered to act as the chef while I'm aboard the *Glory*. This means that I get to stay below deck as much as possible, which works for me as I absolutely hate being topside. I hate seeing the endless expanse of the sea, the reminder of how far away I am from everything, from anything.

I'm cooking three meals a day for six people—between prepping, cooking, serving the meal, and then cleaning up afterward, I'm working from sunup to sundown, for the most part, with my only downtime being after the last meal has been served.

In a way, I'm grateful to be so busy, to have so little time free. Because free time means time to think

And time to think means remembering.

It's a bittersweet thing, remembering. I try not to, I try to stay busy, so busy I collapse into bed at night and fall right asleep, but even then, I'm not safe from Memory.

There's just no escaping my memories. Because, as I said, they're all I have left, in many ways.

Currently, it's dawn. The boat is never quiet, never still—the engines always rumble in the background, water slaps against the hull, and there are voices at all hours in the hallway outside my tiny berth—literally just a cot attached to the wall in a room barely big enough to stand up in. Dawn is the rousing hour. Shifts change, the nets are readied, and the scent of brewing coffee fills the ship. I'm not an early riser, never have been, but living on the *Glory* has forced me to become one. When the ship wakes up, so must I.

I'm woken by my alarm, put on yoga pants and a hoodie, and set about making a fresh pot of coffee and preparing breakfast for the crew—those going off the midnight shift and those going on all pause at sunrise to eat together and discuss the voyage and fishing conditions and weather. Once everyone has eaten and I've cleaned up, I gather shower supplies—a towel, my small bag of toiletries, and a change of clothing—and trudge to the shower, which is, thankfully, empty. Another fun part of living on a ship with a bunch of men: the shower room is always closed, and there's a pretty good chance I'm going to walk in someone in the shower, which doesn't faze them, but it does me.

I lock the door—something almost no one else

does—then turn on the taps until the water sprays hot, strip, and step in.

I lose myself in the steam and the heat, and feel Memory taking hold.

Two weeks before Thanksgiving, three years earlier

"Mom and Dad have invited us to their house for Thanksgiving, Chris," I say, and then take a sip of wine. "I think we should go."

Christian sighs, pressing his fingertips to the base of his wineglass and swirling the rich red liquid. "We went last year, and look how that turned out."

I cut a bite of the chicken cordon bleu I made for dinner. "I know. But they're my parents."

"I get that, but I'm just not a fan of getting pulled into family arguments, you know?"

I wince. "It doesn't have to be like that again."

"But it will be." He takes a bite, washes it down, and then gestures at me with his fork. "There's a reason you don't visit them very often, Ava."

I set down my fork and knife, dab at my mouth with the napkin. "I know, I know, I just—"

"You hope, every single year, that it'll be different, somehow?" Christian suggests.

I nod. "Yeah, basically."

He smiles at me, somewhat sadly. "Unfortunately, babe, I just don't think things will ever change."

I take hold of my wineglass, but don't drink from it. "So, what? We just stay here, this year? Do the holidays just the two of us?'

He nods. "Yeah, exactly. We get a turkey and all the fixings, and we cook it together, and we watch football and cheesy movies and we don't leave the house."

"So, a pants-optional Thanksgiving is what you're suggesting?" I ask, with a smirk.

He winks at me. "I was thinking more along the lines of a naked Thanksgiving."

I feel my cheeks heat and my thighs clench together. "Cooking naked sounds risky."

"I might allow an apron. Just while you're cooking, though."

"While *I'm* cooking? What are you going to be doing while I cook our Thanksgiving dinner?"

"Smoking a pipe, reading the newspaper, wearing a wool cardigan, and calling you my little woman."

I frown at him, but it's hard to hold it in place, as a giggle threatens to escape. "I see. So I'll be barefoot, wearing nothing but an apron, cooking us dinner. And after we've eaten, I'll bring you your slippers, I suppose?"

"Followed by knitting in front of a fire. And then we'll retire to separate beds in the same room."

I can't help laughing. "You're such an idiot."

He quirks an eyebrow at me. "I really do plan on

keeping you naked as long as possible."

We finish our meal in silence, but it's a tense, sexual silence, now. His eyes fix on mine, hot and intense and suggestive, and he doesn't miss the way I rub my thighs together, doesn't miss the way my nipples poke through the fabric of my bra and shirt.

When we finish, I move to begin clearing the dishes from the table; Christian reaches out and touches my wrist, stopping me.

"Let me," he says.

He clears our plates and silverware, loads them into the dishwasher—without rinsing them, which irks me, but I let it go—and pours the last of the bottle of red into our glasses. He moves to stand beside me at the table and stares down at me. Neither of us needs to speak.

He sets his glass down, kneeling in front of me, twisting me so I'm sitting sideways on the chair. I'm wearing a red skirt, knee-length, and a white shirt. This is one of his favorite skirts of mine; I wore it specifically because I know how much he loves it, and I knew he'd appreciate me wearing it. He'd returned just this afternoon from a three-day trip to New York to meet with his agent and editor, which is always exhilarating but stressful for him. Thus, the meal, and the skirt, and the wine.

He kneels, cupping my ankles and slides his palms up my calves. "I love this skirt on you," he says.

"I know. That's why I wore it," I murmur, biting my lower lip as his touch slides upward.

"I hate New York."

"I thought you loved it."

"I love it, and I hate it." He reaches my thighs, his fingers traipsing and traveling over my quads to my hip-bones, underneath my skirt.

"How'd your meeting with Mark and Lucy go?" I ask.

He hooks his fingers into the lace of my underwear, a pair of black, lacy little things that cover pretty much nothing, and are meant for immediate removal. "Eh. It was fine. We discussed my ideas for the next book, nailed down what they would like to see in it, and a delivery time frame. We went over basic contract details. The usual. The bigwigs and muckety-mucks from the publisher took me to a fancy dinner, where I got overpriced steak and overpriced wine, and pretended I knew or cared which fork to use first."

"Sounds…boring, actually."

"It was. I wished, the whole time I was there, that either I was here at home, or you were with me." He tugs my underwear down, and I lift up so he can slide them past my buttocks. "New York just isn't as fun without you."

"I'm behind schedule on my book, or I would've gone with you."

"I know." He slides the underwear to my knees, and then pulls them off, tossing them onto the dining room table. "Did you get your chapter finished today?"

"I did." I let him nudge my thighs further apart. "Four thousand words on my book, and another thousand on the blog. It was a good day."

"Good girl." He leans in, kissing the inside of my thigh. "You should get a reward for being so productive today."

"Oh?" I breathe. "What kind of reward?"

He pushes my skirt up and I lean backward, holding on to the table with one hand and the chair back with the other, as his mouth travels up my thigh. "The kind where you scream my name."

"I approve of this reward."

"I thought you might." His lips find my core, wet and waiting, and I gasp as he feathers his tongue over me. "I have a proposal."

I throw my head back and whimper as he lavishes his attention on my sensitive flesh. "Oh? What…what's that?" I ask, and then laugh. "Quid pro quo? You go down on me, I go down on you?"

He mumbles a laugh. "That's a great idea, but that's not what I was thinking."

"Then do tell."

He slides a finger inside me, and I feel myself beginning to come apart. "We stay here for Thanksgiving, and spend Christmas Eve with your folks. Then we come back here that same night so we can have Christmas Day together in our own home."

"God, oh god. Are we really—ohhh, oh god—are we

really having this discussion while you're going down on me?"

He doesn't answer right away; he's too busy bringing me to the cusp of climax. "Yes we are."

I grip his hair and scream as he sends me over the edge.

When I come back down, still shuddering, Christian is kneeling in front of me, watching, a pleased grin on his face. "So. How does my proposition sound?"

I laugh shakily. "You're so strange."

He smirks. "I like to challenge your focus while you orgasm."

"I see." I slide off the chair, my legs trembling, and then pull him to his feet and lead him to his favorite spot, the corner of the couch, where he sits. "Well, then, quid pro quo. You challenge me, I'll challenge you."

He knows exactly what's happening, now, and when I undo his jeans, he's already hard. "I think you'll find my focus razor sharp."

I grip his length and caress him, taking my time, until his chest is heaving and he's grinding into my hand. "So. Christmas Eve at my parents, hmmm?"

"Yes. We head down either early that day or probably the day before. Spend a day or so with them, and come back late Christmas Eve."

"Why Christmas, though? Why not Thanksgiving? What's the difference?"

He groans as I wrap my lips around him, swirling my

tongue, tasting him. "Shit, shit—Ava, god! Thanksgiving is just a lot of sitting around, eating, and watching TV. Christmas, at least, there are presents to exchange. Things to occupy us besides making conversation. If you and your parents are left to yourselves, you'll start arguing about something, usually the past, and that never goes well for anyone."

I have him at the edge now. "What's the real reason, Chris?"

He's groaning, grunting, short of breath, thrusting into my hand. "Thanksgiving with your parents reminds me of Thanksgivings growing up. My parents would argue, Dad's parents would be in town, and Mom's parents as well—oh shit, ohhhh god—plus Mom's sister and her bratty kids who I was expected to play with. No one got along with anyone else. It was horrible, and I just...I hated it. Sitting around in a hot, stuffy sweater, stuck at the kid's table with Aunt Marjorie's shitty kids, eating Mom's shitty turkey, and her shitty stuffing, and her shitty mashed potatoes, listening to the adults bicker. I hate Thanksgiving. Always have. I don't want to spend it with your parents, doing the...the stupid usual traditions."

His focus is beginning to slip as I use my hands to tease him close to the edge, and then back him away from it.

"Jesus, Ava," he growls, hips bucking. "You're making me crazy, babe."

"Good. I like it when you're crazy." I have him there,

right on the verge of letting go, nearly unable to hold back any longer. "So, we stay at home and start our own tradition."

"Exactly."

"Which, according to you—" I pause, here, to tease him with my mouth again, until he's groaning and cursing, "—which according to you entails naked cooking and sex?"

"Can you—ohhhhh shit, I'm so close, Ava—can you think of a better way of spending Thanksgiving?"

I laugh. "No, not really, now that you put it that way."

"Ava, *please.*" His voice is ragged.

With hands and mouth, then, slowly, deliberately taking my time, I bring him over the edge, bring him to a gasping, cursing, shuddering finish, taking every drop he has to give me and swallowing it like the finest wine.

I refasten his pants and perch on his knee as he gasps, recovering. I take a sip of my wine. "I'm noticing a pattern, with us and holidays."

He gazes at me blearily, his eyes dull and spacey. "Unh. Pattern? What pattern?"

"Birthdays, we usually have dinner out somewhere, but we never make it as far as a movie. We always end up back here, fucking. We give each other presents naked, in bed. Valentine's Day we also spend largely naked and horizontal, and wasted. Fourth of July we spend on the beach, and usually end up naked under a blanket on the beach, fucking as the fireworks go off." I dab at the corners of my mouth with my thumb. "And now Thanksgiving, instead of going to my parents' house like usual, we're going to stay home, stay naked, and probably spend most of the day eating, getting drunk, and fucking."

Christian is slouched in the chair, his head resting against the back, his eyes recovering their sharpness and heat. "Again I ask you, can you think of a better way to spend a holiday other than getting naked and making each other feel good?"

I curl up on his lap, resting my head on his chest, and his arms go around me, cling to me, tugging me tight against him, and I hear his heart beating under my ear.

"No," I whisper. "I really can't."

A knock on the door jars me out of my thoughts.

"Ava, you gotta give up the shower." Dominic, his deep voice gruff.

"All right, sorry. Be right out!" I shout back.

I shut off the water and make quick work of dressing. Normally, I'd spend twenty or thirty minutes on my hair and makeup, even if I'm not leaving the house—a long-ingrained habit learned from Mom; one week spent living on a ship has taught me the value of time, specifically that spent in the bathroom on one's appearance. There's only one man on this earth whose opinion about my appearance matters, and that is Christian, my husband. Who, for all I know, may very well be dead. So, I've quit bothering with hair and makeup. I towel-dry my hair, brush it out with quick, economical jerks of the brush, and then tie it back, and that's it. No makeup, not even lip-gloss or concealer or anything, despite the flaws in my complexion from the poor water quality and lack of time and effort spent on proper self-care.

It just doesn't matter.

The men on this ship are barely acquaintances, seen only briefly during the day and during meals. Dominic is the only one I would consider a friend.

I exit the bathroom—which Dominic refers to as the "head," a term I can't seem to remember to use myself.

Shawn and Tom are both sitting in the galley, side by side at the table, cupping mugs of coffee. Shawn is just staring into space, thinking who knows what, and Tom is idly flipping through an old, well-worn men's magazine. I pour a cup of coffee and sit at the table opposite Shawn and Tom.

Shawn is broad-shouldered, head shaved completely, with a short, grizzled beard, his dark skin weathered to leather and brown eyes that give away nothing of his thoughts; he could be thirty, or he could be fifty, it's nearly impossible to guess. Tom is sixteen, and an orphan. Blond haired and blue-eyed, sweet, energetic, and a little prone to staring at me when he thinks I'm not looking, which is understandable considering I'm the only woman he's spent any real time around...like ever. Tom's parents died when he was young, and the only kin he had who could, or would, take him in was his great-uncle, Mack, who is a lifelong sea dog, which means he brought Tom with him aboard *The Glory*.

I'm sitting, sipping, and thinking.

Tom clears his throat, sets the magazine aside, and I feel his eyes on me. "So, Ava."

I glance at him. "So, Tom."

"Captain Dom was pretty vague about why you're on board. You're not crew, and we don't take passengers, and Dom was always pretty clear about not being willing to waste space or money on a dedicated cook. Not to mention, he'd never hire a woman. He runs a male crew, he says, since it keeps things simple."

I consider the best way to answer. Eventually, the truth is the only thing that makes any sense. "My husband went missing at sea, and I'm trying to find him. I need transportation across the Atlantic, and I also need Dominic's connections and knowledge of the sea and the various ports."

"And, in return for having you aboard, we get food we haven't had to cook, plus, you know...it's nice having a lady around."

I snort a laugh. "Everyone benefits."

Tom leaves the table, fetches the carafe of coffee, brings it back to the table, and refills our mugs; Shawn accepts the refill with a silent nod. With a fresh cup of coffee, Tom eyes me speculatively.

"How did your husband go missing?"

I shift uncomfortably. This is deeply personal territory for me, and it's hard to talk about to anyone, let alone a sixteen-year-old kid. "I…it's complicated."

Tom opens his mouth to say something else, but Shawn taps him on the shoulder with a thick, blunt forefinger, and then shakes his head at Tom.

Tom's mouth snaps shut, and he lets out a breath. "Sorry. I ask too many questions."

"It's a difficult situation," I say, "and it's hard for me to talk about it."

Tom only nods; he tosses back the last of his coffee and leaves, depositing his mug in the sink on the way. Shawn remains, and his unwavering, unreadable brown gaze meets mine. He nods, once, slowly.

I smile at him, a wobbly grin. "Thanks."

Another nod.

I'm tempted to ask him why he never speaks, but I don't. It's his business, not mine. I know I don't care to be pushed into subjects I don't want to talk about, and I'm not going to do that to Shawn, despite being intensely curious about him.

After a few minutes, Shawn finishes his coffee and I'm left alone in the galley. I finish my own coffee and get to work prepping lunch and dinner. This occupies me for most of my day, leaving only the occasional handful of spare minutes throughout the day.

Once dinner is finished and the galley is clean, I retreat to my room. I brought very little with me when I stepped aboard this boat a week ago: a single duffel bag stuffed full of clothes; a wallet with an ID, my passport, a credit card, a debit card, and cash; a new cell phone, which I was told would work globally. I also brought several leather-bound journals, and a box of gel-tip, fine-point pens, so I would have some kind of outlet for my thoughts and feelings…

And Henry's blanket.

For the first time since coming aboard, I sit down on my bunk with a journal and a pen, and try to put my thoughts into some kind of order:

From Ava's handwritten journal; November 2, 2016

I have no idea where to even begin. It's not that I have writer's block; it's the opposite, whatever that might be called. There's too much in my head, too much in my heart to even know how to start putting it on paper.

First things first: I hate the ocean. I hate living on a boat. It's never quiet—there's always, ALWAYS someone awake, someone talking, someone clomping down the halls in thick boots, the engine is always on, grumbling away in the background of every waking and sleeping moment. It sounds as if there is a giant trapped in the hull, grumbling, humming, and snoring.

Why am I here? Why did I come aboard this god-aw-
ful, godforsaken boat? Why?

Christian. That's the short answer, the easy answer.
I'm out here to find Christian.

But just yesterday morning Captain Dominic
showed me our position on the GPS, up in the wheel-
house. The coast of the US was a mammoth squiggly
line on the left, extending from the top of the screen to
the bottom, and our position was marked a few scant
inches away from the coast. A week of constant travel,
and we're only barely off the coast of the United States!
I stood on the deck late yesterday evening, just as the
sun was setting. I watched as the last of the orange-red
ball descended below the horizon. It hit me, then, as it
hits me now, writing this—the world is huge. It's SO big.
It's easy to think the world is small, in this age of instant
messaging and emails and the Internet. You can get a
DM on Twitter from someone across the globe, speak to
them in real time, FaceTime them, Skype them. Instant
communication. You can hop on a plane, and in a few
hours be across the country, a few hours more and be
across the ocean, on a different continent.

I've done that, sat with my face to the airplane window, watching the landscape, writ miniature, pass underneath. It doesn't feel real, does it? You're in a cap-
sule, locked away from reality, and it feels like magical
transportation, time suspended in that dim, quiet tube,

maybe a movie to occupy the time, or a book, or sleeping. And then the tube opens, and POOF, you're somewhere else. Even looking out the window at evidence of travel doesn't make it any more real. Lakes are just silver-blue stains, mountains are ripples and bumps, and cities are messy clusters of yellow lights. It's not the real world—there are no lives down there. It's just...an illusion. Part of the mystery of air travel.

But not this.

Not on board this boat. I'm aware of each moment. Each mile passes slowly, deliberately. Even asleep, I'm aware that we are moving. The engines rumble underneath me, around me, and there's the movement of the waves, our ascent and descent, the bobbing, the swaying—hard, physical proof of travel. It's not smooth, it's not magical, it's not mysterious. I'm aware of the physics of it, whereas on a plane, it's just...magic. Even if you understand how several tons of metal can fly thirty thousand feet in the air, it still feels...magical. This? On a boat? Not so. You are at the mercy of the ocean...of the Sea, deserving the capital letter. She rules all, out here. Those old tropes from Grecian poetry—the caprice of the wine-dark sea, all that—it's all so much more real to me, now. The Sea carries you on her back, and the waves can dwarf you. She is all, she is endless.

Her moods can kill you.

We have traveled nonstop, night and day, for a week, and there is nothing around us but water, nothing but the Sea, endless, just a rippling azure field as far as the eye can see, curving away into nothing. A week of travel, and it feels as if we've gotten nowhere.

How am I supposed to find Christian?

I have no way of contacting him, obviously—no answer to my calls, texts, or emails. I've tried, and it all goes unanswered—even assuming he's alive, his laptop and cell phone would be on the bottom of the ocean.

What if he's dead? But no, he's not. He can't be. I feel him, still. Maybe it's hope, maybe it's wishful thinking, but I FEEL Christian. More than a gut feeling, more than an instinct or a hope or anything, it's just this bone-deep, unshakeable KNOWLEDGE that my husband is alive.

Somewhere.

Somewhere in this wide, wide world.

The Sea took him from me. She stole him, the bitch.

Memory, and the Sea—they're both bitches.

The Sea stole my Christian from me. How do I find him? Where is he? Africa?

Dominic showed me something the other day: a map of the US, drawn to scale, and a map of Africa, drawn to scale, without the Mercator projection: the entirety of the United States of America can fit easily into Africa with room to spare for all of China and most of Europe; Africa dwarfs the US by several orders of magnitude.

To say Christian is somewhere in Africa is nearly meaningless. Trying to conceive of the size of that continent is mind-boggling. And that's IF I can reach Africa.

IF the Sea lets me get there. IF, after days and weeks of travel, I manage to reach Africa. And then, god, and then? I have to find him, on that massive continent. But how? How do I do that? I don't speak any language but English. I don't know where to even start looking. Christian's shipmate, Jonny, only had a basic idea where they were when the storm hit, and he says they got blown way off course during the storm, so there's no way to know exactly where they were when Chris was swept overboard. How did he survive? Where did he end up? He could have been taken aboard a freighter and ended up in China, or Jakarta, or England, or anywhere on the globe. He's been gone for months—what if he's been traveling this whole time? He could be anywhere.

God, I'm dizzy just thinking about it.

How do I find my husband?

I'm so angry with you, Christian.

But I love you. I miss you. I need you.

I'm in so far over my head. I'm lost. I don't know what to do. All I know is, I have to find you, Christian.

Conakry, Guinea, Africa; date unknown

I spend a lot of time pondering the nature of Time.

There is very little to do around here, but sit, and think, and try to remember. James, the doctor, brought me a book, in English. A gift. *Ulysses* by James Joyce. As I read, parts of it feel familiar. Mostly the beginning. It is a thick book—thick, in terms of sheer size, but also thick in terms of...feel. It is dense. Impenetrable. I read a little every day, usually just a few pages, but it often makes very little sense to me, and I skip over sections. It is a gift from the only person who seems to know me or care about me, so I keep it, and I attempt to read it.

I don't think I like it very much.

When I grow tired of reading, and trying to

remember, and writing, I sit, and I think and it often feels as if Time is a ribbon, but a stretchy one. The sun beats hot on my head and face and shoulders. A fly will buzz around my head for hours. A beetle, black and bulbous and iridescent, will crawl through the dust at my feet for many hours more. Time is stretched out thin like a rubber band stretched near to snapping, so thin it's almost translucent.

And mere minutes will have passed.

I know this, because as I sit on the screened-in porch, I can twist in my chair and see a clock. It is old. A grandfather clock, the kind that used to sit in my own grandfather's house. In his foyer, near the front door. This clock, in this place, is very much like the one in my grandfather's house. It ticks slowly with the same dull, endless *tock...tock...tock...tock*, as if it has been endlessly keeping time, as if nothing could stop that tarnished brass disc from swinging side to side, side to side.

I would sit, as a child, on the floor of my grandfather's foyer, watching the clock. Hours and hours I would spend, just sitting there, watching the clock. I don't remember why, though. Was I waiting? Was I fascinated by the clock? I don't remember.

All I remember is sitting cross-legged on a threadbare rug, the front door to my right, sunlight shining through the window at the top in a brilliant golden river of light, illuminating dust motes like particulates of heaven. The clock would stand in front of me, up against a wallpapered wall. White wallpaper, with blue flowers in vertical lines, roses climbing a trellis, in repeating patterns. To my left would be a long hallway, ending in an oil painting of Jesus, blond hair and blue eyes, serene and somewhat sad, making that weird sign with the fingers of his right hand, staring vaguely Heavenward. Beneath the painting, a small table. On it, a thick white candle. A cut-glass dish full of butterscotch candies, which I was allowed to have, but which always sounded more appealing than they ended up tasting.

I remember this vividly. Sitting there, on the floor, staring at the clock. Waiting. For what? I don't know that. I can't remember. Why do I remember this? Is it an important memory? Did I do this frequently? Does this memory hold some significance? I don't know.

But the clock, here in the hospital, it tocks, tocks, tocks, and sometimes, as I think, I can count the individual seconds as they pass:

Tock…

Tock…

Tock…

Each moment separate, disparate. My thoughts fill those taffy-stretched moments like water rushing into an empty cistern—

*whoamI? WhycantIrememberanything? Whoisshe? Where-
isshe? Whereishome? WhyamIhere? WHYCANTIREMEM-
BER?—*

All those thoughts are jumbled, twisted, gnarled, tangled. Too fast. Rushing through me, too fast to catch, thoughts too dense and painful to think about. If I could catch those thoughts, it would feel like gripping one of those spiny, spiky balls dropped in your yard by the trees. Like squeezing a burr plucked off a dog's coat.

Then, sometimes, especially when I'm writing, scribbling in my notebooks, I won't be aware of anything except the scritch of my pen across the white paper, blue ink smudged on my hand, blue ink leaving trails of thoughts and half-memories and fictitious, desperate wishful memories across the page. I'm writing, and I'm writing. The pen moves of its own accord. The words flow like a river. Endless. A flood. And then, suddenly, the grandfather clock behind me tolls balefully—*DONG... DONG...DONG*—and hours have passed.

I have filled four notebooks with my scribblings.

Some are just stories I am telling to myself, to pass the time. These are easy and light and meaningless. The harder, sharper, darker, more difficult and painful stories are the ones possessed of some element of truth, or history.

More painful yet is my constant need to write to and of this woman, this Ava. She is in my thoughts constantly, but I can't remember more than fragments of her. She must have been my wife, or my lover. It is maddening, to know I have loved someone as much as I must have loved this Ava, to have her in my memory so fiercely, so indelibly, when all else seems lost, even my own name.

I write to her. As if she could hear me, as if she might ever read the mad scribblings in these pages. I write to her as if she is with me, as if she is real, as if I will see her again. None of this is a surety. I gain fragments of memory, but they are few and obscure and vague and small.

So, because it helps alleviate the boredom, and because I simply *must*, I write to Ava; I pour myself out to her.

Sometimes, the line between story and letter becomes blurred, even to me.

Dr. James visits often, to check on me, to talk, to listen.

Today, he manages all three at once. He probes my head wound—which caused my memory loss—a wound sustained in what I've been told was a shipwreck, though I don't as yet remember the event itself. I was shipwrecked, lost at sea, and found through sheer luck by local fishermen, and brought to this hospital in Africa—outside the city of Conakry, in Guinea, to be more accurate, which I'm dimly aware is a country on the western coast of the African continent. I only know that much because Dr. James has told me as much—it's certainly hot enough to feel like Africa, and the other nurses and orderlies do not speak English, only various dialects and languages native to this country and this part of this country, and a little French, which I know a few words of, somehow. So, Dr. James is my only source of real conversation, as he's the only person I see regularly who speaks English.

Today, he looks over the casts on my arm and leg, probes my head, and probes conversationally.

"You have been writing today?" he asks, glancing at the notebook on my lap.

He is older, in his fifties or sixties. Dark black skin, portly, with graying hair trimmed close. He dresses in slacks and short sleeve button-downs, his belly straining against the buttons, no belt. He wears glasses, which he puts on as needed and takes off again, stuffing them in his shirt pocket.

I nod. "Yes."

"Did you remember anything from the writing?"

When I first arrived, I could remember nothing, nothing at all. And then Dr. James told me I'd been saying a name—Ava—and that name prompted a flood of memories and images, none of which inform me about myself. I have temporary amnesia, Dr. James insists, and claims I will eventually remember. And in the meantime, to prompt the return of memory, he provided a stack of spiral-bound notebooks and a handful of pens, and suggested I write whatever ideas or images or memories occur to me. It may help jog loose memories, he claims.

So far, he's right. I remember—I remember Ava.

Not everything, but enough to know she's someone

vitally important to who I am. Enough to know I want to remember more.

And so I write:

From a handwritten notebook; date unknown

We broke up, once. Do you remember that, Ava? It wasn't for very long, and it was when we first began living together.

We broke up over, of all things, peanut butter. Peanut butter. You see, I prefer creamy peanut butter, and you prefer the crunchy, organic kind which requires a cement mixer and power tools to mix properly, and which always leaves a smear of oil on everything the jar touches. You went shopping for groceries, a chore I know you dislike. I offered to go for you, with a list made by you, but you only laughed, somewhat caustically, and asked me if I remembered the last time you sent me shopping. I confessed I did, but insisted I'd learned my lesson. You only laughed all the harder, and left, list in hand; the last time I'd gone shopping for you, I'd come back without half the items on the list, and the ones I did come back with were, in some way or another wrong—the wrong brand, or kind, or variety. Scented bathroom wipes as opposed to unscented; Palmolive dish soap versus Dawn; off-brand 1% cow milk as opposed to the CORRECT brand of vanilla almond milk; creamy peanut butter versus a particular brand of organic crunchy. We'd had a quarrel about that trip, wherein you lambasted me for not knowing what foods we eat and what brands we buy, and I'd tried to insist that it really didn't matter all that much, did it? Apparently, it did.

So, yes, I understood why you laughed, and why you went anyway, that day. I didn't want to grocery shop—I hate it more than you do—but I loved you and just wanted to at least make the overture of offering to do it.

You came back with all your particular brands and varieties, and all seemed well. Until the next morning, when I went to make breakfast. Scrambled eggs with jalapeños and cheese, half a package of bacon between us, and toast with peanut butter. There wasn't any peanut butter. Or, rather, it wasn't *my* peanut butter, it was the impossible to stir organic bullshit kind, impossible to spread, always separating, hard to eat, sticky, thicker than clay. So I asked you if you'd gotten me my peanut butter. I asked nicely. Just wondering if perhaps it had gotten put away somewhere I wasn't looking. You'd stared at me for a moment over the top of your laptop and remarked, somewhat snidely, that you'd gotten *real* peanut butter, not the nasty, sugary, fake shit.

Which led to what was at first a civil and tongue-in-cheek discussion about the merits of the different kinds of peanut butter. When it became heated, I tried to diffuse it. I asked you—reasonably, in my eyes—to please buy both kinds next time. A good compromise, right? I thought so. We both get the kind we like, and since

I always made breakfast, I'd be the one responsible for making sure you got yours and I got mine.

But no.

You insisted the organic was the only real kind of peanut butter, and the other stuff—and here, you spat the brand name as if it were a swear word—was sugary, awful death, and is to *real* peanut butter what Sunny Delight is to real orange juice. You wouldn't buy it, you said.

Again, my attempt to defuse the situation, which was quickly becoming a rather ridiculously heated argument, fell on deaf ears. I like a certain kind of peanut butter, I said, and there were very few things about which I had a particular opinion in terms of groceries. I didn't even care which brand, just that it was creamy rather than crunchy. Didn't seem to be too much to ask, I thought.

Maybe you were stressed about something else—an exam, perhaps. This was at the very beginning of our relationship becoming serious—we'd been together for two years, had just moved in together, and we both had a few months left to finish our degrees. So maybe you were stressed about an exam, or a paper. Maybe you hadn't slept well. Maybe peanut butter really was that important to you. I don't know.

I just know that you refused to give an inch. No, no, no, no. Until the discussion passed from being a merely heated discussion to being an argument, and then you said something like "I won't have that shit in my house" and I, unwisely, took the bait—I allowed myself to be drawn in. Your house? What about OUR house? Didn't I get a choice?

Aha, no. I didn't.

I admit, freely: I could have simply stopped letting myself be involved it in. I could have given in. Accepted that I just wouldn't have the peanut butter I preferred. But, god, that seemed so emasculating. To be overruled in my own home, by my girlfriend, about PEANUT BUTTER? How stupid.

It's just peanut butter, it doesn't matter.

Which cuts both ways, I realize. I knew it then, but sometimes, as people, I think we get into a fight with a loved one and we just can't seem to make ourselves relent; once we've got it in our teeth and our blood is up, we just can't let it go.

We couldn't release it. Neither of us was prepared to lose. Is it really about winning? I don't know. In some ways, yes. Sometimes it's just about the principle of the matter.

Soon, our kitchen echoed with shouts. You trotted out every single wrong I'd ever committed, and I did the same, and we got in each other's faces, and we slung words we had no business slinging, insults, vehemence neither of us was used to feeling.

I think, perhaps, in shouting matches like that, a small, deep, dark part of us enjoys it. We enjoy letting go of our anger, letting ourselves scream and shout. We know it's wrong, but it feels good, in that deep, dark, secret part of us, to give in, to give vent to that simmering inferno.

I think after a while, we'd forgotten what we were arguing about. At that point, it was the argument itself that mattered. Too many words had been slung, too much nastiness had been thrown about. It was our first real fight. Oh, we'd quarreled before, obviously. Many times. But it was usually about minor things, quickly solved and even more quickly forgotten. Nothing like this. Nothing real, nothing that spawned such anger.

Which is what was weird about this argument: it was over something so stupid, so unimportant, so not worth fighting over. But with most fights, I think, the spark that sets off an inferno is very rarely the real, deep down catalyst. The spark just touches off the tinder, which has already been piled up, dry, hungry for that spark. When you cohabit with someone, day to day, life tends to slowly and subtly build up that pile of tinder and, sometimes, all it takes is a tiny little spark to ignite a blazing fire.

We fought, Ava. Oh, we fought. How long did that quarrel rage? An hour? Two? Until we were both exhausted from the intensity of it. I don't remember what we said, only the feelings of anger and the vision of you pointing at me angrily, jabbing a finger at me, cursing at me, eyes blazing, hair flying.

I think you said it just to end the fight— "Fuck you,

I'm done. I'm leaving." That's the only thing I distinct-
ly remember you saying. It stunned me silent. Which,
again, was the real purpose of it. To get me to shut up,
to end the fight decisively. Well, you accomplished it.
You were out the door, purse on your shoulder, keys in
hand, before I could gather my wits, before I could fathom what you'd said, or what to do about it. You were in
your car—that old Civic, you remember it? Black, but
always so dirty it was almost brown, with the rip in the
cloth of the back seat and the broken windshield wiper,
smelling forever of cigarettes from the previous owner.
You were gone by the time my brain kicked into gear
and reminded me that my girlfriend had just walked out
on me. Broken up with me, possibly.

That moment, when I watched your car pull out of
the driveway of our apartment complex and make that
left turn, was when I realized, really, truly, and deeply,
that I loved you. How deeply, how fiercely? Watching
you drive away, and not knowing if you'd be coming
back, drove it home for me. Hammered into my heart
the reality—that you were *mine*, and I was yours, and
that we belonged together.

And that I was terrified of losing you. That, most of
all.

I lived in utter terror for several hours. I tried to
reason with myself, tried to convince myself you'd be
back, you just needed to cool off. Go shopping with a
girlfriend or two, maybe get drunk and call a cab home

in the wee hours. I made it six hours before I gave in and texted you—the cowardly approach first—because I was too afraid of your anger and your final, parting words to risk a phone call.

So I texted you, asking you where you were.

It went unread. Unanswered. Another hour.

I sent a second text, begging you to just tell me you were safe.

Another hour without a response. It was after four in the afternoon by this time, and you'd been gone since shortly after nine in the morning. I'd gotten no work done, couldn't read, couldn't write, couldn't focus, could barely even watch TV. Fear and worry and even a little anger at you for vanishing like that ran through me. Ruled me. Owned me. Those emotions rotated, twisted, took turns ravaging me.

I called you, and called you, and called you. No answer.

Finally, I had to go look for you. I went to your old dorm, where a lot of your friends still lived, but they hadn't seen you. I went to the mall, another of your favorite places, and searched all your favorite stores, questioned cashiers and security guards. Nothing. I went to your three favorite hangouts, but two had only just opened and the other hadn't seen you. Where could you be? I roamed the beaches and back alleys, even called hospitals. I searched everywhere I could think of.

Finally, after ten p.m., I headed home.

It was a complete accident—fate, or fortune, I don't know which. But I happened to glance to my left as I sat at a left-turn light, the one right before our complex, and there, in the parking lot of a run-down cantina, was your car, less than a mile from our apartment. I knew it was your car at one glance—I knew the dent in the back left fender because I'd put it there with my truck eight months before, and I knew the exact, off-center, slightly sideways placement of your University of Miami bumper sticker in the rear windshield, on the right side, down low. I pulled a slightly reckless U-turn through the red light and into the parking lot. Parked across two spots like an asshole, and jogged over to the bar.

And there you were. Hunched over at the bar, your hair a frizzy, tangled mess from running your hands through it a million times, playing with it as you do when you're agitated. There was an electric bell on the door of the cantina; it dinged as I entered, and you turned, saw me, and tried to pretend you hadn't seen me, that you didn't know me.

You were the only native English speaker in that bar. It was probably not the safest place for you, especially alone.

But there you were. Ignoring me, still angry with me. You'd probably been sitting there all damn day, drinking yourself into a stupor, talking yourself into a rage about how much of a dick I was.

I sat down beside you, and when the bartender came

over, you waved at him dismissively. "Don' serve him, José. He's an asshole, and we hate him."

José just quirked an eyebrow at me and poured me a Dos Equis anyway, and then vanished somewhere. Before he vanished, he met my eyes, gestured at you, and gave a subtle hand signal: a chopping motion at his throat, signifying that you'd been cut off. Indeed, as I glanced into your glass, I realized you had what you thought was a margarita, but was mostly just margarita mix, ice, and a lot of lime, with just enough tequila to make you think it was a real drink. You had no idea. You were babbling at the person sitting next to you, an older man who glanced at you every now and then, silently, and kept his eyes otherwise on the TV, sipping his cerveza, ignoring you. You didn't care. You didn't care that he probably didn't speak a single word of English. You just wanted to rant. About me.

I sat beside you for three more beers; enough to take the edge of my own mood, now that I knew you were safe. After thirty minutes of ranting as if I wasn't there, you finally let your head thunk forward onto the sticky top of the bar, groaning.

"What do you want?" you asked me.

"For you to come home."

"Why? So you can scream at me about fucking peanut butter some more?"

"No, because I love you, and because you've been gone for twelve hours and I was worried sick."

You giggled. You reached into your jeans pocket and produced your phone, which was lit up as if it were on, but the screen was blank, and swirled with rainbows. "I got sick of ignoring your calls and messages, so I accidentally on purpose dropped it in the toilet."

I sighed. "Nice."

"You wouldn't leave me alone! I just wanted to get drunk in peace!"

I couldn't help a laugh. "I get that, but it would have been nice to know where you were, or if you were safe."

"Like you care."

"That's not fair."

"YOU EAT CREAMY PEANUT BUTTER!" you shouted.

I laughed again. "I'm not arguing with you about this again, Ava."

"Why not? It was fun the first time, right?"

I realized, then, that you weren't capable of reason. Your eyes would cross and uncross as you looked at me, and sometimes you'd just drift off into silence in the middle of a statement.

So I tried a new tack. "Ava, can we just go home? We can figure this out tomorrow. It's time to go home, okay?"

"You go home. I'm fine here. I need another margarita anyway. If I can talk, I'm not drunk enough."

I wanted to tell you that you'd had enough, but didn't dare—I knew exactly how that would go down.

"How about this—if you come home with me right now, I swear I'll never say another word about peanut butter again. Okay?"

You snickered. "And you're still arguing with me about peanut butter. Go stick your dick in your creamy peanut butter, you fucking dick."

I sighed, and rolled my eyes. "Actually, I'm just trying to get you to come home."

"Why? So you can try to seduce me with your wicked ways?" You leaned close, and I felt a flare of hope. "Not…gonna…happen."

I was tempted, then, to just sit here and feed you straight tequila shots until you passed out, but I didn't. For one thing, I had no idea how many margaritas you'd had, and I was afraid of giving you alcohol poisoning, and for another, I knew from experience that you were capable of putting away a startling and somewhat absurd amount of tequila and stay something akin to conscious and upright. Which meant that plan might backfire.

I tried every way I could think of to get you to come home, and you shot them all down.

Finally, you had to pee. You stood up, stumbled into a nearby table, but shook off my hand. So I followed you to the bathroom and stood outside waiting for you to finish. After five minutes, I was worried. So I went in, and found you passed out in the stall, jeans around your ankles, leaning sideways against the stall wall.

I stood you up, leaned you against me, and with a lot

of effort, got you dressed. You sort of came to, and I was able to mostly carry you out to my truck. I set you on the passenger seat and buckled you in. Then I drove home as slowly and carefully as I could.

Got you in bed.

Put Tylenol and water on your bedside table with a note saying that I loved you. That nothing mattered to me but you, and us.

I was woken from a fitful sleep. I was bleary and disoriented and half dreaming. You were in the bed behind me. Your presence woke me up the rest of the way, and I rolled over to face you. Expecting a confrontation. Expecting…I don't know. Something. Anything.

You were asleep.

Mouth open, a soft snore soughing gently from your parted lips. Fully clothed, And god, the sight of you in bed, sleeping, snoring…it slayed me. Erased, in that moment, at least, all my anger.

Reminded me of my love. Reminded me what you meant to me.

So, I went back to sleep.

And when I woke up, you weren't in bed. A dozen emotions seared through me—anger again, confusion, panic. I left the bed, and found you sitting at the kitchen table, laptop open, headphones on, as if nothing had happened.

Only, on the island, side by side, were two jars of peanut butter, one creamy, one crunchy. You'd printed out photos of us and taped a photo of me to the creamy, and a photo of you to the crunchy; the photo had been a selfie of us, arms around each other, on that vacation to Iceland. The way you taped the photos to the jars made it look like the jars were embracing. A peace offering.

I made us breakfast: fried eggs with melted cheese on top, breakfast sausage…and toast. Creamy for me, crunchy for you.

We never talked about it.

I learned the depths of my love for you, how desperately I needed you.

I learned, in those hours you were gone that survival without you is possible, but it is sheer and utter Hell, and I never wanted to do it again.

Which begs the question, my dear mystery love, my Ava: how did I end up in the Atlantic Ocean, injured and alone, without identification, hundreds of miles from the nearest land?

Where are you, Ava?

I set the pen and notebook aside and let my mind wander, perusing what I just wrote, and what it means.

I'm conflicted.

How can I remember all those details, but not my name, or where I'm from, or how I got here? How can I remember the exact wording of a text message from myself to Ava, but not how old I am? How do I know Ava and I met at the University of Miami, but not my parents' names, or where I grew up? How could I describe the fight in that story so accurately, but do not know how I ended up drowning in the Atlantic? The details in the story—are they real, or are they invented?

I think I am a writer, for the telling of stories comes easily to me. A little too easily, perhaps, because it is increasingly difficult to tell fiction from fact.

Dr. James says that the human memory is a strange creature, one that we know very little about, and that we seldom remember things as they truly happened, that we invent details and fill in gaps unconsciously, and we cannot tell the difference. Even modern, fancy Western medicine knows very little about how memory works, even with all the fancy machines and gizmos.

Dr. James has a theory, though:

Ava is so crucial to me, to who I am, that even memory loss cannot erase her from my psyche. She's woven into the very fabric of who I am. So even though the trauma I suffered has possibly been blotted out—either permanently or temporarily—my memories of myself cannot completely blot Ava from my mind.

I suppose that makes a kind of sense.

Ava.

I whisper her name, and the hot African breeze snatches the syllables from me and flutters them across the courtyard.

I imagine that a bumblebee hears me whispering Ava's name and carries it out to the shore, whispers it to a passing gull, who carries it in raucous, playful, mischievous circles out to sea, and then the gull calls out her name to an albatross, winging slowly on a warm updraft, far, far out, where the waves reach Heaven and there is nothing but Sea and her moods. Then the albatross carries her name for thousands and thousands of miles, across the ocean, where a tern hears the name being sung in the swirling wildness of a thunderstorm ravaging the southern coast of the United States. And then, I imagine, the tern alights on the sand of a beach, somewhere. A little white thing with black on its wings and quick, orange feet, and a shrill voice. And this tern will hop along the sand, and it will find Ava. She'll be on the beach, sitting on a blanket, sunglasses shielding her vivid blue eyes, and her face will be tilted up to the sun, and the tern will whisper Ava's name in a quiet, ethereal voice, and Ava will hear it, and know it is me. Whispering to her from across the sea:

Ava.

Ava.

On board The Glory; The Atlantic Ocean;
November 9, 2016

Y ou'd think this would be a great adventure, leaving the safety and comfort of everything I know to board a fishing boat and sailing across the open Sea in search of my husband.

But for the most part, it's boring.

I cook, and I clean, and I write in my journal, and that's pretty much it.

I avoid the deck, and the men. I avoid their mundane conversations, their vulgar jokes, their nose picking and farting and spitting. It's an all-male crew, so such things are to be expected, and I avoid it.

My life is more insular than it has ever been.

Which…is really saying something, I'm realizing.

My life has always been insular, but I seem to have reached a new plane in this respect.

My head and my heart are screaming at me to avoid going down this path of thought; it's like a sore tooth, aching, painful, but you can't quite seem to stop probing it with your tongue.

If I'm going to throw my entire life into a sequence of change, throwing literally everything I know out the window, then I might as well try and do some serious introspection, right?

Right.

So, despite the pain, which will accompany an examination of my flaws, failures, and faux pas, I'm not going to shy away from this.

I have lived a sheltered, privileged life—fact number one.

I grew up in St. Pete, in a solidly middle-class home, the daughter of two parents who loved each other and who have been married for many, many years. They were not wonderful parents, but they got the job done. They provided for Delta and me, they didn't hit us or abuse us, they got us to school and made sure we kept up our grades, got us presents for birthdays and Christmas. They checked off all the parenting boxes. Really, when you compare the way some people grew up, the things some have endured in childhood, I had an easy life. I went to school. Came home. Acted in a few plays here and there throughout middle school and high school, had a decent circle of friends with me from elementary school through high school, and a couple of friends who stayed with me through college, but no one I remained in contact with after we graduated and started marrying off. I was never bullied. Everyone gets picked on or made fun of once in a while, but I experienced nothing that really stuck with me, or affected me long term.

I lived in the same home from birth through college, and only ventured as far away as Miami for college, which was four hours from home. Close enough to head home for laundry and a home-cooked meal on the weekends. But, as I got older and more independent, Mom and Dad eased into retirement and started vacationing more and more. They stayed in touch, mostly, but once I graduated high school, it seemed like they just figured they'd done their duty as parents, got us to college, and were done parenting Delta and me.

I was never close to them. They were Mom and Dad, and I loved them, I suppose, and they me, but they always just seemed to be just so…wrapped up in each other, I guess. More concerned with their own lives than Delta's or mine. As soon as Delta was old enough, they'd leave me with her and go do…whatever. Party? I don't know. By the time Delta left home I was old enough—in their eyes, at least—to be on my own, so Mom and Dad were gone even more.

It wasn't as if I had *bad* parents, I just wasn't close to them.

I've gotten off topic, I think.

My point is less about my parents than it is about my insular life. I lived in Florida my whole life. Lived in a middle-class neighborhood, never struggled for money, never experienced significant trauma. Never wanted for anything.

I got partial scholarships to UM—one for academics, and several grants for various essays. I paid for the rest of my college tuition with loans, which included my living expenses. I was never a broke college student. I had a decent car, a dorm room to live in, a roommate I liked, a circle of friends, enough money to eat, and some savings from working at a diner during high school and throughout college so that I could go out with my friends.

When I met Christian, and gradually began spending more and more time with him, he just naturally began taking care of me. He often treated me to meals, tickets to movies, and the like. And then, over the summer between my junior and senior year, we moved in together. We lived on his boat, at first. And then, when I decided I didn't really enjoy the cramped quarters of his sailboat's cabin, I convinced him to get an apartment with me. He was already writing by this time, had sold a collection of short stories and his first novel, which had brought in enough income that Christian had put the deposit on the apartment himself and paid for the utilities, and I made sure we had groceries; we had a system that worked, a system in which Christian took care of me.

I kept waiting tables at the diner through my senior year, but then Christian's father died, which required us to take an extended leave of absence in Illinois, where Christian grew up, and rather than asking them to hold my spot on the roster, I just quit my part-time job. After that, I never went back to any kind of full-time work; I didn't have to.

The death of Christian's father had been traumatic for him, and had been emotionally devastating for him. Not because he was close to his father, but rather more the opposite. It was relief, perhaps, which in turn made him feel guilty, I think. I don't know for sure. I just know that instead of going to counseling or something, Christian locked himself in his study when we finally returned home, and had written a full novel in three weeks, pouring out his emotions into a book. The book sold hundreds of thousands of copies and ended up getting him a film deal, which officially cemented our financial position in life as "doing really well."

Meaning, I never had to do a damn thing after that. Christian was perfectly happy for me to stay home and write. I had a novel I was working on, and a growing audience for my blog. It was a life of leisure. We spent a lot of time together. Went out for long lunches, dinners and movies, long weekend trips and extended vacation, and I lived a life wherein I did...

Essentially nothing.

God, now that I put my life in perspective, I'm coming to a horrible realization: I've accomplished absolutely nothing in my life.

My book did okay, but the idea for a follow-up never panned out, and then I got pregnant and had Henry, and became a mom, and that was my life. That was the only thing I've ever done which had any real meaning. And then he died of a brain tumor when he was just shy of eighteen months old.

My meaning, my purpose in life, my son, was taken from me. And look where that led...

God, I don't know if I can go there, just yet.

Let's just take this brutal self-examination one step at a time, shall we?

I've never been alone.

I've never taken care of myself.

I've never done anything crazy or daring.

Never, never, never.

My life had gone from being taken care of by my parents, to a brief period of quasi-independence at college before I met Christian, and then I was taken care of by him.

And now? What is my life, now?

Apart from my sister and these guys on the trawler I am completely alone.

My home is gone.

My life as I knew it is gone.

My Henry is gone.

My Christian is gone.

I am gone. I am nowhere. I am no one.

In searching for Christian, am I searching for myself? For a semblance of a life that once was?

In an attempt to make sense of it all, I sit on my cot in my cabin, and I write:

From Ava's handwritten journal;
November 11, 2016

I had a dream last night.

I woke sobbing.

I was at home in the condo in Ft. Lauderdale. I had Henry in my arms. Alive. Warm and wiggling. Cooing. A baby, not quite newborn, but still a baby. He had on his little blue hat, and he was all burritoed up in his SleepSack. That was it. That was the dream. I was just... holding him. Staring down at him. His eyes, still the innocent pale blue of a baby, were gazing up at me. His mouth was open, working, gurgling. He'd gotten one little hand free of the swaddling, and he was reaching for me. That clean baby scent was in my nostrils, and his weight was tiny and yet so significant. The sun was shining in through the open sliding door, so the sound of the ocean could be heard as it crashed constantly. The sound was in soothing, shushing, mesmerizing.

The sound of the sea has always been a constant in my life. In St. Pete, in Miami, in Ft. Lauderdale. Always, always the sea, always near.

Henry in my arms...god...it didn't get any better than this.

I woke, and my arms were empty, and my heart was empty. I sat up in my bunk and cradled the emptiness in my arms, and sobbed Henry's name quietly, because the last thing I needed was to answer questions from the crew about why I was sobbing so hard.

It was the silent, breathless sob, the kind where you can't catch your breath because the grief is just so fucking razor sharp. And when you do catch a breath, it's a shuddering, a quavering wail hidden in a pillow, and then more breathlessness, shaking, shoulders heaving.

Thinking about Henry is too painful—I've been avoiding thinking about him as much as possible. Unhealthy, perhaps, I know: how am I to heal from his death if I can't even think his name? But I just can't. It's too hard. It hurts too bad—almost as much even now as it did the day he died.

Finally, I fell back into a fitful, restless sleep.

Which became another dream.

This one was about Christian.

I think it was informed by the movie I watched last night, before falling asleep: <u>The English Patient</u>, one of a small number of DVDs on this boat.

In my dream, Christian was sitting in a wheelchair, an old one with a wicker back and wide tarnished wheels and wooden handles. The footrests were too short to properly support his long legs. He was wearing loose blue scrub pants, and a dirty white T-shirt. He was unshaven, an unkempt, untrimmed beard obscuring his handsome jaw. There were palm trees waving in a constant breeze, and it seemed hot in the dream. I don't know how to put it—there was just a feeling of heat, an awareness of it, rather than actually feeling it myself. His hair was too long, and his eyes were...vacant. He was staring into nothingness, but seeing something. His lips were moving—just his bottom lip, lifting, curling in, tucking into his upper teeth, and relaxing. Whispering something?

My name—

Ava...

Ava...

There was a flash, in the dream—a jump from one image to another. Suddenly Christian was above me, staring down at me. His eyes were full of love and he was whispering my name. Not just whispering it, though. It was...a benediction. A prayer. I was his goddess, and he was worshipping me.

Another flash-jump and the dream went back to Christian in the wheelchair. He was hurt—injured, but healing. Casts on his left leg and left arm, covering the entirety of both limbs, and a smaller cast on his right arm from elbow to wrist, the casts dirty, aged, smudged.

He had a notebook balanced on his right thigh, secured in place with his left hand. In his right hand he held a pen, a blue ballpoint. He stared into nothingness, whispering my name—I heard nothing, there was no sound, just a vision of him. In an old, rickety wheelchair, somewhere hot, with palm trees all around.

It felt…real.

So real.

TOO real.

It felt like I was seeing him, as he was, in that moment.

I don't believe in mystical, fairy tale, fantasy novel bullshit like clairvoyance or anything like that. It's fun fodder for stories, but in reality? No. You can't hear thoughts; you can't see in your mind someone thousands of miles away. It's fiction, stuff for stories.

But in that dream? It was *real*. That was Christian. Evidence of him, alive. There was not a thought in my mind, no question in my heart, no doubt in my soul. That was him. My husband, my Christian. Alive. Real. Whispering my name, as he so often did when making love to me.

Upon waking, I lost the surety.

Could it be real? Could I truly have seen him in my dream as he was right now?

I've never wanted to believe anything so desperately in my life; I did not want to doubt that it was real, that it was possible. But doubt, like rot seeping into wood, slow, subtle, almost unnoticeable, tainted the beauty of the dream.

It had been a lovely dream—I remember very clearly the sense of love emanating from him as he whispered my name. I remember very clearly the relief I felt when I saw him in the dream: it was him! He was real, he was alive!

Then I awoke and the love and the relief disappeared.

A million thoughts coruscated through me as I woke, and pondered the dream.

Where is he? Even injured, could he not come to me, could he not find me? Contact me in some way?

But how? Our Ft. Lauderdale home is gone, and we never had a landline, and he hasn't tried my cell phone, hasn't tried my email. Delta, breaking out as a country music star, is away on a national tour and is unable to respond to communication frequently. How could he possibly find me?

He could, if he wanted. He's Christian: he has been all over the world, knows people everywhere, knows all the ports of call where ships with passengers are most likely to go. He knows how to find people.

And then I doubt the dream. I chide myself for being ridiculous, to think a dream could bear any resemblance to reality. It was just a dream. It was my longing for my husband making itself known in my dreams. It was just a dream, and nothing but a dream.

BUT...

WHAT IF…

The idea that Chris could still be alive plagues me.

From Ava's handwritten journal;
November 12, 2016

I miss Darcy and Bennet, the puppy and kitten Christian gave me before he left on his sea journey. They went missing during the storm. I remember hearing Darcy yowling and barking, and Bennet meowing, and then the roof fell in on me as I took cover in the bathtub.

When the storm started intensifying and I realized I had to take shelter, I tried to get them to get in the tub with me, and managed to get Bennet in with me for a few minutes, but he jumped out, and Darcy flat out refused to get in with me. After the roof caved in, I heard a bark, Darcy's sweet voice, but it was distant. And I may have hallucinated it, or imagined it, but I thought I heard little paws ticking and scrabbling across the chunk of drywall imprisoning me in the tub.

I like to imagine that Darcy and Bennet are still out there, somewhere in Ft. Lauderdale, safe and happy. Maybe they stuck together and found a family who adopted them. Like in…what's that movie with the pug and the cat? Milo and Otis.

I have an entire story made up in my head.

They found each other in the storm and took shelter together under an overpass. Wet, shivering, and missing me, they huddled there until the storm blew out, and then they went out looking for me. But the way back to the condo was blocked, and by the time they found a way there, the building was mostly rubble. And in the process of looking for me, a kindly older man found them, and brought them home to feed them, and wash them, and he gave Bennet a saucer of warm milk—even though cats are lactose intolerant and shouldn't have all that much, except as a rare treat—and he gave Darcy a rawhide bone. The old man, whose name would be Roger, and his wife, Tabitha, used to have a cat and a dog, but they both passed away from age, and now the couple have Darcy and Bennet to love and take care of, and though my kitty and pup miss me, they're glad to have someone to cuddle with. And maybe Roger and Tabitha have grandchildren who come over and play with them, little ones to lick and snuggle.

That's what I like to imagine, anyway: my kitty and pup, alive and well and safe. Home, and loved.

Everything I'm not. Well, I'm alive, I suppose.

Sort of.

Am I, though? Technically, I am alive. I draw breath, my heart beats. But life—LIFE—isn't that something more than breathing, something different?

I don't know.

Have I ever known what Life truly is? Is it just having

a home and a husband? Is it accomplishments? Is it being a mother? Is it...I don't know. Is it something I haven't considered, something I don't understand?

Right now, life feels futile. Empty. Pointless.

But the dream of Christian, fucking haunts me.

HE haunts me.

I wake up thinking I've heard his voice, and that he's whispering my name.

I'm coming, Chris. I'm coming. I'm looking for you. I'll find you. I swear, I'll find you.

Where or when, I don't know. But I'll find you. I promise.

From a handwritten notebook; date unknown

A gladness sparks in me,
   A fragment of madness,
   A particulate of joy.
It is a small thing, a tiny thing, elemental, wild, tremulous, and fragile.

There is frost on my heart, a crackling coldness at the edges,
   spiderweb cracks reaching hungry fingers inward.

The spark, it warms me, pushes at the edges of the ice.

Whence comes this gladness?
Whence, the mad fragment?
Whence, the fractal iota of joy?

I know not,
I know only that it judders and shakes inside me,
singing a nearly silent song,
trembling in the shadows of my soul.
Does it come from the cool breeze on my skin,
which awakens some shiver of memory?
Does it come from the shiver of memory itself,
from the slither of knowing
coiled deep in my fallow, fertile mind?
If Memory slithers, it is a silent, sneaking serpent,
Which craves to remain unfound.
But the slither, I feel it,
I feel the glide of scales,
feel the smooth skin in hints,
feel the questing hiss of the tongue.
Memory is a serpent,
And I seek it in the tall grasses,
watch the grass as it moves against the wind,
evidence of that which I seek.
Is it thence from which comes the spark of gladness?
I think no.
Because it is a false joy.
Think of the madman,
clad in straitjacket and chains,
howling in his padded cell.
He laughs, does he not?
He ululates, and drools, and gibbers.
But through it all, he laughs.

A wild cackle.
A crazed guffaw.
A manic chortle.
Thus am I.
Minute by minute,
Hour by hour,
Day by day,
Week by week,
Month by month,
I sit in this be-damned imprisoning chair,
rickety, ancient, and creaking,
staring at the swaying palms,
suffering the heat, batting at flies.
Scribbling.
Hoping my scribbles will form a net,
which will ensnare that wily serpent:
Memory.
I cast my net wide.
I weave it with strands of madness,
Threads of fiction,
Filaments of truth,
All part of the warp and weft of my tapestry,
Which is my net.
Which is all that I am, all that I have of myself,
whatever sense of self I possess
in this mad, waiting time.
So,
This spark of gladness…

What is it?

It is momentary, at best.

Easily devoured by the cold,

Drowned in the shadows

Which obscure my mind.

I want to cup that spark in my hands,

frame it with my palms,

protect it, nurture it.

Breathe gently upon it,

catalyze the spark into a flame,

Fan the flame into a blaze,

Pour accelerant on the blaze,

Make it a pyre,

A wildfire,

An inferno,

Brighter than the sun, hotter than an African noon,

So bright it sheds light upon me, banishing the shadows,

Illuminating the serpent,

Which is named Memory.

I wish to be free of this place.

Rise from this wheeled chair which is my prison,

Free from the plaster binding my arms and my legs,

Free from the pain in my ribs,

Free from the throbbing emptiness of my knowledge of self,

Free to venture forth,

And find

ME.
Find the ruins of the life I led,
And resurrect them.
Rebuild them.
Or, failing that,
Build anew.

From a handwritten notebook; date unknown

I see us in a million montages.

My pen flies, scratching and scritching and scribbling fast and wild, and I have no control over the words that emerge. I feel them, a pent-up flood. They are dammed inside me, and they must spill out, must find vent—I am a steam engine under too much pressure, and if I do not vent, I will explode.

I feel these words, the images and the sorcery that now trickle down to my pen. They are dark, and they are fraught with tragedy and tears, and they roil uneasily inside me, seeking a path outward.

I cannot stop them, and so I write what I see in my mind—

You and me, Ava, in a million vignettes. Visions of us.

I am trying to weave them into a choate formation, a string of pearls each of which is laden with imagery, and memory, and truth.

A memory, whole and yet incomplete, without context or frame:

A sward of green, the hue so vibrant the eye begs relief from the intensity of it. Beneath us, a quilt—one of the very few childhood possessions which I treasure; this quilt was handmade by my great-grandmother, passed down and passed down and passed down, eventually to me. It is made from squares of flannel, patches from wool shirts, canvas coats, and calico dresses, scraps of rags and tatters of cloth, all pieced together in an abstract pattern, with a white rim around the edges, which family lore claims are the remnants of a sail from a ship a forebear once captained. This quilt upon which we lie is warm from the sun. On it, beside us, an empty bottle of Sangiovese, a closed pocketknife, a slivered remnant from a block of cheese, the butt end of a large summer sausage, and an empty sleeve which once held crackers.

I am on my back, my head pillowed on my backpack, and you are lying beside me, curled up against me, your head on my chest. You have your phone in your hands, the bottom of it resting on my stomach. You are supposed to be studying notes from your literature class in preparation for an upcoming exam, but instead you are scrolling through social media, sniffing out gossip and commenting on it to me, which I only half hear. I am reading from a dog-eared paperback: <u>Out of the Silent Planet</u>, by C.S. Lewis—the second and third books in the trilogy are in my backpack, waiting to be reread for the dozenth time.

We are replete, content, happy. We need not talk, and indeed, we have been lying here, silently, and I have nearly read a third of the book already.

There is a strain of something running between us, a tension, a tremor of awareness: it is revealed in the way your hands, holding the phone, slowly creep toward my belt line, and in the way my hand, once resting easily on your arm, now slides to cup your side and hip to begin slow affectionate circles on your backside.

We allow the tremor to grow, allow the tension room to breathe, space to grow. We are in no hurry to let that spark grow into flame; we know it will, and soon, and we enjoy the buildup as much as we do the event of mutual release.

Another memory:

You, beneath me, naked; I know your body intimately, every inch of it.

You have a spray of freckles on the round of your left shoulder. A thin white line on your right hip, a scar from scaling a chain-link fence in pursuit of your sister. Another spray of freckles on the right globe of your ass—these are a favorite of mine. Afterward, in the delicate silent postcoital glow, you sometimes lie on your stomach, head pillowed on crossed arms, dozing, and I trace patterns between the freckles on your buttock, as if I am creating new charts in the stars. You have dimples in the sides of each butt cheek. Fine hairs on your forearm, which you bemoan but which I find adorable. A mole on your back, low, on the right side. A single freckle on your right breast, on the inside, where your breast just begins to curve around underneath—I often lick and kiss this freckle on my way to your nipple, and you always gasp when I do so, in anticipation of my lips suckling around the erected, sensitive flesh.

You are beneath me. You stare up at me. You gaze, lovingly, into my eyes, and you do not look away as you come apart. I see this moment, over and over and over again, the way your eyes widen even as your brows lower, and your mouth falls open, and your eyes betray your burgeoning ecstasy. Your legs are wrapped around my back, just above my tailbone, toes hooked around ankle. Your hands slide up my spine, furrow into my hair, and then claw downward once again as a silent scream shivers your mouth.

You whisper something, as the shudders rack you—

The words you whisper are lost to me.

I want those words—they mean everything.

What is it you whisper in the moment of our most intimate completion?

My name, surely.

Yet, I cannot hear you. My face is buried between your breasts and my chest heaves and my hips crash into yours and your name soars freely off of my lips, drowning out the syllables, which you whisper in the moment of your release.

What is it you whisper, Ava?

Please, tell me. Whisper those sounds to me again, even just once, I beg you.

Come for me, and come with me: I will hear those sweet, dulcet syllables blooming from your lips and I will know myself, and I will know I am home.

Conakry, Guinea, Africa; date unknown

Dr. James sits beside me, one ankle crossed over his knee. I have been writing, lost in the flow of words, conscious of his presence but ignoring him. Now, he clears his throat, and then speaks.

"It would not do, I think, to become obsessed with this writing, my friend. You must not force it."

I shake my head. "You don't understand."

"What is it I do not understand?"

"It's there. It's there, all of it. I just...I can't reach it. I can't grasp it."

"It will come," Dr. James says, his voice deep and calm and reassuring, his accent adding an exotic lilt to his words. "It will come to you, I tell you."

I shake my head again. "No, no. You don't get it. You don't get it." I look up at him, twirling the pen between my fingers in an idle gesture of pensive energy. "There's…there's something there, just beneath the surface. Something happened, Dr. James." I'm whispering, now. "I feel it. Something happened. Something bad… very bad."

Dr. James rises slowly to his feet, with a soft grunt of exertion. "Well, I will leave you to it, then. But remember that I am here to help you. If you need to talk, remember that I am here. Okay?"

I nod. "Okay. Thanks."

And then Dr. James is gone, and I return to writing:

from a handwritten journal; date unknown

Two sounds rule our world: the intermittent beep of the heart monitor, and the rush-hiss of the oxygen machine.

Henry's hospital room is dark. There is no clock, but inside me there is the vague ominous weight that one only feels at three in the morning. We know this hour, and we know it well: we have sat like this, awake, at three in the morning for…too long. We are intimately familiar with how three in the morning feels.

You sleep fitfully in a hospital chair, your brows

furrowed. There is no need to wake you; you've slept little enough in the past weeks.

There is a window behind me, blinds levered closed, curtains drawn. The heart rate monitor casts a dull glow, the lines blipping up, falling, blipping up, and falling in even intervals—intervals that are too slow. I know the number that should appear on the screen, and the number that IS there...it is far too small. The oxygen machine, on the wall beside the crib, is a green accordion within a transparent cylinder, and the green accordion squeezes downward, whooshing, and rises upward, hissing. It does this steadily.

Clear tubes run from the machine and into the crib. They loop and twist and tangle, and lead, at last, to the small still form within the crib.

There is a hook above the crib, and from it hang two bags of clear liquid, one nearly empty, the other half-depleted; one is saline, for hydration, and the other contains high-dose painkillers.

Palliative care. That is what those drugs mean. Dull the pain into manageable submission, until the end arrives.

Two more clear tubes lead from those bags, into a rectangular machine with orange numeral readouts, and then emerge once again, looping and tangling into the crib, to an arm, a tiny, frail, stick-thin arm, the needles hidden and held in place by tape and gauze.

I sit in a hard recliner made from institutional faux

leather, and I stare at the crib.

At the form inside it.

The body.

The patient.

The child.

My child.

My son.

Henry.

The doctors—oncologists, the experts in this gruesome waiting game—have finally uttered the words we have expected for weeks: "You should probably begin saying your goodbyes. It won't be long now."

These words and phrases are meant to lessen the awful meaning behind them, beneath them:

It will not be long—he is going to die soon; say your goodbyes—whisper words of love and farewell to your child…whisper them to the small, unconscious, unmoving form…whisper them, and wonder if he can hear you.

The beeping of the heart rate monitor pauses. A long, baleful, vicious silence…and then it resumes, but more slowly.

His chest rises and falls, but barely. And so, so slowly. So shallowly.

Is this it? The crushing burden on my chest tells me it is.

You are in the other recliner, curled up, knees drawn, brows furrowed in fitful sleep. I have to wake you up.

I draw a shuddering breath, let it out slowly, and it

emerges as a half-muffled sob. I touch your shoulder, just two fingers barely brushing you, and you jerk awake. Blink up at me. You see the torment on my face, and you lurch to your feet, stumble to the crib. Glance at the monitor, at the slowing numbers, the growing space between beeps.

The sob that escapes you, then, is the single most heartbreaking sound I have ever heard, and hope to never hear again.

"Henry, no…please, no." You sag against the hospital crib, shoulders shaking.

I crowd against you, my arm around your waist, holding you up. I thought I had wept all my tears already, but it seems I have not. They fall, but silently. My eyes sting and my nose runs and my chest aches so badly it feels as if an anvil is crushing me. My stomach clenches. My heart pounds. My mind is absent of all thoughts except a silent scream of agony.

The beeping slows yet further.

You reach into the crib, take his tiny, limp hand in yours. I cover both of your hands with mine.

Moments pass, heavy, each passing second crashing upon us like two-ton stones.

BEEP… … … BEEP… … … BEEP… … … BEEP… … …

"It's okay, baby. You can go now," you whisper, your voice ragged, hoarse, shattering. "Mommy—Mommy and Daddy love you. I love you. It's okay, baby."

Those words break me.

And then, and then…

Henry's chest lifts, pauses…falls. And does not lift again.

The monitor beeps once, and then intones the flatline.

Normally, there would be a flurry of activity, the rush to resuscitate.

There is no rush. No hurricane of nurses, no paddles.

We are left alone in our fractured, ruined silence, alone in our sorrow.

You sag against me, and I have to lift you and carry you to the chair.

Someone comes in on silent feet, pushes a button to cease the tone of the monitor, and they vanish again.

We can only sob.

I soak your hair with my tears.

How much time passes, I know not. After a time, you rise up on shaky knees, and creep over to the crib, as if to not disturb him, as if he is only sleeping. You bend over the crib, lean in on tiptoes, and press a shuddering-lipped kiss to his forehead, and then collapse to the floor.

I kiss him as well.

His flesh is already cooling, dispelling the notion that he is merely asleep.

He is gone.

Frame it as it is: Henry is dead.

My son is dead.

I want to scream, but cannot. Want to weep, but cannot weep any harder than I already am.

If you slice open your finger with a very sharp knife, after the initial slice of pain, there is a brief pause of numbness, before the blood begins to well up and run free, and then the true throbbing fiery ache begins.

This moment, after the initial racking stab of agony, is that pause before the ache and the blood begin.

Soon, the real sorrow will take over.

I do not know if I will survive it.

I do not know if you will survive it.

If WE will survive it.

How can we?

Dear god.

I sit on the veranda of the hospital, the late afternoon sun beating hot on my face through the screen, notebook and pen on my lap, and I cry.

Those words, that story about Henry... just poured out of me. In the moment, in the grip of the flow of words, it was as if I was writing a story about something that happened to someone else, but I know...I *know* in my bones and in my blood that it happened to me.

I had a son, and he died.

I scream, then. A bellowing wail of raw, shattered agony as I feel that sorrow all over again. I scream, and

I scream, and I scream, and I throw the notebook across the room. It flaps and flutters, white pages rustling like the wings of a dove, and lands on the floor. My cramped, all-caps scrawl in blue ink neatly follows the red lines across the page, upside down. I throw the pen, too, and it thumps silently against the screen of a window. I want to break something, as I am so freshly broken, but there is nothing to break, and so I scream again.

A nurse arrives, a short, rotund woman with inky black skin and white teeth and worried brown eyes. She coos at me, trying to calm me. I have no idea what she's saying as she speaks in a complex mixture of Susu, French, a few words of English, and Malinké. The words don't matter; her tone communicates worry and compassion, and then a query.

I am incoherent. Shouting—*No! No! No! Henry!*—screaming. Sobbing. Shaking my head and clutching at my hair, yanking at it until strands rip free.

She grasps at my hands, trying to stop my barrage of self-harm, and then she shouts something, calling for help most likely, and another nurse arrives with a syringe.

I am mad. Utterly mad.

A sharp poke, and I blink, and my screams and shouts fade.

Darkness snatches at me, reaching up from the shadows beneath my wheelchair to tug me down, down, down. I hear voices, Susu words, Malinké phrases, French. Then…nothing.

I don't fight it.

When I awaken, I am in my cot. I hear a rustle, a flap of paper, and a deep cough, a snort. I roll my head, still dizzy and foggy and drowsy and weak.

Dr. James sits in a chair nearby. He is tall, thick of shoulder and burgeoning at the middle. He has enormous hands, the palms slightly pinker than the rest of his dark skin. His eyes are brown, and kind. He wears spectacles—and I say spectacles because they are very old, deserving the anachronistic term, thin gold wire frames with thick lenses that distort my view of his eyes. He is wearing chocolate brown slacks and a pale blue, short sleeve, button-down shirt with pens in the breast pocket, and a stethoscope casually forgotten around his neck.

He is reading my notebook.

I am angry at this, at seeing my writing in his hands. That is my soul, my very heart, the naked essence of me. I am exploring myself in those pages, and it feels like a violation to see someone else reading it.

He notices I am awake, and peels off his spectacles, a sideways tearing motion, turning his head the opposite direction as he pulls them free, then folds them and puts them in his breast pocket, next to the pens, one arm hooked over the pocket.

He lifts the notebook. "My apologies. I only read this to know why would you cause such a scene. Such strong emotion from you…it is most unusual." He speaks with a thick, lilting accent, and his voice is deep, with a mellifluous timbre.

I roll my head away, resume staring at the ceiling—his words require no response from me, and I am still nursing anger at him for the invasion of my privacy.

"You remembered something, I think? Something most full of sorrow."

"Yes." I jerk my chin at him, intending the gesture to mean the notebook. "You read it."

"I only look quickly here and there to determine the nature of the writings. Until I come to the most recent entry." He pauses, leaning forward to rest his elbows on his knees, fingertips steepled together, touching his lips. "Would you tell me what you remembered?"

I shake my head. "You read it, damn you. Don't make me talk about it."

He nods, a slow bobbing of his head, shaggy graying hair glinting in the dusky golden afternoon glow. "Yes, very well. Perhaps it would be too much." He leans back again, perusing the final entry once more. "This is a true memory? We have spoken sometimes about not knowing for certain if you remember truly or if you invent memories."

I sigh. "It's real."

"You are certain?"

"Yes it's fucking real! Why would I freak out like that if it weren't real, if I didn't feel how real it is? I had a son, and he died of brain cancer."

"And your name? Your past?"

I shake my head. "Nothing but that." I reach out my hand, and he gives me the notebook. "I think it'll come, though. I remember so much about...about *her*, Ava. About us. I remember so much about us." My words come slowly. "I'll remember. I feel it all, it's in there—" I tap the top of my head with the corner of the notebook, "I just have to get it out."

Dr. James is quiet a while. "I am so sorry you have endured such a great loss," he says. "But I am also glad you have remembered. Strong memories will bring with them many smaller ones, I think."

"What if—what if there's something I don't want to remember?"

Dr. James sighs deeply. "You cannot fight it. You can only accept it, and let it be. You are very strong, very resilient. You will be good as new before you know it." He pats his knees with his hands twice, and then pushes himself to his feet. "Well. Get some rest. It will do you good."

And then Dr. James quietly walks away, leaving me to my thoughts.

Which I'm not sure is a good thing. I don't know if I want to be left alone with my thoughts. With the memories of Henry that are now, as the doctor predicted, bubbling up, one by one.

I write them. Sniffling, throat raw from screaming, scalp aching, fingers cramped, I write the memories as they come:

from a handwritten journal; date unknown

Ava, rounded belly leading, climbing laboriously into bed beside me, clad in a voluminous nightgown which is too big around the shoulders and arms, tight around the belly, and loose around her thighs. She would breathe heavily for a few moments after getting in bed. I loved the way she would curse and complain about being pregnant one moment, and then rub her belly with her hands and coo lovingly the next.

Ava giving birth is something I will never forget it; it was one of the most important moments of my life. I remember her hunching forward, hands gripping the bed railings in a white-knuckle grip, teeth gritted, snarling rather than screaming, and then collapsing back against the pillows, gasping, sweating, hair smeared against her forehead. Breathing, just breathing, until the next contraction came, and then she'd lean forward again, growling past bared teeth, vulpine, lupine. I would slowly count to ten as she bore down, and on ten she would stop, fall backward, gasping.

Finally, the wet, bloody, effluvia-smeared wiggling form slipping out of her, and I wept and laughed at the sight of such a miracle. The doctor placed our baby on Ava's chest, still messy, and Ava laughed and wept and called him precious: "hello my love, yes, hello; hi there! Welcome to Life, little one."

The bustle of activity as he was cleaned and weighed and measured under the heat lamp, and then he was diapered and swaddled in a blue and white blanket, and handed to Ava, who cradled him to her breast, which he latched onto immediately and began suckling hungrily, nuzzling and crying and quieting as he found her nipple.

Then followed all the sleepless nights at home, the vile, yellowish, seedy diapers at four a.m., handing him to Ava to feed, her on her side and him cuddled up against her ribs, one hand resting possessively on the outside of her breast, long little fingernails scratching now and then. Bringing him over to the crib, his tiny warmth resting on my shoulder, patting his back gently until he burped. Rocking and bouncing him to sleep, and ever so gently snugging him, all swaddled with his little hat on, in his bed.

Then, amazingly, he began to crawl, wobbly at first, and then there was no stopping him.

His joyful babble as he lay on his back on a play mat, batting at the large, colorful plastic shapes dangling over his face.

He was so sweet. So perfect. So joyful, except when he was hungry, or had messed in his pants.

The moment I saw him, the very instant he emerged from Ava's womb, I knew he was the most important thing that could ever happen me. He became, in that instant, my reason, my purpose, my life.

Ava's, too.

He was our everything.

From Ava's handwritten journal;
November 16, 2016

It's four in the morning. There's a storm raging outside, and it has been raging for so long that I've lost track of the hours. I thought for sure it was a hurricane, the kind of thing that slammed Ft. Lauderdale and nearly killed me—the thought of going through another hurricane actually caused me to have a minor panic attack.

Dominic only laughed at me. "This is just a little squall. Nothin' to be scared of."

It doesn't feel like a little squall, it feels like a damn hurricane. The boat is getting tossed around like a toy in a bathtub, rocketing down the side of one massive wave only to course up another. We twist and tilt this way and that, and my heart is pounding in my chest fit to burst. If I close my eyes, I'm back in the bathtub all over again, trapped in by rubble, hearing the storm howl like a maddened god. I don't close my eyes.

I don't dare.

I haven't slept in I don't know how long.

I've watched every movie on the boat, one after the other, on the tiny, aged TV in the common room of the boat—I don't know the terminology of boats, but I'm sure there's a nautical term for it. I watched all those movies, and then tried to read to distract myself, and then I tried cooking—I've baked three batches of cookies, made a giant pot of stew, and another pot of soup. The men are working through the storm, taking turns to catch sleep, and the ones on shift make frequent trips to the galley to wolf down bowls of soup or stew, and to shove cookies into their mouths chased by gulps of coffee—the coffee pot on this boat is never, ever empty, which is the first thing I learned when I came aboard.

And now, it's four in the morning and I'm scared and bored at the same time, which is a bizarre mixture of emotions.

So, I'm journaling.

I don't want to. I feel a million thoughts and feelings simmering just below the surface, things I've put off, buried, bottled up.

I want them to stay there, repressed down deep.

I don't want to deal with them.

I don't want to think about them.

I don't want to let them out.

But yet, here I am, in my quarters, sitting cross-legged on my hard little cot, a blanket around my shoulders and another across my lap, with my notebook on my thigh and a thermos of green tea nearby.

Fuck.

Fine.

Here it goes.

I'm going to write down five letters, which I have not written nor thought nor spoken—through constant and intentional avoidance—for many, many months.

H E N R Y.

Fuck. Fuck.

I'm fighting sobs as I sit here, staring at those letters, struggling to see the page through tears.

I haven't allowed myself to think about him almost at all in the nineteen months and thirteen days that have passed since his death.

Weird—I didn't have to stop and think, stop and count, I just knew, instinctively, exactly how many months and days it has been since Henry died. He was admitted to the pediatric oncology ward on Valentine's Day, twenty-one months ago.

We buried him nineteen months and eleven days ago.

I couldn't think about him.

I still can't.

Just writing those five letters of his name has taken everything I have. My pen is shaking in my hand. My lips are pressed tightly together. I'm breathing hard—my lungs refuse to inflate all the way. My eyes burn. Sting. They're hot. The page is blurry.

I haven't allowed myself to really cry in…God, I don't know how long. I cried—I sobbed, shattered, utterly broken—the day he died. A few tears trickled down my cheeks now and then, in the days that followed—slow, dripping, single tears. Like a leaky faucet—DRIP… DRIP…DRIP. I couldn't cry, though. Not really. After that initial shattering, I couldn't really cry anymore.

Why?

I'm not sure. I haven't cried since then.

Wait—no. That's not true: I cried when I discovered Christian had left.

Have I coped? Have I grieved? Have I mourned?

I don't know.

I saw a therapist—I saw two, actually. The first was Craig, who ended up referring me to a female therapist who actually was able to get me to open up a little, in a way Craig never could. Because with Craig, I only saw him as a man, a MALE, rather than someone to whom I could trust my innermost turmoil. I told him I needed a different counselor, and he referred me to a colleague. I liked her immediately upon our first appointment, and she really did help me to come to terms with the tragic loss of Henry, to some degree at least.

Craig called me a few weeks later to ask me to go out on a date with him.

And then there was a second date, and a third, and a fourth. On the fourth date, something happened: he kissed me...and I liked it. A lot. I was so needy, so vulnerable, and so lonely. So angry, so consumed by—I don't even know what. A million burning emotions, and when Craig kissed me, they all exploded, the sweet relief of physical touch—something I craved, something I needed—something that was consuming me. I never even stopped to think. I just—I ACTED. I let myself have it. Christian had abandoned me, and I was alone and needed comfort. So I took it.

Craig got me naked, and I got him naked, and we were kissing and he was touching me, and I was touching him. It felt GOOD. I liked it. But it wasn't...it just wasn't RIGHT. He wasn't Christian. He didn't feel right, didn't sound right. Didn't touch me the right way. There was nothing wrong with the way Craig kissed or touched me or sounded or felt, it was just...WRONG. I don't know how else to put it.

So I stopped it.

I cried when he left.

And I think that was the last time I truly cried.

Why am I thinking about this, using journal space on it? Maybe because that moment with Craig showed me that I NEEDED Christian. That even when I try to move on, I can't.

When was the last time I thought about Henry? I don't even know. Part of me feels horrible about that... like I've betrayed him, as if by refusing to even think his name, or call his sweet little face into my mind's eye, that I've forgotten him—

As if I COULD forget him.

I just...I think I instinctively knew that if I let myself think about him, I'd start crying and I'd never stop. There'd be no end to the sorrow that would emerge from me. It would just...devour me. Consume me. Drown me.

Even now, I'm afraid of that.

I'm afraid of thinking about Henry too much, because I'm afraid I'll start crying and never stop.

My hand is cramping, I'm exhausted, and the storm is finally starting to die out a little. Which means, maybe, I'll be able to sleep.

It's worth a shot.

I don't know how long I slept. I haven't even really gotten up yet, haven't checked my phone, haven't looked outside, haven't even left my bed, yet. It feels like I slept a long time, though. I've got that groggy, disoriented, sluggish feeling you get after sleeping for something like eighteen or twenty hours, you know?

I woke up sobbing again.

I dreamed of Henry again.

I saw him. I felt him. I smelled him. He'd be a little over three by now, but in the dream he was alive, and he'd never died, and he was just as I want to remember him, as he was before he started showing signs of being sick—a sweet, happy, warm, joyful little bundle of perfection. Those blue eyes, so bright. His little hands, chubby and reaching for everything, grabbing onto everything. His cheeks and chin, so much like Christian's. His hair, dark like mine.

He was *real*. He was alive, in my arms, and it was pure joy, for those few moments.

And that's when I woke up—with the realization that it was just a dream crashing through me, the knowledge that Henry was gone.

How long did I sob, before I got it under control? I don't know. Too long, and not long enough. I had to force myself to stop. Had to growl at myself to be quiet, had to clamp my teeth down on the sobs, had to wipe the tears away and sniff the snot away and blink and breathe until I could pretend like I'm in control.

But I'm not in control.

At all.

I think it's a good thing this is a dry boat—meaning there's no alcohol on board. Not a drop. Dominic says it ensures the crew is always in control and sober and ready for anything, and it makes putting into port and getting free time all the better for everyone. If there were alcohol on this boat, I'd be drinking it right now. I'd probably be drinking it all the time. Every moment.

Which…is a problem.

There's a period of time I genuinely just don't re-member—the weeks after I finally forced myself to start eating again, forced myself to leave the bed. Which I think I only did because I realized I couldn't will myself to just die.

That's what I wanted, I think: to die.

To just…stop being alive, so I could be with Henry, and so I could escape the pain.

When I finally realized I wasn't going to die, I started eating…and started drinking.

Christian and I both hit the bottle pretty hard, during that period.

It was the only thing that could numb the pain.

I still worry I'll use that coping mechanism even still. But, I haven't allowed myself to drink, not since the hurricane.

Up until then I'd been drinking myself to sleep every single night. Was it low-key alcoholism, maybe? I don't know. Self-medication, certainly.

Where am I going with all this?

I don't know. Nowhere. I don't have a point. I don't have anything specific I'm trying to say, this time.

It's all a mess inside my head. Even with all I've writ-ten so far, it's just the tiniest little scratch on the surface.

It's like being a diver free-swimming with fins and a tank and a wet suit, swimming down and down to the limits of human endurance, which is the nothing at all, not in comparison to the true depths of the ocean.

That's me.

That's what's within me.

What I've dredged up so far is just a tiny sliver, and lurking beneath it all is a Marianas Trench of heartache and sorrow and anger and guilt.

It's easier to pretend it's not there, to just go through the motions of being alive. On board this boat, it's far too easy. But I can't do that.

I just cannot allow myself to do that any longer.

Because really, that's what I've been doing so far, isn't it? Hiding? Running? Pretending?

How much longer can I do it? It's festering inside me. Rotting. Fermenting.

I can't go through the motions anymore.

I can't keep burying and repressing and hiding and running and bottling.

I am in flux—in life, and as a person:

Who was I? Who am I now? Who will I be? Who do I WANT to be?

I hear Dominic outside my cabin. He's knocking, telling me the storm has passed and they need me to put together more food—the stew and the soup and the cookies are all gone.

I'm needed.

There's that, at least.

Conakry, Guinea, Africa; date unknown

All of my writing, so far, has been about me, or Ava, or Henry. About us, about my life— events, memories, and images; vignettes of my life, remembered without context. Today, however, I feel like I need…a break. A brief respite from constantly thinking about myself and Ava and everything.

And so, I'm going to write something different. What it means, I don't know. What relevance it has, I don't know. I just know that there's significance to what pours out of me, this time. I feel it inside me, this story. Words. Ideas, images, themes. Not directly about me, but still about me in some indirect way.

I don't know.

So I let it out. Let it emerge.

Sitting in my usual place on the veranda, in my chair, notebook balanced on my knees, I write:

From a handwritten notebook; date unknown

THE LIGHTHOUSE AT THE END OF THE WORLD

It is a barren, windswept island. A few scrub pines grow on it here and there, some tall, sharp-bladed grass. The entirety of the island is hilly, rising and falling, curving around and carving in, full of divots and caves and hidden folds in the granite. It looks and feels like what it is—an outcropping of rock protruding from the angry, wine-dark sea.

It is a place of importance to sailors; it marks a channel, alerting ships to the presence of nearby rocks. There is a lighthouse upon it. A residence. A barn. An acre or so of grass fenced in for a cow and her calf and a few goats. Some chickens cluck in scattered clumps around the house, and a path of uneven stone flags mark the way from the residence to the lighthouse. A small fenced-off garden grows behind the house with vegetables growing in neat rows.

The sky above is almost always clear blue, except when storms blow in, and when those storms come, they rage with all the fury of the gods.

Connor Yates is the lighthouse keeper. He is a sullen, terse, unhappy man. Prone to bouts of heavy drinking—there was a war, and the memories of it haunt him, driving him to drink in an attempt to drown them out. It doesn't work, and he will give up the bottle for a time, only to go right back to it when the nightmares and waking moments of memory become too strong.

He has been alone on the island, tending the lighthouse, for too long—years. So long he has forgotten how to speak, he sometimes thinks. The shipping company which owns the lighthouse sends a ship twice a year, laden with supplies—haunches of dried beef, sacks of potatoes, canned fruits and vegetables, bags of corn and flour and sugar, pouches of smoking tobacco, cases of whiskey, months' and months' worth of newspapers bundled together in heavy squares and tied with twine, books, casks of ale, sides of mutton, tins of coffee and tea, bales of hay, barrels of oats and grain and seed for the animals, bullets for his rifle and pistol which he only uses for target practice as a means of passing the long boring hours, a myriad of other sundries necessary to support a man alone on an island in the middle of the ocean.

Connor is lonely, but mostly content in his solitude.

The solitude is the only balm he has found for the ragged wounds to his soul; he came away from the war unwounded in body, and this too is a source of unending guilt for him. He likes the isolation—when he wakes screaming from a nightmare, there is no one he will awaken or frighten, no one to ask him what's wrong, no one to try and wake him and perhaps be accidentally wounded, for he can become quite violent when roused from a nightmare. Which, long ago, is something Connor discovered the unhappy way, and is the reason for his self-imposed exile to this distant, desolate place: he doesn't trust himself around other people.

For all of its desolation, for all that it is far, far from anything like humanity, it is a beautiful place, wild and brutally lovely. Connor can see hundreds of miles in every direction from the tiny rim of a balcony encircling the glass of the lighthouse, which is a hundred feet tall and built upon the very highest promontory of rock on the island, another two hundred feet above sea level.

Connor finds the greatest peace—the only peace—standing on that narrow, ledge gripping the brass railing and staring out at the rippling marble field of the sea, veined with streaks of silver and jade and azure, twinkling with diamond glints on sunny days and hard and leaden on gray, stormy days. He stands facing east to watch the dawn, and returns at sundown to face west, watching the sun drown itself beneath the horizon. He is capable of standing there, forearms on the brass tube of the railing with the wind in his beard, for hours on end. The wind is always blowing, up there, hard enough to howl past his ears, hard enough to sometimes require him to grip the railing to keep from being blown off balance.

Sometimes, he thinks he could bound up onto the railing, crouch there a moment, then spread his arms like wings, leap into the sky and catch the wind and be carried away. Sometimes, he has gone so far as to grip the railing and tense his legs and prepare to leap, but then he remembers the ships, and that without him, the light would go out and the ships would crash, and more lives would be laid at his feet. More blood would coat his hands. And he then forces his hands to unclench and forces himself to relax against the rail and watch the sun, to close his eyes and feel the wind in his hair.

Time is a fickle mistress. The days and weeks and months pass unevenly. Sometimes an entire month will pass and he'll only realize it with a start, and wonder where the time went, and then he will think surely half a year has passed already, and he'll consult the calendar affixed to the wall in the kitchen, and realize only a week has passed. Time plays the same game on him with hours and minutes. Units of time are interchangeable, to Connor, in some ways.

The only way he has of marking the passage of time at all, really, is the arrival of the ship with his supplies in spring and fall, reminding him of the existence of the world beyond his little island.

The ship, in the years Connor has lived on the island tending the lighthouse, has always been captained by the same man—Elijah McKenna, a hard, swarthy man with a black beard long since gone mostly silver, skin like old

leather, eyes like chips of granite, a man almost as tersely uncommunicative as Connor himself. Elijah pilots the
lighter from the ship to the tiny dock himself, and helps
Connor unload the supplies and then helps him haul
them up to the residence. Once the work is done, the
men will tamp their pipes and tipple some whiskey and
sit and smoke on the porch of the residence, and Connor
might remark on recent storms, and Elijah might remark
on events from wider world, but on the whole, both men
are content to sit and smoke and drink. They may play
cards, or they may pass back and forth the pages of the
most recent newspaper—many weeks and months old
by this time, usually. Elijah is the only person Connor
has had any contact with at all in at least three years; if
there is anyone in the whole world whom Connor might
call a friend, it would be Elijah.

Then, one spring, the ship arrives, and the lighter
scuds up against the dock. Connor is there to accept
the line and tie it off; he does so slowly, his movements
listless and fumbling. His attention is not on the rope,
nor the pylon to which he is tying it, but on the lighter.
Instead of Elijah—stout and leathery and solid and silent, clad as always in faded dungarees and a thick wool
sweater and heavy boots and an old slouch cap—there
are two people; neither of them is Elijah.

One is a man on the older side of middle age, but
trim and tough looking, with broad shoulders and fierce
eyes, smartly dressed in a suit, with an unmistakable

air of a man used to command. The other is a woman. Young. Soft. Hesitant of movement as she climbs out of the lighter onto the dock, but with confidence in her gaze, which lands on Connor and remains there, unwavering, openly curious; she is more than just pretty, or lovely; she is, truly, the most beautiful woman Connor has ever seen, and he knew many women before the war, when he was an eager young man in a sharp uniform, when the world held only possibility. She is fair of skin—her skin looks to him like cream just before it is poured into a mug of coffee. Her hair is dark, twisted into an effortlessly elegant knot behind her head. Her dress is pale green, accentuating her creamy skin and dark hair. It is not the gown of a high-born lady, but a sturdy, sensible thing, allowing her easy movement. But yet, for all that, she carries herself with an air of elegance and sophistication, which makes Connor feel uneasy and dirty and hesitant.

Once both the man and the woman—obviously his daughter, for they have the same eyes and a similar cast of feature and similar bearing—have climbed from ship's boat to the dock, Connor only stands there, staring, silent.

"Well?" the man says, his tone hard and impatient. "Best get the supplies unloaded. I'm Captain Robert Kinross, and this is my daughter, Tess. You are Connor Yates?"

Connor only grunts an affirmative, at first, then

remembers his manners in the presence of a lady. "I mean, yeah. Yes. I'm Connor." He reaches down into the lighter and hauls out a bag of potatoes, one in each hand. "Where's Elijah?"

Captain Kinross checks his pocket watch, and offers no assistance. "He took ill a few months ago. He is retired, now."

"Took ill?"

"Something to do with his heart."

"Oh." Connor stacks bags of wheat and corn. "Good man."

This is more than he's spoken all at once since the previous fall, and his voice feels rusty, the use of words an unfamiliar taste in his mouth.

The lighter is full of supplies, sagging low in the water, and even with Elijah helping it usually took the two of them half a day to unload and haul all the supplies up the island to the residence; if Captain Kinross is disinclined to help, it will take Connor the entire day and then some.

Still, he says nothing of this, only moves with slow and methodical and tireless economy, stacking all the goods on the dock and taking inventory as he does so; Captain Kinross has withdrawn a small notebook from his breast pocket and is taking notes of some kind, and Tess has found a seat on a bag of potatoes. She too has a book in hand, but hers is larger, a sketchbook, and she is busily sketching the scene. As he works, Connor takes note of her sketches—she is very good. She draws the growing stack of goods, the house up on the hill, the lighthouse high up on its perch. She draws the lighter, rocking emptily now against the dock. The ship away in the distance, sails reefed, masts and spars thin dark lines against the pale blue sky.

She even draws him. In the sketch, he is turned partially away from her with a barrel of whiskey on his shoulder and a sack of nails in his other hand. She captures in a few quick strokes the line of his jaw and the scruff of his unkempt beard, the breadth of his shoulders and the dark hollows of his deep-set eyes.

She notices his attention, and turns the book so he can see the sketch properly. "It isn't a very wonderful likeness, of course, only a hastily done sketch." She shrugs modestly. "I could do a proper portrait, if you like."

Connor only stares, unsure of a response.

"No time for that, I'm afraid," Captain Kinross says, not looking up from his writing. "We must be away soon. Time and tide wait for no man."

"But Papa, we've only just arrived," Tess says. "I should like even a short break from the ship, and besides, I want to see the lighthouse. Could Mr. Yates show me, once the supplies are in?"

"We really must be away, soon, Tess."

"Then why don't you help poor Mr. Yates with the supplies? It would be done in half the time, wouldn't it?"

Captain Kinross's eyes narrow over the top of his

notebook, and then flick from Connor to Tess and back. And then, moving slowly and reluctantly, he pockets his notebook and the stub of pencil, and begins helping Connor.

Together, the work progresses apace, and soon the supplies are stacked on the dock. Connor has been doing this long enough to have a system in place: he always unloads the items from the lighter first, and in so doing takes inventory of the incoming supplies, and compares it against the inventory of what he currently has in stock on the island—this running tally is kept in a small thick ledger wedged in his back pocket, which he hauls out and consults now and again, marking a note on this item or that, making sure nothing has been forgotten. When he is sure all the supplies brought in match his needs, he writes down on a separate sheet of paper the items he will need on the next ship in, and how much.

The first trip up the stairs from dock to residence, Tess follows the men up and makes herself at home on the porch. She takes a seat in a rocking chair and immediately opens her sketchbook and sets to work sketching the new vista—the island beneath them, the dock and the lighter, the stairs, the ship like a toy in the distance.

Several hours and many trips later, the supplies are all in and put away. Connor isn't winded at all and is barely damp with sweat, but Captain Kinross is huffing and dripping, and it is he who suggests, now the work is done, that a brief respite and refreshments would not go amiss.

And so Connor finds himself clumsily attempting to make sandwiches and coffee. He has made rather a mess of the sandwiches and the coffee has been percolating and bubbling, and it is just then, as he is beginning to feel flustered and overwhelmed at the unfamiliar task of preparing food for more than merely himself, that Tess appears in the doorway.

"Your coffee is burning, I believe," she remarks.

Connor just grunts—an alternative to the curse he wishes to let loose—and snags the coffee off the top of the wood-burning stove. He burns his fingers, only just managing to not drop the pot, but in so doing knocks the sandwiches to the floor.

Shaking his hand, he snarls a curse, and then blushes with a glance at Tess. "Apologies, ma'am."

Tess only laughs. "Don't be silly. I live onboard a ship, surrounded by sailors. There's nothing you could say that would shock me." She surveys the mess he's made. "Would you like some help, Mr. Yates?"

"Ain't no mister. Just call me Connor," he grumbles. "Guests aren't supposed to see to their own refreshments."

Tess laughs again. "Yes, well, I don't mind." She makes quick work of sweeping and binning the mess on the floor, and then sets to remaking the sandwiches. "I am hungry, and this is work I'm rather more suited to than you, it would seem."

Connor watches as she accomplishes in moments what it took him minutes to do. "Don't get people round here often," he says by way of explanation.

"Twice a year, as Father explains it. From what I understand, you've only had Captain Elijah to visit twice a year for the last several years."

Connor manages a noise of affirmation.

"Don't you get lonely?" Tess asks.

He lifts a shoulder. "Some."

She arranges the sandwiches onto a plate, but doesn't move to carry them out to the porch yet. "I should think I would be dreadfully lonely here, all by myself for months on end."

"Used to it," he murmurs, rinsing out coffee mugs so long unused that they're dirty with dust. "Ain't really much for company anyhow."

She looks at him with an odd light in her eyes. "I don't think I'd mind it here at all, so long as I had one other person to talk to."

He catches something in her voice, some potential for hidden meaning. "Ain't no place for a lady, Miss Kinross. This place barely counts as livable, except for a solitary fella like myself."

"I think I'm rather capable of determining for myself what is and is not livable to me." She smiles at him. "Most would say a ship full of coarse men out on the open sea for months at a time is also no place for a lady, yet such is where I have lived the last ten years of my life."

"Ain't got no kin? Nowhere more decent to live?"

She frowns. "I've a very distant aunt or cousin or some such, living in Suffolk, or somewhere like that. I'd rather be with Papa. I like the sea, and I like the open places. I feel confined and constricted when we visit cities."

He wonders about her mother, but doesn't dare ask. "Last time I was in a city, I damn near stopped breathing 'til I got clear of it. Too many folks and not enough air." He winces, and rubs the back of his neck. "I shouldn't curse. Hard habit to break."

This is more than he's said all at once since the end of the war.

The strange conversation ends then, when Captain Kinross calls out a query regarding refreshments. By the time the coffee has been drunk and the sandwiches eaten, it is dark. Elijah never cared much about having to row back to the ship in the dark, but Captain Kinross is a different sort of man entirely, and to expect a woman to make such a trip is unthinkable. There is one extra bedroom, which Tess takes, and Captain Kinross takes Connor's bed; Connor tries unsuccessfully to sleep on a chair in the sitting room. He knew the moment he closed his eyes that he would suffer from the dreams again, and with company in the house didn't dare risk waking them up with his screams; he abandons all pretense of sleep.

Instead, he puts on a pot of coffee, pours himself a mug, and carries it with him up to the lighthouse.

He settles into his usual place, leaning against the railing, watching the moon arc across the sky.

He hears a noise behind him, but dismisses it as the settling of the building, so unused is he to company. Thus, when a hand alights on his shoulders, he is badly startled, cursing viciously as he whirls and steps away, spilling coffee as he draws a knife from a sheath on his belt, his teeth bared.

Tess, candle in one hand, backs away, frightened. "I'm—I'm sorry, I—I didn't mean to startle you."

Embarrassed, he turns away. "I'm the one to apologize, Miss Kinross. Told you, I ain't much used to havin' folks around."

She tiptoes cautiously onto the balcony, moving slowly, clinging to the railing with her free hand, peering over the edge nervously. "We're very high up."

"Some four hundred feet above the sea, where we're standing. Thereabouts, leastways. Less directly to the ground, though."

"Don't you get frightened? The wind is so strong. I'm afraid it'll just pluck me up and carry me away."

Indeed, the wind is very strong. It whips her hair behind her in a straight black line, and plasters her nightdress against her body. Connor notices this, tries not to stare and is only partially successful.

"Sometimes, I think I could just fly away," Connor

hears himself say. "Just…let the wind take me wherever it is the wind goes."

"If I wasn't so scared of falling, I'd think that was a lovely sentiment indeed." A rough gust of flattering wind pushes at them, and Tess shrieks and shrinks against Connor's side. "Oh, how frightening!"

Connor lets her weight lean against him, keeping a strong grip on the railing with one hand, nursing his coffee in the other. "Forget I said that. The wind ain't gonna hurt you none. Just hold on tight and you'll be fine."

She holds on tight, all right, but to him rather than the railing. "I'd rather you held me, Connor." The words are daring, put out there in the open like that, so boldly.

"You don't know a durn thing about me, Miss Kinross. I ain't fit company for a lady like yourself."

"I'm the daughter of a sailor—I'm no lady. I've spent more time on the deck of a ship than among proper society, and I can read the sea more easily than I can the newspaper." She pulls away, then, straightening her spine and turning to face the sea. "I know myself, Mr. Yates. I know what I want."

"You've been here not even a day. Come winter, the storms have real teeth. And there wouldn't be anyone around, not anyone at all 'cept me. Not for months and months at a time. No way to change your mind once you see how things is."

"I've weathered hurricanes and typhoons, helped fight off brigands, seen men hung, keelhauled, and thrown overboard. We've been becalmed several times, nearly sunk twice, and I once ordered a man flogged for rape when my father was ashore conducting business." She turns to face Connor, then. "I know myself, Mr. Yates."

Connor has no idea how to respond to this, and so he doesn't. Silence breathes between them, and Tess seems content to let the silence be, rather than needing to fill it with chatter, as he'd have expected.

After a while, she turns to Connor again. "Will you walk me back down?"

"O'course."

The walk down the stairs is long, and she seems to push ever closer against his side as they descend, and her hand continually brushes against his. This, for some reason, makes his heart pound worse than the first battle he fought, in the moments before his line rushed the enemy.

Tess pauses at the bottom of the stair, plucking at Connor's sleeve. "Wait a moment, please."

He stops, turns back to face her, the door behind him. "Yes, Miss Kinross?"

She stares up at him. "Call me Tess."

"All right."

"I like you, Connor."

He just blinks at her. "Not rightly sure why, ma'am." He rubs the back of his neck. "I ain't good company."

"You seem like perfectly agreeable company to me."

"The war, you see. It…did things to me, here and

here." He taps his temple, and then his heart. "You saw what happened when you startled me."

"Not all of the men on my father's boat are chosen for their skill as sailors, Connor." There's a subtext to her words, which Connor reads easily. "I'm not afraid of you."

"We just met, Tess."

"I know. But I know myself. And I know what I want."

"What is it you want, then?"

"A quiet life, away from the crowds and the cities. A home near the sea. Solitude, and a good man to keep me company. A child, perhaps, someday."

Connor's collar suddenly feels too tight, and his chest wouldn't expand all the way. "I—Tess, I—"

She just smiles at him. "Think about it, perhaps?" Her hair drifts across her face, hiding a smirk and a burst of soft laughter. "You'll have several months in which to consider the idea, after all."

She's passed him, then, out the door and tiptoeing across the stone flags, her candle guttering in the wind. He watches her lithe, lush form, an uneasy, unfamiliar rush of something sharp and hot and tense filling him at the sight of her body, highlighted by the way the wind blows her nightdress against her curves. She stops at the back door, and the wind shifts, pushing the night-dress against her breasts and between her thighs, and his mouth goes dry and he feels dizzy and the sharp hot

tense feeling intensifies, until he recognizes it as desire
and lust and something deeper, something more.

He has a small cot up at the top of the lighthouse, in
case a storm blows up and he has to doze by the light, to
keep it lit the night through. Here, Connor sleeps, fitfully. He dreams odd dreams, full of desires he thought he'd
forgotten long ago, in his quest for solitude.

Next morning, she is awake before he is and bustling
about the kitchen, preparing a more hearty breakfast
than any he'd had even before he joined the army. She
smiles at him at odd moments, brightening a face already so beautiful it makes Connor's heart ache.

Her father notices, Connor is certain.

When it is time for Captain Kinross and his daughter
to return to the ship, Connor walks them down. Captain
Kinross goes ahead a few steps, and Tess walks in stride
with Connor.

"I had hoped you would take my hand yesterday
night, as we descended the stair," she murmurs to him,
as they walk together. "Or that you would have kissed
me, there at the landing."

"I don't know if I could be so bold," Connor says.
"You're so beautiful, I'd think I was…taking airs above
my station, or somethin' of the like."

"Don't be ridiculous," Tess says. "I don't think THAT
for stations, or airs, or any of that nonsense." On the
emphasized word, she snaps her fingers. "But I do thank
you for your compliment."

Connor walks a few paces more in silence, considering his words carefully, as he always does. "I'm not a clever man, nor an ambitious one, Tess. This is what I've chosen for my lot in life. I don't know that I'd be good company for a woman, nor a child. If you're having me on, then leave off the game. And if you're serious, then you as well have many months to consider if this is really the life you'd like."

She seems to drag words out of him, great floods of words he didn't know he possessed.

Tess just smiles at him, and presses something into his palm, discreetly. "I am not a woman to play games, Connor, be assured of that. And furthermore, I neither need nor want cleverness nor ambition in a man. Only truth, protection, and love. And, perhaps...passion." Here, she gazes up at him, and her eyes are full of innuendo he doesn't miss, which makes his heart pound and his chest feel constricted. "Do you think you could possess those qualities, Mr. Yates?"

"I think—I think I could learn, if a body was patient in the teaching."

They are interrupted, then, by a call from Captain Kinross. "Tess, darling. We must go." To Connor, then. "Mr. Yates. A word."

The men pace away from the dock, out of earshot of Tess, who sits in the lighter. "This is no place for a woman, Mr. Yates, and certainly not my daughter. Nothing said against you, mind, but—"

"I've expressed much the same to Tess myself, Captain. You've a headstrong daughter on your hands, sir."

Captain Kinross laughs good-naturedly. "Indeed I do, Mr. Yates. Indeed I do." He claps the younger man on the shoulder. "Well, we'll be off, now. And if she's still interested when we come back for our fall visit, well...I'm not sure I could stop her if I wanted to, and by all accounts, you're a good man."

"She's a rarely fine woman, Captain. I wouldn't ask her to choose this life...but if she did? Well, sir, I'd consider it a greater honor than a man like me deserves."

Connor watches the ship depart, standing at the rail of his lighthouse. He can't see nearly so far, but his imagination provides for him a vision of Tess, standing at the stern, wind tossing her hair sideways and her dress against her thigh; perhaps, to her, he is a speck near the top of the white spire. He wonders if she will be back.

He hopes, for his sake, that she will be; and for hers, that she won't.

As she'd said, Connor has all the months of spring and summer to wonder. He thinks of the moments spent with her at the top of the lighthouse, and the descent down the stairs, her hand brushing his, and the words they exchanged at the landing. He thinks of the things she'd said on the way down to the dock, that last day, and the way she'd looked up at him. As if a creature so lovely and elegant and wonderful and angelic could look at a man like him and see him with anything like the desire he feels for her.

As such things go, he plays in his mind the few moments they'd shared together over and over again, until each individual second with her is imprinted on his mind like a tintype image. He imagines the things she might say if she returns, and what he would say. Sometimes he chastises himself as a fool, wasting his time on romantic notions which could never see fruition, and sometimes he thinks perhaps she might arrive on the next ship, and he would be there on the dock waiting as the lighter drifted slowly from ship to shore, and she would alight from the vessel and she would be in his arms, and her eyes, so like the color of the Caribbean sea at high bright noon, would fix on his and neither would have to say anything—they would just know.

Time, ever the miscreant, ever the mischievous mistress, plays its usual tricks upon Connor, dragging days out to feel like weeks, and weeks like months, then compacting months into the space of a week, and he finds himself watching the eastern sea for signs of the ship. He finds himself consulting his calendar and marking days off, when he used to barely care for the arrival of the ship at all, except that it meant fresh food and new spirits and the occasional batch of news from beyond his island, and perhaps the silent company of Elijah.

Now, though, he finds himself waiting for the ship with impatience he'd never known before. It bothers him, his impatience. His hope. That hope frightens him—to survive alone in so desolate a place requires a certain numbness, an apathy, a willful lack of concern for the company of others, disdain for what the future might hold.

Until Tess, each day of Connor's future held the same as the day before; now, though, the future holds something else: the unknown. Possibility.

It is a tantalizing thing.

He still spends much of his time at the railing of the lighthouse, watching the sun rise and set. In his hands, he holds the small square of paper she'd handed him upon her departure, now wrinkled and thin from much folding and unfolding. The wind plucks it, trying to snatch it away, but he holds it firmly. On the paper are written a few words in a neat, looping, feminine script:

I SHALL BE A VERY PATIENT TEACHER, MR. YATES.

—TESS

He reads this over and over again, thinking back to that conversation, and hoping that her note means she will return, and that she will want him.

Folded into the square of paper had been a scrap of lace, which smelled of perfume, of woman. He isn't at all sure where the lace had come from, and his imagination plays tantalizing tricks on him, suggesting all kinds of possibilities. It really is just a scrap of lace, a few small inches of fabric that could have come from a handkerchief or a bedspread or the rags of an old dress. But it smells of her, the way he remembered her smelling.

He keeps this piece of lace folded into a scrap of cloth and tucked away in his Bible, a generations-old keepsake handed down from grandfather to grandson. The note he keeps in his pocket, and withdraws to read often.

And so, he waits.

He lives the life he's always lived, there on the remote island, going about his daily chores the way he always has; nothing has changed. But yet…all is changed. She changed things just by existing, by offering even the faintest ray of hope.

No, he tells himself. Don't be absurd. You are a silent, sullen, soldier prone to nightmares, he tells himself. You drink too much. You live on a remote island far from civilization. You have nothing to offer anyone, let alone a vibrant, funny, beautiful woman like Tess Kinross—

She said it herself, though, he argues back: she knows what she wants. And she made rather clear what she wanted—

Unless you were imagining that—

The note referring to our conversation doesn't leave much room for misunderstanding, though—

And so, around and around it goes.

Days, weeks, and months more, stretching and

compacting. The air grows cooler and he harvests his vegetables—he knows from the inventory tally in his ledger that the ship is due soon.

He is in his garden, turning over the soil so it will go fallow for the following spring. His back aches, and his hands are blistered from the rough handle of the hoe. He straightens, stretching his lower back, resting the hoe against his shoulder and rubbing his stinging palms on his trousers.

There, off in the distance, is the ship. Anchored, sails furled. He can almost make out the bustle of activity on the deck, tiny specks hustling to and fro, the shadowy outline of the lighter as it is lowered.

His heart pounds.

Is she on that lighter?

Will eight months of the wide, complex, interesting world beyond this isolated shore have changed her mind?

He turns back to his work, knowing it will be quite some time before the lighter is loaded and longer yet before it can make the trip from ship to shore. He finishes turning over the garden, washes his hands at the well pump, goes inside to change his shirt. Pausing at the mirror by the front door, he examines his reflection—his wild, long, tangled hair, his unkempt beard.

He stumbles hurriedly to the bedroom, finds a comb on the bureau, drags it through his hair and his beard. His reflection, then, is somewhat more presentable—but his shirt is buttoned wrong.

He curses his foolishness, and takes a deep breath. Considers stopping in the kitchen for a slug of whiskey to fortify his nerves, but rejects the idea—Tess would not want to shackle herself to a drunkard.

He is a mass of jangling nerves by the time the lighter arrives, and his heart sinks when only Captain Kinross is in the boat. Tying off the line, Connor begins immediately retrieving supplies, without a word. Captain Kinross helps him, handing up bags and sacks and barrels and crates. Not a word is spoken until the lot is piled on the dock and tallied, and then Kinross ascends to the dock, wipes his forehead with a kerchief, and settles his weight on the top of a barrel.

"You were hoping to see Tess, unless I'm mistaken," Kinross says.

Connor just nods.

"She took ill in the weeks before we departed." Captain Kinross delves a hand in the breast pocket of his suit coat. "A dreadful case of influenza. She would have taken berth for this journey even ill, but I feared for her life, and forbade it."

"She will recover, then?" Connor asks.

"Oh, most certainly. Her anger at me may not, but her health will." Kinross hands Connor an envelope. "She bade me give you this."

"I see." Connor takes the letter, slices it open with his knife then and there, and withdraws the letter.

MY DEAREST CONNOR,

CURSE THIS ILLNESS, AND MY BODY FOR SUCCUMBING! I HAVE MISSED YOU MUCH THESE PAST MONTHS. I HAVE SPENT NEARLY EVERY WAKING MOMENT THINKING OF YOU, AND I LOOK FORWARD MOST EAGERLY TO OUR REUNION. I DO NOT DARE LEAVE SUCH WEIGHTY MATTERS AS OUR FUTURE TO THE VAGARIES OF TIME AND THE CAPRICE OF THE SEA, AND SO I RISK ALL WITH AS MUCH FORWARDNESS AS I POSSESS:

IF YOU SHALL HAVE ME, I WOULD BE YOUR WIFE.

I KNOW WELL THIS IS NOT HOW SUCH MATTERS ARE CUSTOMARILY ARRANGED, BUT I AM FAR TOO IMPATIENT TO WAIT. IF YOU DESIRE THIS UNION, ASK MY FATHER FOR MY HAND WHILE HE IS THERE, AND TELL HIM I HAVE ALREADY AGREED. THEN, I WILL, WHETHER SICK OR HALE, JOIN YOU ON YOUR—NAY, ON <u>OUR</u> ISLAND—AS YOUR WIFE. IF YOU SHOULD AGREE, I WILL BE MRS. CONNOR YATES BY THE COMING SPRING.

WITH ALL OF MY LOVE, AND MORE YET TO COME,

SOON TO BE YOURS,

TESS

Connor reads the letter through a dozen times before the meaning and the import of the contents truly sink into his head and his heart.

"Well?" Captain Kinross grumbles. "What does she say?"

Connor blows out a breath, considering his next words with great care. "She regrets her absence, and curses her illness."

"Is that all?" Kinross's voice betrays doubt, and not a little amusement. "I seem to see more words upon the page than that."

Connor nods, reading it through yet again. "She bids me—" He stops, teeth clicking down on his words. "What I mean to say, sir, is that I humbly beg you for your daughter's hand in marriage."

Kinross is quiet a moment, considering. "Well, I do admit this is not momentously shocking news to me. You were, these past months, nearly all my daughter would speak of."

"Sir, I—"

Kinross interrupts. "Connor—Mr. Yates. Answer me this: is this marriage your idea, or hers?"

Connor just blinks. "Both."

"You told me, last we spoke, that I have a headstrong daughter on my hands. You little know how much so, I fear. I would not want to see her suffer for getting what she thinks she wants, and coming to regret it. Your isolation here is total, for the majority of the year."

Connor nods. "I said so to her myself, back in the spring. I believe I love her, sir, and will love her all the more every day, if I should be so honored as to have her as my wife. I would never begrudge her the chance to change her mind. If she were to ever want to leave, if she grew to hate this place, I would see her gone on the next ship, so she could find her happiness elsewhere. But yet, as long as she willfully desires to be my wife, I will love her and protect her with all that I am." He is nearly panting with exertion, having used so many words all at once, and so properly.

Captain Kinross nods. "I believe you. You have my blessing."

The rest of the visit passes swiftly—without Tess, the men find little to speak of, and so waste little time transferring the various goods to the residence and packing them away. There is a pot of coffee, a little food, less conversation, and then Captain Kinross makes his departure.

Standing on his lighthouse, Connor watches the ship vanish over the horizon. He finds it little coincidence that the ship vanishes from sight at the exact moment of sundown, when the last orange slice of sun sinks under the horizon, and he takes it as a portent of good fortune when the rim of the bright yellow-orange-crimson orb flashes green.

Another moment, and the sun is gone.

Now comes the long, cruel winter. Storms, and

bitter cold. Endless wind, sharper than razors. Deep nights, dull days.

It is, in every way possible, the longest and most lonely winter Connor has ever known.

Eagerness to see Tess consumes him, and stretches the passing of the weeks and months out to unbearable agony. It is worsened by the fact that there could be no letters in the meantime, even if could he find the words to put on paper. He tries, just for practice, but his penmanship is so awful and the few words he did manage so clumsy that he burns the scraps of paper.

The waiting is torture, and with the storms raging so frequently and the cold so brutal, there is little enough for him to do besides sit in the lighthouse and tend the light. He very nearly lives up there, that winter. He has a stockpile of bits of wood of odd shapes and sizes, and he whiles away the time whittling, carving little figures, likenesses of horses and wolves and bison and whales and dogs and roosters, until he has enough to fill a crate.

The storms fade, flowers bloom, and warmth returns.

His inventory tells him the ship is due soon—he's nearly out of coffee, sugar, tobacco, and wheat, which he very carefully rations.

Then, on a sunny but cool evening, he spies the ship cresting the horizon, spurring a freshet of panic in him.

He quells it, with difficulty.

As the lighter approaches, he combs his hair and

beard, changes into fresh clothing; he considers attempting to trim his hair and beard, but decides against it—she claimed a desire to marry him as he is, so why attempt to change himself into something else? If she wants his hair and beard trimmed, perhaps she will do it herself.

He does, however, find himself waiting on the dock, impatiently whittling away at a block of wood, slowly revealing the shape of a flower.

He finishes the flower when the lighter is still only halfway between ship and shore, and so he pulls out a scrap of sandpaper out of his pocket and sets to work smoothing out the edges. He has little enough to offer Tess, and this, at least, is something of his own doing which he can present as a token of his affection.

At long last, the lighter comes to rest against the dock. Within the lighter, aside from the supplies, are Captain Kinross, Tess, a black-clad priest or minister—Connor is not a religious man, and little knows the difference—and a handful of men who must be ship's crew—the first mate, the bosun, and the quartermaster, most likely.

Connor's nerves thrum into life, then, at the sight of so many people. He has not encountered so many people all at once since the war, and he finds his heart squeezing and clotting in his throat, his pulse hammering wildly, irrational fears racing in his mind.

Then his eyes land on Tess, and all quiets within him.

She is wearing a yellow dress, and it is not designed for practicality this time, but for allure. The neck is scooped almost indecently low, and it hugs her waist and hips, and when she steps from lighter to dock, Connor sees a glimpse of her calf. Her eyes dance merrily, happily, as she drifts across the dock to where Connor stands, one hand in his trouser pocket, the other clutching the carven flower.

Tess stops mere inches from him, gazing up. "Why Connor, you've combed your hair and beard."

"Probably needs a bit of a trim," he mumbles.

She only smiles. "Nonsense." She reaches up and runs her fingers through his beard. "You're quite handsome just like this."

"Your dress is…" he hems and haws, and tries again. "You're the loveliest woman I ever saw."

"Thank you, Connor. I purchased it especially for this day."

He just stares down at Tess, drinking in her face, the black luster of her hair, the vivid azure of her eyes, the pale cream of her skin. "You're here. Felt like you'd never get here, some days."

Her hand rests on his chest. "Oh, the voyage here was absolutely interminable! And Papa even says we made excellent time. I just…I couldn't bear a single minute apart from you."

"Thought I'd dreamed it all."

"So did I."

"You…you really want to be here? With me?"

"There's nowhere I'd rather be, and no one I'd rather

be with, than here, with you."

"Why?" He can't help the question. "Why me?"

She combs her fingers through his beard again, her touch gentle and affectionate. "My heart chose you. The moment I stepped onto this dock and saw you, I knew. And when I stepped off the dock the last time, I knew I'd be back. And now that I've returned, I just know…"

"Know what?"

"I shan't be leaving again. I'm home, now."

"I'm not much for pretty talk, Tess." He steps a little closer, so he can almost feel her body against his, a tease, a ghost of a touch, a promise. "But if you're patient, and you're willing, I'll learn how to love you. That's about the best I can promise."

"I don't care overly much for fancy words. I can get those in books, if that's what I want." She takes his hands in hers. "I just want you, Connor. Just as you are. Gruff, and quiet, and dependable."

"Don't deserve you, Tess."

"That's the thing about love, Connor—it's not something we earn, or deserve. We have only to accept it, and give all we have in return."

He hesitates a moment, and then shows her the flower he carved for her. She takes the carving and examines it with surprise and joy.

"Why, Connor! I had no idea you were such an artisan!" She tucks it into the valley of her bosom, and then returns her gaze to Connor's.

"It's just…I just wanted to have something to give you."

"It's lovely. I shall treasure it always."

Behind Tess, the other men were unloading the goods, but for once, Connor let himself stay still, let himself just stand and hold the woman who had decided she was his, and he hers.

"I got one question, though," he murmurs.

She smiles softly up at him. "Which is what?"

"The lace, that bit of lace you gave me with the note." He hesitates, and then continues. "Where's it from? What'd you cut it out of?"

Her smile is less soft, and more playful. "Well, Connor, I'm not sure it's proper or decent that I tell you." She tugs on his beard, an eyebrow quirked up. "You'll have to wait until after we're married to find that out."

His face heats. "Oh. The wondering has been eating at me, these months."

"You won't have to wonder long." She glances at the minister, who has remained in the boat, perusing a passage in his Bible. "Reverend Galloway can marry us today."

"Today?"

She nods, and then eyes him quizzically. "Unless you've a reason to want to wait?"

"No!" he protests, a little too suddenly. "No." He eyes the cluster of men standing around the pile of supplies. "There's no one else you want with you for the wedding?"

"My mother died many years ago, and I've spent most of my life aboard ship with these men. They're nearly as much my family as Papa." She pats his chest. "And really, all I need is you."

"You have me." He gestures at the island. "This place…it's all I have to offer, Tess."

"As long as you're here, I shall be more than happy."

He shakes his head, not quite able to dislodge the lingering doubt and disbelief. "You're sure, Tess? I know I've asked this more than once, I just…I need you to be sure. About me, and about this life."

She laughs, then. "I've had a year to think on this, Connor—a year to consider the hardships, the realities, and the dangers. I've thought of little else, all this time." Her hand comes to rest on his cheek. "I am absolutely sure this is what I want. I have not a single doubt. Not one." A glance at her father, and the other men, huddled together, trying to light their pipes despite the wind. "Now. Kiss me, quickly, while they're distracted."

Her lips are softer than velvet, and warm, and damp, and she tastes of something sweet. It is a moment only, a promise of a kiss, lips on lips for mere seconds, but Time plays its trick on Connor, and he feels the kiss to last a lifetime, and more.

They are married just outside the garden, with the sun setting. Tess clutches a spray of daisies and gardenias

Connor has grown, and she wears a white dress, which leaves Connor's breath coming short and pulse hammering hard, and he wears his only suit. There is a time of conviviality afterward with the captain and the other officers, a bottle of wine brought by Captain Kinross for the occasion is opened and shared, and then, with a few tears on the part of Tess, and a gruff, huffing hug by the captain, the lighter departs. Connor and Tess watch it shrink across the water, watch it be drawn up into the ship, and then the ship's sails drop down and belly out in the stiff wind. A cannon blasts once, a farewell, and then the ship slowly dwindles over the horizon.

"Well, husband?" Tess, finally, turns and rests her hands on Connor's chest, and her eyes betray a myriad of heated emotions Connor has trouble believing are real, and meant for him. "We are alone, now."

"So we are."

"I bet if you explored a bit, you might find out where I cut that bit of lace from." She brushes a lock of his hair away. "You'd have to make rather bold in your exploration, however."

"Should we…" he glances up at the house, "should we go up, first?"

Tess lifts a shoulder in answer. "We could. But it is a beautiful and warm evening, and your coat upon the dock would make a fine cushion, and there is, after all, no one around to see us."

"Here?" He is surprised.

"Anywhere, Connor. Everywhere."

"Will I ever cease to be surprised by you?"

She unbuttons the top of his shirt. "I most certainly hope not, my husband."

His fingers are clumsy, seeking the buttons of her dress, at her back, but she is patient, and allows him to fumble.

She is patient, indeed, as he spends long moments freeing her from her many layers, and eventually, she is clad in only bits of silk and lace, there on the dock, and he discovers that she'd cut the lace from the inside of her most intimate unmentionable, where the lace lay against her skin.

He gazes at her for long moments.

She reaches for his clothing, and removes it item by item, until he is clad as she—that is to say, nearly not at all. And then she smiles up at him. "There is clothing yet to remove, Connor," she says. "I've dreamed of this moment with you more than I dare admit."

"I didn't dare dream of this at all."

"Then touch me, my love, and find out that this is not a dream."

"You'll always be my dream, Tess."

"And you said you weren't one for pretty words." She breathes a laugh of delight as he finally, finally, runs a hesitant, questing hand over her skin.

Later, lying tangled together on the dock, she gazes at him, happy, replete, and full of joy. "I don't think passion is something I'll need to teach you, Connor. You seem to have quite a firm grasp of that all on your own."

He laughs with her, and shows her again all the things he feels for her, which he doesn't have the words for.

He doesn't need words, he discovers. She is eager and willing to learn in other ways, and shows him her own love, thus.

In the years that follow, the dreams loosen their grip on him. When a nightmare does rack him, Tess never wakes him, only clings to him when he does awaken, screaming, and she is quick to soothe him with kisses and words of comfort and love, and soon even the dreams are as distant a memory as the war itself.

With Tess at his side, the island becomes truly home, somewhere to LIVE, not just subsist.

Conakry, Guinea, Africa; date unknown

That story...it feels familiar somehow. It poured out of me unbidden, spewing from my pen in an unbroken stream of scribbles, from midnight through the dawn, until my hand cramps and my eyes swim. Even as I finish it and set the notebook aside and lie in my cot, the fan swirling slowly overhead, flies and mosquitos buzzing beyond the screen, I think of the story and wonder over and over and over why it feels as if it is a story I have somehow known before.

Is it a story I've written before? Is it something from my life before I lost my memories? A book I've read or a film I've seen? I don't know. I just know it feels familiar. Certain elements strike me as...not quite *déjà vu*, but something like it. The lighthouse in the middle of nowhere, the quiet, stern, gruff man, the woman who brings him to life, the ship coming only so frequently… did I invent these elements, or did I bring them over from a hazy, forgotten corner of my past, brought alive and made new? Is it a metaphor?

My mind often works like that, I think, telling stories in an attempt to make sense of my life and my circumstances.

What does it mean?

Am I the island? Am I the man alone upon it, barely surviving day to day, each day a twisted gnarl of sameness and boredom and loneliness?

The woman…she is, clearly, Ava—at least, the Ava I am remembering, assuming she truly exists, and is alive. If my Ava were to have been born in the nineteenth century, she would have been like Tess, forward, lovely, elegant, impatient with nonsense, eager, full of life and love and affection.

I didn't want to write the rest, I wanted to keep it for myself, hidden and private in my mind—but I saw Connor and Tess together, on that island. He learned to whisper, at least to her, the truths deep in his heart, and she healed him of his pain, and accepted that which could not be healed. She bore him a child, a son. They raised him together on the island, until he became old enough to require school, and then Connor took a position at a lighthouse nearer civilization, where Tess could have friends and their son could be educated, and Connor even formed a friendship with an old barkeep…

Am I Connor? Scarred and haunted, and in need of my own Tess to come and bring me to life?

That feels true; it slices at me, probes deep, stirs dark, shadowy memories in my soul.

There is a cauldron of pain roiling beneath all this, I think.

I am honestly frightened of remembering.

Sleep claims me as I think on all this, and my sleep is haunted by ghosts and dreams and memories—if those are indeed disparate entities.

Part 2

From Ava's handwritten journal;
November 17, 2016

I feel as if I've opened Pandora's Box. In allowing myself—or forcing myself—to delve into things I've long avoided thinking about, I think I am dredging up a lifetime of repression and avoidance. It makes sense, though. Mom and Dad were…flaky, and self-absorbed. They didn't want to be parents. I think I've journaled about this recently, but I don't care. They had Delta and then me, and got us to the point where we were mostly self-sufficient and that was that. Hands-off. They provided the necessities, but they had their careers and their friends, parties on their friends' yachts and at their friends' country clubs, bridge nights and bowling nights and book clubs and poker nights, and Delta and I were left to our own devices. Get our own lunches, get ourselves up and ready for school.

I remember being walked to the bus stop for kindergarten and first grade, and then in second grade I was waved at from the front door, and after that it was a kiss from the kitchen, and as I got older barely even that. It was just life, and I didn't realize it was even unusual. Maybe it's not, I don't know. But…especially as I got into high school and Delta had left home, my parents and I were like roommates more than anything. They didn't charge me rent or utilities, but I bought my own food because they ate a bunch of shit I didn't like. They gave me Mom's old black Civic, which she'd driven for years until they were ready to upgrade it. It was in decent condition, but they'd bought it used themselves from a guy who had smoked in it, so it was thirdhand for me and stank forever of cigarettes. It was mine, though, and I paid insurance on it and put gas in it.

So I grew up in a very odd, in-between place, I think. If the upper end of the spectrum is a fully intact, happy, affectionate, loving nuclear family and the bottom end is pain and abuse and abandonment, I'm somewhere in limbo between the three. I grew up with both parents, and they loved each other—I never doubted that. I grew up always knowing where my next meal would come from—but more often than not, from fifth or sixth grade on, I was the one who prepared it, or Delta when I was younger. I grew up being provided for, I had a roof, clothes, a safe neighborhood, all the safety and security boxes checked. And for that I'm grateful. But…

I raised myself, with some help early on from Delta, until she left to chase her dreams—which I have never and will never harbor any ill will toward her over; it was what she had to do, and I knew it then as well as I do now. I wasn't abandoned, exactly. But close to it. It was kind of like I was given a house to live in, with this kindly older couple that lived there too, who I sometimes interacted with. By the time I was in junior high, I was totally independent.

I've never explored how I felt about all this. Not really. I mean, clearly I'm a little…disillusioned with my parents, at the least, since I rarely see them. But is that disillusionment? Is that anger? Resentment? Apathy? A mixture of all of it? I don't know, I've never examined it. I just…went on with my life. Graduated high school, moved into the dorms in Miami, met Christian, married him…

God. See? That right there, that last line, it leads me down a whole different path of self-examination.

I was independent, yes, sort of alone, yes, but I never lived totally alone. I never had to completely provide for myself. This is where that in-between space pops up again, because I was putting myself through the paces of day-to-day life and survival from a very young age—the basics were always just…there. I got a job in high school mainly so I could buy groceries I wanted, but if nothing else, the basics were always there. I went from that home to a dorm, where room and board were included in the tuition. I was surrounded by other people my age who didn't really care where I'd come from or what my background was. They weren't deep or meaningful relationships, but they were friends I could party with, study with, hang out with; it was wonderful, honestly. It felt like a sort of surrogate family in some ways. And besides, what was there to be deep about? Chemistry class? Boys? The latest sorority party? It was college, and none of us were looking for depth.

I know I wasn't. Not even when I met Christian. I certainly wasn't looking for anything serious with him, either. He was just a hot guy I was interested in, at first. He was intriguing, very different from anyone I'd ever met. And it just sort of grew up around us, this love. I don't think he was expecting it any more than I was. It just...happened. One thing led to another; hanging out led to sleeping together, sleeping together led to sleeping together regularly, which led to spending all of our time together, and then moving in together, and then getting married. It just all flowed from one thing to the next without much of an intervening transition or discussion. We never had a "what are we and where are we going as a couple" conversation. We just went from one thing to the next, and we both wanted it and it was fine and it didn't matter where we were going as a couple, because we were together and the future was what it was, and would be what it would be.

Is that how we saw it? I don't know. Like I said, we never really discussed it.

But Christian took care of me. I didn't expect it, or even want it or understand it at first, but he took care of me.

God, I'm rambling. I know this is a journal, but it's not like me to ramble with such little focus or direction.

Where am I going with this? What am I trying to discover about myself?

What questions do I have about myself? About my past, and my future?

Something to think about, I suppose, before I put pen to paper next.

All I know is, right now...I'm scared of letting myself grieve for Henry.

I'm scared I'll never find Christian. And if I never find Christian, what will I do?

Who will I be?

God, there it is. There it is, right there. The $64,000 question. Who will I be?

Which begs a question even more difficult to consider...

If I don't know who I would be if I never found my husband, then...who am I now?

The question, now that I've framed it in so many words, tolls inside me like the throb of a war drum.

God, I never used to be so melodramatic. I used to make fun of Chris for using similes like that, and now look at me, writing all purple prose and shit. Missing him so badly must be making his writing style rub off on me. Writing like him, trying to sound like him as a means of comfort?

That melodramatic prose is kind of fun, though.

Because dammit, I miss him.

And I don't know who I am.

Have I ever?

Conakry, Guinea, Africa; date unknown

The days and weeks I've been here in this hospital are a blur. They smear together, bleed together. How long have I been here? I don't know. I haven't kept track, and there is no way to measure the passage of time. There are no clocks, no calendars. Each day is the same, and today is like all the rest which have gone before: I wake to the hot African sun shining in through the dirty window facing my cot, stare up at the aged, yellowing popcorn ceiling above me, just breathing, watching wicker fan blades spin lazily, stirring the hot morning air around; eventually a nurse comes by.

"Help you into chair, now," she says, each word

thick and carefully pronounced. "Cast come off soon."

I slide from the bed to the wheelchair. Settle in, and she wheels me to the bathroom, which is nothing but a toilet and a steel sink in a closet. I manage my morning ablutions alone, the little bit of privacy I'm afforded. And then the nurse wheels me down long corridors, popcorn ceiling above, dirty white unpainted drywall to either side, an occasional door on this side or that. A pained moan from behind a door, a snore from behind another, voices speaking low in a dialect I don't understand from behind a third. There are no windows in this corridor, only the buzz of yellowish fluorescent tube lighting. Into the cafeteria, which is a cavernous room with tall ceilings, exposed rafters covered by a corrugated tin roof. Several picnic tables like you would see at a public park, the benches attached to the table. The food line is short, a single row of trays offering rice and beans and oatmeal, suspicious-looking meat of some kind, and fresh fruit harvested locally, all served by a short, fat old black man with a hair net and not enough teeth. He's kind, always serving me extra fruit. There are about a dozen other patients in this wing of the hospital, most of them locals, and all of them either terminal or unable to leave for some reason—I'm in the long-term care wing, I've deduced. None of the other patients have tried to befriend me, mainly because of the language barrier. I've learned a few phrases of Malinké and Susu, the predominant local languages,

according to Dr. James, and a little bit of French—
enough to be able to make conversation with the nurses
who tend to me.

I eat, and then take a Styrofoam cup of weak, burnt
coffee out to the veranda, to my spot in the corner.
The veranda is my favorite place in the hospital—it's a
screened in porch, facing a stand of palm trees, through
which I can see hints of the ocean. It's hot out here,
but it's quiet and solitary, since few other patients ever
spend time here. As I sit facing the screen, to my left is
the bulk of the rest of the hospital, low, long, and squat,
made of old crumbling brick in some places, with
newer additions more hastily built of cheaper materials.

There's a wicker fan overhead, spinning fast enough
to create at least an impression of moving air; it creaks
as it rotates, and wobbles. I sit out here for hours,
sweating, writing, thinking. Remembering, and trying
to remember.

Today, I'm out of sorts. Irritable, sullen, and
uncomfortable. I need...something. It's hotter than
usual today, and I feel a strange sort of longing inside
me.

No, longing isn't the right word. I don't know. I
can't make sense of how I'm feeling, and so I turn
again to the one thing that can ever help me make
sense of myself and my feelings and my thoughts: my
notebooks, and the outpouring of words from my pen:

From a handwritten journal; date unknown

I feel…

I don't know. For once, I don't know if I have the words.

I feel pregnant with memory. It is THERE. It is WITHIN me. But I just cannot reach it. Cannot get it out. I need desperately to give birth to it. It is painful. I am stretched out with it, weighed down by it, but it will not emerge.

Sometimes, like a lovesick teenager, I write your name over and over and over again. I fill pages with it.

I think the nurses think me mad in truth, although I know deep down this is only temporary. Mad with need. Mad with grief? Mad with desperation. I know not what all. Only that I am mad and cannot stop it.

I write your name, Ava.

Ava.

Ava.

Ava.

Ava.

Ava.

Ava.

Perhaps I hope that by writing your name so many times, I will jog loose another memory.

I simply must know, whether for good or ill, who I am and what I have done and how I came to be here. I must KNOW.

The madness I feel, it is from the not knowing.

From the burgeoning, swollen belly of memory I feel growing in me, through me. Ready to explode, but never quite doing so.

I write like a madman now. Some of it is nearly illegible, hastily scrawled, the penmanship cramped and crabbed and messy from hours of clutching a pen. I write from the moment I awake to the moment I fall asleep, out of desperation to disgorge the monstrous thing lurking inside me.

I can't take this much longer, or I will very truly careen willingly into full, gibbering, frothing, straitjacketed madness.

Dr. James finds me on the veranda, dragging a chair over to sit beside me. I set my notebook aside, and use the end of the pen to dig underneath the cast around my wrist, scratching an itch.

"I think we can remove those casts very soon. This week." Dr. James gestures at the notebook. "Have you remembered anything?"

I shake my head. "Not since the memory about my son."

"How do you feel about that memory?"

I sigh. "I don't know. I feel a little…crazy, to be honest."

Dr. James leans forward. "Crazy? How do you mean?"

I shrug, and fiddle with the pen. "Just…like…" I groan. "Fuck, I don't know how to describe it. Like there's so much inside me, just beneath the surface, and no matter how much I write, it won't come out. Not to be too graphic, but it's like being constipated, or something."

Dr. James nods understandingly. "Do you remember anything about your son, besides the memory you wrote about?"

I don't answer for a while. "It's hard to think about." I try to picture Henry, my son, and an image bubbles up; I try to describe it for Dr. James. "If I picture him, I see him as a baby. Old enough that he mostly sleeps through the night. He's got Ava's hair, lots of dark hair. My eyes, dark brown. Chubby cheeks. Grabby little fingers. He was always clutching at my face."

Dr. James lets the silence breathe for a moment, and when he speaks his voice is soft and probing. "Tell me more about Henry."

"I remember…I remember waking up. It was late. I went into his room and he was lying on his back, feet kicking as he cried, little fists shaking. He was *pissed*, like just so angry. So I picked him up, and realized he had a poopy diaper. So I changed him. He was still fussy, so I carried him out into the kitchen and made a bottle of some formula. It was a beautiful night outside. We lived on the beach—I don't know where, California or Florida, maybe? I can't remember. I just have this image of looking out of a sliding glass door and seeing a beach, and the ocean, and a huge full moon hanging just over the horizon, reflecting on the rippling waves. I have this feeling of peace, of joy, of happiness."

I swallow hard, and keep going.

"I remember taking Henry outside onto the back porch. It was just this little square concrete slab surrounded by some fence, separating our porch from our neighbors on either side, with a gate so we could go out to the beach. We had a table and two chairs out there, and I remember sitting with Henry in one of the chairs, feeding him the bottle and looking out at the ocean. He was awake, staring up at me as he guzzled down that bottle, and his little hands would—" my throat catches, and I have to start over. "He would grab at my hands. Squeeze my finger with his hands as he drank. Just blink up at me. He'd smile, sometimes, and milk would dribble down his chin." I laugh, and it's half sob. "That's what I remember."

Dr. James is quiet a while. Eventually he nods slowly. "It is a good memory. Yes?"

I nod. "Yeah. It's a good one."

"Hold on to it, my friend. You have been through very much, I think. Remember the good things. There is sorrow, to be sure, but there is also joy." He stands up, and pats my shoulder. "Let the sorrow pass through you, and cling to the joy. It is all we can do, sometimes."

"Thanks."

"But of course."

"No, I mean for getting me to talk about Henry."

Dr. James just smiles at me, waving. "I will return tomorrow. Perhaps we can see about those casts, yes?"

It will be wonderful to be free of the casts, to have mobility again.

But…there is still so much I don't know about myself, and my past.

From Ava's handwritten journal;
November 18, 2016

Our first Christmas after we moved in together was the most wonderful and memorable holiday of my life.

We agreed a month ahead of time that we would give each other two gifts, one expensive and one inexpensive—the first no more than $250 and the latter no more than $50. We agreed no pressure, no extravagance, just something meaningful and heartfelt.

I got Chris a waterproof, shockproof tactical chronograph, because when in doubt, getting a guy a nice watch probably won't go unappreciated, even in this age of smartphones and always knowing what time it is. Chris wore that watch every single day for years; that was the expensive gift. The inexpensive one was actually the more meaningful one: I found his camera, stole his memory card, went through the photographs, and found a bunch of the best and most artistic ones he'd taken, compiled them into a photo book, which I had printed on glossy paper and bound in a fancy hardback with his best photograph as the cover. It had, secretly, cost more than the fifty dollars we agreed on, but it was worth it, because he had been visibly moved and emotional, seeing the photographs of his travels bound like that, and had barely been able to get out words of thanks and appreciation.

He'd given me a Coach purse I'd heavily hinted at several times, and had printed and bound into a small paperback all the poems and prose he'd written about me, including the love notes and cute Post-It Notes we'd shared.

Honestly, those two items, the photo book and the book of poems and prose he'd written are the only two items that were in our Ft. Lauderdale condo or on Chris's boat which are irreplaceable. I treasured that book as dearly as my wedding and engagement rings, and opened it to read his words of love whenever I needed the reminder or encouragement.

But it was the gift of time shared with Chris that was so important to me. On Christmas Eve, we had put on our comfiest pajamas and curled up together under a blanket, turned off all the lights so the cheap pre-lit

Christmas tree with our handful of ornaments provided the only light. We'd shared a bottle of wine, and we watched Christmas movies until we fell asleep there on the couch. I'd woken up briefly, in his arms, as he carried me to our bed, and then I was snuggled back in his arms. There was Christmas music playing somewhere as I fell back asleep.

I'd woken again to dawn streaming in through the windows, and Christian already awake. He was still in bed, staring at me with love in his eyes. We'd been together for several months at that point, had moved in together a few months prior, and we would say things like "I love that about you" but we'd never said the words "I love you" to each other. Not outright. It wasn't a game, we weren't waiting for the other to say it first, I wasn't scared of saying it and I don't think he was either, we just...it hadn't felt right. It was there, the idea that we weren't just together, weren't just dating or living together, but were truly in love—the knowledge was there, waiting to be expressed at the right time.

When my eyes flickered open and fixed on his, he'd smiled at me, shifting closer.

"Merry Christmas," he'd whispered, nuzzling my cheek with his.

"Merry Christmas," I'd whispered back, smiling up at him.

And then his lips found mine, and we'd gotten lost in a kiss, a long, slow, searching one. Christian had been the first to break away. He'd dragged his mouth away from mine, staring down at me, breathing raggedly. Lifted the edge of my pajama top and kissed my belly. My ribs. I'd arched my back and extended my arms over my head, and he'd shoved the top up and over my breasts and ripped the garment off and tossed it aside, and then he'd resumed kissing me…but not my mouth. He kissed my neck, my chin, my throat, my shoulders, my breasts, and I'd buried my hands in his hair and moaned his name as he kissed his way south, hooking his fingers into the waist of my pajama bottoms. He removed those as well, dragging them down my legs, following their path with his tongue, and then when they were gone and I was naked, he kissed and nipped back up to the juncture of my thighs. He'd gone down on me, then. Slowly. Unhurriedly, leisurely. His tongue and fingers brought me to orgasm again and again, until I was shuddering and shaking and breathless and screaming his name, and then I'd shoved him away and pushed him to his back and climbed astride him.

I'd just sat on his thighs for a moment, gazing down at him, my hands cupping my breasts, presenting them for him. He'd lifted up and nuzzled them, licked his hot tongue around one nipple, and the other. I had held his face to my breasts, spine arched to press them into his mouth, and I watched in love and rapture as he devoured them, kissing and nuzzling and licking until I could bear it no more. I'd risen up, reached between our bodies and gripped his erection, and slid him inside me, gasping his name as he filled me.

We made love slowly.

We never rushed, exactly, but sometimes sex was faster than others. In books and movies it's always endless, entire nights of passion. We had those, too, of course. But when you live together and have busy lives, sometimes all you really have time for is ten or fifteen minutes together before sleep, or in the morning before you get up, or whatever. That's just real life. You're not in a hurry, exactly, but you have things to do and you want each other and you need the renewed intimacy, but you just…you've got shit to do.

That Christmas morning was…it was just…

I don't know.

Crazy intense, and so deliberately slow.

I'd braced my hands on his shoulders and smiled down at him and hoped he saw how much I loved him, and he moved in me, his hands caressing my ass in affectionate, possessive circles as his hips pivoted with achingly tender thrusts, as slowly as he could move and still consider it movement. My love for him blossomed and expanded and exploded with each slow incremental slide of his cock into me, and my love grew even more with each agonizingly beautiful inch of withdrawal. Slow, and slow, and slow. No words. No screams or growls, no curses or chanting names, just our physical connection, his body inside mine, our union. His eyes on mine.

My hair was draped around his face, and the sun was shining, and there was only us in the whole wide world, only this moment.

Only my love for this man, a love so deep and wide and full and fierce that I knew in that moment that it would never end, would never stop growing, would never die, could never be replaced.

Our climax wasn't a nuclear detonation. No, this time, it was something else. A syrupy-slow slide into desperation, his sweat-slick arms wrapped around me, my hands clawing down his chest, leaving marks, our bodies heaving together, writhing, our breathing ragged and synched, the orgasm lasting and lasting until we were left limp and collapsed together.

When it was over, I lifted up, my hands in the pillow on either side of his face, my hair curtained on either side of his face. I know my face must have shone like a beacon, then, with my unutterably enormous love.

A long, silent moment, then, like that—him gazing up at me, his love as clear on his face as on mine, our bodies still joined.

"Christian…" I murmured.

His palm cupped my cheek, and I nuzzled into it.

"Ava."

"I love you," I'd said.

"I know." This, with a ridiculous smirk.

I slapped his chest. "This isn't <u>Star Wars</u>, you geek," I'd said, but I was laughing when I said it.

He rolled us over, then, so he was above me, his body hard and large and beautiful, his hair shaggy, scruff on his jaw; he'd palmed my cheek and he kissed me, a hot demanding kiss, one he controlled, claiming my mouth and showing me exactly how he felt, as if his expression and our lovemaking hadn't already accomplished that.

When he pulled away, it was only far enough that his lips were free from mine so he could speak. His nose was against mine, his weight on me, and I felt his words against my mouth.

"I love you, Ava."

And then he'd wrapped me up in the blanket from our bed, cradled me in his arms, picked me up and carried me out of the bedroom and into the living room.

He'd gone to find my presents, and when I saw him with his for me, I went to get mine for him, and then we sat together on the couch, both of us still naked, wrapped up together in the blanket from our bed, and opened the presents together.

We eventually made breakfast—chocolate chip waffles and bacon—and drank a pot of coffee, and watched a movie. Took a shower together, wherein Christian pushed me up against the tile underneath the spray and filled me and fucked me hard and fast and I got myself off in synch with him, my fingers flying around my clit as he fucked me.

And then we watched another movie.

Ate leftovers for lunch, and each other for a snack,

there on the couch.

That was what we did, all Christmas Day: stayed naked, tangled up together on our couch, watching Christmas movies, snuggled under a warm blanket.

We spent later Christmases other ways: at my parents' house, them at ours, and we went out to Illinois to be with his mother the year his father died. But my favorite Christmas was always that one. Because an entire day spent watching movies and making love is always a perfect day, but mostly because it was the day Christian told me he loved me.

He didn't just say it because I said it first. He didn't say it back. He made sure of that—the kiss, rolling us over so he was above me, that was his way of making sure I knew he wasn't just saying it back, but saying it because he meant it.

When I think of Christmas, I think of that day.

Conakry, Guinea, Africa; date unknown

"You are not well, are you?" Dr. James asks.

I shake my head. It's all I can manage. I'm reduced to rocking back and forth. Unable to write, because I would only write that moment out, again and again. I have written it so many times I have filled half a notebook with it, until my hand cramps on the pen so badly a nurse must force my fingers to release it.

"What is it you have remembered?" he asks.

I only hand him the notebook, and he reads:

From a handwritten journal; date unknown

It's the same dream, the same memory, over and over

and over again, driving me mad.

I see her, above me. Hair draped around my face like a dark curtain.

No…not HER—

You.

Ava.

I see you above me, Ava. Your hair is an inky black curtain around my face, obscuring the sunlight, which is glimmering and glinting through the strands in brilliant scintillating refractions. Your smile…it is an expression of the purest love possible on this earth. It is beyond comprehension, beyond description. Your eyes are the vivid cerulean of the High Sea, and they pierce into me and see my soul and somehow, see something within me worth loving with such purity. Your skin is flawless cream and ivory. Your lips are redder than the most scarlet apple.

This is all there is to the dream. Your hair, the sunlight peeking through it, your red lips and pale skin and blue eyes. And that look of the purest love that could ever exist.

Again, and again, and again.

No words, no sound, no sensations or smells. Just that look on your face, and the upwelling of raw ecstatic joy it causes in me. I cannot fathom it. I cannot pierce the memory, nor dredge it for more. I dream it, every night. I close my eyes as I sit on the veranda in the hot sun. I see you, waking and sleeping, and I am mad with the seeing of it, desperate to know you, desperate to know if I have truly seen such a look directed at me, desperate to know...you—

And myself through you.

Who was I that you could gaze at me like this? That you could love me, like this?

I have but the tiniest fragments of myself, so far: a capacity for the written word; a vague notion of unhappiness as a child; the sea; a son, Henry, who died, and the icy ghost fingers of dread the knowledge of his death engenders within me, though I know not why; and you, for you are truly an intrinsic part of me, Ava, in a way I do not know if I can even now comprehend.

The dream, the dream, always this dream.

You, you, you.

Sometimes I wallow in the madness the dream catalyzes inside me. I linger in it. Allow myself to be mad with it. Allow myself to chant your name and allow the vision—the dream, the memory—to repeat in my head like a looped GIF, the splice between frames perfectly married in an endlessly repeating moment: your head drawing down to mine, your hair draping around my face and pooling on the pillow, your lips curved in that secret smile of purest love, your eyes flicking back and forth as you gaze down at me.

I want to drown myself in that moment.

Am I truly going mad? For days now, that vision has been in my every thought, laced through every moment, awake and asleep. I dream it, and when I awake with a start, lonely and mourning the loss of such love, I close my eyes to steady myself and yet there you are, staring at me, all over again.

There is no escape from it.

WHY?

Why must I be taunted with it? Why can't I make it stop? Or remember more?

What came before? What comes after?

Did you kiss me? That look, that smile, did it morph into a kiss, into more? Into us, drowning in each other there in the sunlight? Or was that moment what came after we made love? Was that the look you gave me in the moments after we both climaxed together, clinging together, gasping, and loving each other as fiercely as our bodies would allow?

I don't know…

And I want more than almost anything else in this world to know, to KNOW.

That vision is taunting me, haunting me. Teasing me. It is a cup of water just out of reach of a man dying of thirst.

Sometimes I'm so mad with it I nearly wish I could dig it out of my head, drive it away from me forever.

Other times I'm so besotted with it I want to live always in that single moment, cling to it like a drowning man to a spar in a storm.

All I can do, however, is endure it.

Dr. James flips back and forth through several pages, and finally removes his spectacles and looks at me closely.

"I can see that the same thing is written over and over many times, this central image of your vision of your wife, this woman, Ava."

I nod.

"Can you explain why?"

"It's all I see. Over and over and over again, awake and asleep—I see her but I can't remember—I can't remember what came before, or what came after." I rock back and forth in my chair, squeeze my eyes closed and mutter her name a few times—*Ava, Ava, Ava.* "I can't remember. I just can't remember."

Seeing that I was becoming agitated, Dr. James said, "You must try to calm yourself. This will not help you remember."

"I *CAN'T* REMEMBER!" I shout. "If I could remember the rest, I know I could remember my name. I just…I *know* it."

Dr. James doesn't argue. Just nods and pats my knee. "You must not try to be forcing it. As we have discussed before—the memories will come when they are ready to come. You can only help them along so much."

"I'm trying, but this is just…it's so frustrating."

"I know, I realize that. Which is why I think you

should take a few days of a break from the writing.
I think you are becoming obsessed with it and I don't
think that is healthy for your psyche."

"I have to remember. I *have* to. I *have* to know her. I
have to remember more of her. I *have* to remember what
happened."

Dr. James leans forward, hand on my knee. "Please,
put the pens and the notebooks away for a day or two,
at the very least. Please. It will help, I promise you. It
will give your mind a rest. Your injuries are healing and I
think it is time for you to do some walking. Let us focus
on the healing of your body, and regaining your mobility.
And *then* you can go back to the writing, and then I think
you will have more luck in shaking loose the memories."

I nod. "Okay."

He claps his hands, pleased. "Very good! Okay. More
walking, more gentle exercise. The staff is here to help
you. The weather is very pleasant and I think you will
enjoy exploring the grounds and breathing in the fresh
air. You will feel like a new man, I promise you this."

And so, when Dr. James leaves to continue his
rounds, I lay aside my writing.

My casts have been off for some time, but for how
long? Days? Weeks? I have no idea. It doesn't seem to
matter, either.

How long have I been here? I have no idea. Forever,
it seems.

For the next week—I count the days, mark them off

in a corner of my notebook—I walk around as much as I can. There is no residual pain any longer, but my muscles feel stiff and sore and weak. I walk around the hospital, and even walk to the shore, under the watchful eye of a nurse, as if I am a child or a prisoner but, in truth, I am grateful for her presence, because I know nothing of their languages beyond a few words.

Once at the shoreline, with the sea in view, something in my heart swells.

Cracks.

Trembles.

I kick off the flip-flops I wear—they are handmade from a piece of rubber and bits of rope, but they protect my feet from the rocks and heat of the earth. I roll up the edges of my trousers, and I wade into the sea. I go in up to my ankles at first, and then my knees, and then to my hips, the water soaking my trousers. The water is cold. I touch a finger to the sea and then to my lips and taste the salt.

A wave slaps unexpectedly against my chest and salt sprays my face, and I am abruptly plunged into memory—

Black sky above. Lightning flashes, illuminating an angry jade wave cresting over my head, caught mid-motion, the tip becoming a spear as it curls, arching over me. Salt on my lips. I am tossed like a stick. A wave slams onto me, plunges me under the surface and I am twisted and rolled and flipped. I am at the mercy of the Sea. I paw clumsily at the water, trying to paddle for the surface, but there is no surface, no up or down, only the angry waves and the sky and lightning and the clap of thunder and the wind.

I feel someone pulling me backward, and I stumble and twist to see the face of the nurse. She's jabbering at me in Susu, scolding me. I am soaked from head to toe and I am shaking from the memory rather than the cold.

She gestures, indicating she wants me to return to the hospital, but I can't go back yet. Instead, I strip out of the wet clothes and leave them in the sand to dry, and lie down beside them—this nurse washed me when I was helpless, so I am unconcerned about being naked around her. I lie there in the sand, eyes closed, and let the sun beat down on my face.

And for a moment, I have a shred of peace.

Perhaps I doze, I don't know.

I awake feeling a bit calmer, and I return to the hospital with the nurse. I feel in possession of myself again, not so mad with the need to know.

The dream of Ava continues, but I find comfort in it now—I choose to believe that she is with me in spirit, and that itself is a comfort.

Another week passes and I continue with my explorations in the area around the hospital, and I even convince Dr. James to take me into Conakry itself. We bump along the narrow streets in his rattling old car with the windows down, the radio playing something melodic and bouncing and fun and light, chatter floating in from the streets.

He points things out places and people of interest. "My cousin, he live there. He sells mobile phones...That is a restaurant which is very good, maybe we go there soon...I had my first flat in that building...My first wife, she grew up just there—oh, she passed on, many years ago, from an illness..."

We drove until we came to a market; he parked and we browsed the market stalls, speaking together like friends; he told me of his second wife, to whom he was married for twenty years, and of her death in the Guinean political protests in September of 2009. I spoke of Ava and shared some of the things I remembered. Speaking of her seemed to jar loose more memories, little ones, which I tuck away for later.

Dr. James drives us back to the hospital, and now the radio is off and we are both silent. The air billowing in from the open windows is warm, smelling of dust and food and exhaust. Dr. James parks near his office and, for a moment, we just sit in the car, listening to the engine tick and pop, watching a group of boys and girls play stickball in the shade of a huge tree.

A thought occurs to me—a question. "Dr. James?"

He glances at me. "Yes? What is it?"

"How long have I been here? In this hospital?"

"Seven months. Almost eight. You came to us in

the beginning of May, and it is now the middle of
November." He checks his watch, a cheap, digital thing.
"Today is November 19, 2016."

Eight months? That is a long time.

"What if—what if I never remember anything else?"
I ask. "What then? What will I do? Where will I go? I
can't stay here in the hospital forever."

Dr. James sighs. "No, you cannot. But we cannot
just send you out alone without even your own name.
What if someone is looking for you? Surely this woman you remember, your Ava—surely she is looking for
you, missing you. But where is she? How do we find her?
We have very little by way of resources here." Another
sigh. "What will you do if you do not remember yourself? I do not know. Begin again, somehow, somewhere,
I suppose."

Begin again.

Choose a new name? Forget Ava? Just...start life
anew, from scratch?

How could I do it?

No, no. I *must* remember.

I *will* remember.

When we return to the hospital, I write once more,
for the first time in two weeks.

I write feverishly, with renewed desperation:

From a handwritten journal; November 20 2016

A memory, which has bubbled to the surface:

I am sitting at a computer, typing—I was a writer, then, I believe, which is consistent with what I feel in myself. It is late at night, the sky beyond the windows dark. Lightning plays far out on the water, visible through the sliding glass door to my left. I wear faded jeans, the knees ripped and fraying, a gray T-shirt, and a thin, faded black hoodie, which I wear superstitiously whenever I write. I am stiff, sore. I have been at this desk many hours. Cans of soda are clustered, empty, on one side of the desk, and a bag of pretzels sits open nearby, mostly gone. Music plays from a sound system, tiny square speakers installed in the corners of the ceiling—solo piano music. The only light is from a pair of floor lamps in opposite corners of the room.

I hear something behind me—the door opening. I know it's you. I don't turn, but I'm smiling at my screen.

"Hey, babe," I say.

I hear you clear your throat meaningfully.

"Yeah, I'm just finishing up."

"You've been working since six this morning. Have you even eaten?"

"I'll grab something. I'm done now." I still haven't turned around, instead saving my work and backing it up to a thumb drive.

I feel your hands on the back of my office chair,

pulling me away from my desk and spinning me around.

"Hey!" I protest. "I wasn't done—"

You stop the rotation of the chair with your foot, and my words die on my lips. "I have something for you to eat," you say, your words low and your voice sultry.

"Oh yeah?" I ask.

You tangle your fingers in my hair, and pull my face toward your leg, your foot propped up on the chair between my thighs. You're wearing a set of lingerie I got you a few months ago, a just-because gift. It's a black lace bodysuit, which obscures and reveals and emphasizes every curve of your breathtakingly sexy body. Stockings, garters. Your breasts are pushed up, and your cheeks are pink with excitement. I can smell your desire.

You pull me closer yet, and my lips graze your inner thigh, just above your knee. "Start there and work your way up," you murmur. "You'll find out soon enough."

I kiss the creamy skin of your thigh, lapping and licking and nipping upward until I reach the apex of your thighs. I inhale deeply, sniffing along the seam of your pussy, covered in lace, soaked with your need. "Smells delicious."

"It does, huh?" You're breathy, now. Your thighs tremble with anticipation—you crave my mouth on your clit.

"So good. It smells so good I think I might just—" and instead of saying it, I do it.

I hook a finger in the gusset of your bodysuit and pull it aside to reveal your slit. Your pussy is soaked with desire, and you smell delightfully, arousingly, of anticipation.

I love that word—pussy; I think of your sex like a pink flower, two delicate petals and a tiny, hard little bud.

I slide my tongue up the damp opening of your pussy, and you gasp.

I flick my tongue against your swollen clit, and you moan.

The sounds you make, Ava...they're intoxicating. I am drunk on you. I devour you. Work you with my tongue into a thrashing fervor, your hands in my hair clutching me hard against you, and your hips pivot and flex and you grind your clit against my swirling tongue, against my suckling mouth. You cry out as you come, hunching forward, legs trembling.

And then you drop to your knees. Gaze at me, still breathless. Keep your eyes on mine as you unhook the clip of the garter from the stocking and peel it off. You use the stocking to tie one of my hands to the arm of my chair. Then the other stocking is removed, and my other hand is bound.

"This is a fun game," I say. "I like where this is going."

"You're going to love what I have in store for you," you say, mischief in your eyes. "I was reading some erotica earlier, and I got a really fun idea."

"What's that?"

You just grin. "Now why would I tell you when I could just show you?" You huff. "Dammit. I forgot to take off your shirt before I tied you up."

I laugh as you untie me, roughly peel off my hoodie and T-shirt, toss them aside, and then retie me. "Now. Where was I?"

"About to tell me what your plan is?"

"No, that's not it."

"I think you were about to bring that sweet, juicy peach of a pussy of yours over here so I can eat it some more."

Your cheeks flame and you step closer. "Hmmm. Tempting."

You sidle up to me, and I frame you between my knees. I kiss your breasts, over the lace, and nibble at the bump of a nipple, until you pull away with a gasp, and I bend lower, dip my mouth closer to your mound.

You let me get a teasing whiff, a brush of lips on lace, and then you pull back. "Tempting, but no. I have other ideas. And I'm not going to tell you. You're just going to have to trust me."

"I trust you," I say, immediately. "Obviously. Go on, then, wife. Have your wicked way with me."

"I think I should blindfold you, though. It'd be more fun."

"If you insist."

So I find myself blindfolded by my own T-shirt, and then I'm truly helpless, which is how you want it. Usually, you like it when I'm in control, when I pin your hands over your head and take you, when I guide your hips with my hands as you ride me, when I bend you over our bed and thrust into you and spank you as I fuck you, when I roll you to your stomach and pull you into doggy-style position and pound into you.

This time, though, is different. You've got a spark in your eyes, a heat in your gaze that tells me this is going to be about you taking what you want—me. How you want me. What you want from me.

I like this. A lot.

I sit, bound and blindfolded, waiting. My cock is bent and throbbing inside my jeans. I smell you, feel you near me.

You spin my chair around a few times, disorienting me. And then I smell you, feel your presence at my shoulder, and then your lips close around my earlobe and your breath is hot and loud, and then you're gone. A nip at my nipple, sharp and sudden. A fingertip trailing from hip to knee over denim, your fingernail tickling my skin in the rip of my jeans. Another spin, then another. I'm truly disoriented now. I feel lace brush against my hand. I hear rustling.

"Know what I'm doing?" I hear you ask.

"No."

"I'm taking off the bodysuit."

"I want to see."

"I'm naked, now."

"Take off the blindfold."

"Nope. You've seen me naked a million times. Use

your imagination." You slide between my knees. "This time, just FEEL me."

I gulp as you press your lips to my chest, and I gasp as you trail kisses down my stomach. I hiss as you pry open the button my jeans, and then hold my breath, tensed, as you tug down the zipper. I dressed quickly this morning, in a hurry to get to writing, and didn't bother with underwear.

"You're commando."

"Yep."

"Normally I'd say that's kind of gross, but in this situation, I approve." You grasp my shaft in your hand, sliding your fist up and down my length. "Easier access."

"God, that feels good, Ava."

"Mmm-hmmm?" I feel you between my thighs, feel your body descending as you sink to your knees; you tug at my jeans, and I lift my butt up off the chair so you can tug them off of me. "You like the feel of my hand on your cock?"

"So much."

Now your naked skin slides against my thighs, and I feel your breasts swaying and brushing against my stomach as you lean close to kiss my chest, both of your hands around my erection. I'm wild with need, groaning and flexing my hips unreservedly into your touch, gasping and huffing laughs as you pepper my flesh with kisses, from chest to stomach, stomach to ribs, ribs to waist, and then to my hipbone and over my thigh. You're not really stroking me yet, just sort of toying with my cock, petting it, caressing, rubbing your thumb across the tip, and I'm shaking with anticipation of your touch, of your mouth.

You do not disappoint me.

There's no warning, no buildup, no teasing. Just your mouth dancing from thigh to hip, hip to stomach, and then the warm wet suck of your mouth on my cock, and my expulsion of breath in ecstatic relief.

"That feels good, too, right?" You pull away just long enough to say this, and then take me into your mouth again.

I laugh. "Fucking amazing."

"Probably don't want me to stop, huh?" Again, you say this and then fill your mouth with my erection.

"No—god no."

"You wanna come in my mouth?" You whisper this to my cock, the words huffing hot on my wet, sensitive skin.

"Fuck yes."

"I might just let you, since you made me come so hard."

"Oh fuck, Ava."

"But not yet." You punctuate this by releasing my cock so it springs free of your hand and slaps back against my belly.

"Aw hell, babe...I was getting close."

"I know." I can hear the grin in your voice. "But...I

think I might need one more orgasm before I give you yours."

I hear my desk creak as you sit on it, and then feel your toe hook around the back of my leg and you haul me across the hardwood floor, the casters loud as I roll toward you. Your thighs are velvety soft as they come to rest on my shoulders, and I nip the flesh hard enough to make you squeak and jump, and then your hands are in my hair and you're guiding me to your slit, pulling me against you. I feel your body arch as I begin lapping at your clit, feel your fingers tighten in my hair. You're on a hair trigger, already gasping wildly, and I've only licked at you a few times, and when I pause to suckle the hard little button of your clitoris into my mouth, you whimper and shift and thrust against me, and then when I return my tongue to you, circling faster and faster, you cry out and gasp and tell me, "YES! YES! Right there! Don't stop!"

As if I would stop—as if I COULD stop. The sounds you make, the erotic whimpers and breathy groans, they're enough to make my cock throb without even being touched. And when you clutch me hard against you and scream wordlessly in your thrashing climax, I nearly do come just hearing the sounds you make.

And then you kick me away, one foot pushing at the chair so I roll backward, and I hear your feet hit the hardwood floor and I feel your hair tickle my thighs and that's all the warning I get before I'm in your mouth and you're sucking hard and pumping my shaft with both hands, and I'm groaning and thrusting.

You don't let me finish, though.

You stand up and I feel you twist around between my thighs, and then your hand clutches my cock and bends me away from my body and you sink me into your slick wet tight heat and you're straddling me, facing away, the angle delicious and tight and taut, and your walls squeeze around me and your ass slaps down on my thighs and I'm trying to thrust but I have no leverage.

"Hold still," you say. "Let me do it."

So I go still, which is difficult. You only have a little leverage, so your thrusts are shallow, just enough to tease us both. Enough to get me close, but not enough to push me over the edge.

"Fuck, Ava—I need to come."

"Yeah?"

"I need to come so bad."

"So come."

"I can't—not like this."

"You can't?" Your voice is teasing. "How sad. Whatever shall we do?"

"Untie me, and I'll show you."

"Unh-uh. I don't think so."

Without warning, you rise up and climb off me, and I slide free of your tight wet slit, aching, dripping, and a single touch away from exploding.

"You know what I've always wondered?" you ask.

"What?" I ask, my voice guttural, tense.

"What you taste like after you've been inside me."

"Oh—shit!"

It's all I have time to say before you have me in your mouth, sinking down around my aching shaft, tongue swirling, and then you're licking me from root to tip and your mouth is sideways on my length, tongue flicking and sliding, tasting our mingled essences. I feel you gather your hair and drape it across one shoulder, and then you take my cock in your hands and wrap your lips around the head and suck and stroke, until I'm grunting and thrusting and begging you to let me come.

You don't.

You let me go, turn around again, and sink me into you, slowly, all the way, and you rock there, hips rolling, driving, until I'm panting with need, and I think NOW, now you're going to let me come, buried deep inside you.

But you don't.

You slide off me again, and you take your time going to your knees, not touching me, giving me time to back away from the edge, and then you're licking your taste off my flesh, and I'm grunting and groaning, and I can't take any more.

"Ava, PLEASE—please. I'm going crazy."

"You want to come, huh?"

"So fucking bad. I NEED it, baby."

"Okay. But I have one demand."

"Anything."

"When you come, I want you to say my name—shout it as loud as you can, and tell me how much you love me."

"Yes—yes, of course."

"Then I shall allow you to have your orgasm."

"How kind, my mistress."

You take me into your mouth and now I know, finally, there's no more teasing, no more games. Your hands curl around my shaft at the base and slide up and down my length, and your mouth bobs down and then you suck hard on the way up, and your hands grind me to the edge, and there's no holding back. No chance of it, and I wouldn't even if I could.

I hit the edge and my hips thrust and you take it, allow me to thrust into your hands and mouth, and my hands tug and test the bonds.

"Ava!" I shout. "AVA! Shit—shit—I'm coming now, Ava. I'm gonna come so hard."

You hum around me. "Mmmm-hmmm!" and stroke me faster and suck harder, taking more of me into your mouth.

"AVA! Oh my god, Ava! I love you, god I love you so fucking much! I—god—oh god oh god, Ava, I love you so much I can't stand it, I love you more than anything in this whole universe—"

I have no idea how I'm managing to formulate words right now, much less say them without stuttering hopelessly. It feels too good, so good—this is heaven, this is perfection, this is—it's everything, and I don't want it to stop, I don't want to come, I want to just feel this forever, your hands gliding and your mouth hot and wet and sucking hard around me.

But I can't stop the orgasm—it's a freight train slamming through me at a thousand miles per hour.

"Ava—I love you—I love you…oh my god Ava, I fucking—I fucking love you—oh god…AVA!"

My shout is so loud it echoes off the windows, and I come so hard I see stars bursting behind my eyelids, and you swallow and suck more out of me, pump it out of me, and you don't let off until I'm going soft and gasping raggedly, chanting, "I love you, I love you, I love you."

I'm left utterly spent when you finally pull away. I hear you pad away, hear a drawer open and close, and I know you've brought out my hideout bottle of whiskey. I hear the cap unscrew and the glug-glug as you pour a measure into the glass tumbler I keep in my office. You put the cup to my lips and tip and I taste the fiery burn of the whiskey as it slides down my mouth, and then I hear you drink and hiss, and then you're untying the blindfold and I'm blinking in the dim light of my office. You take another drink, and then dip three fingers into the whiskey and smear the golden liquid across your nipple and bring your breast to my mouth, and I lick and lap it away, and you groan in delight as I do so.

You feed me another drink, and then take one for

yourself, and then the glass is empty and you set it aside, move to sit astride me. Smash your breasts against my chest, wrap your arms around my neck, clinging to me. One hand drifts away, unties my hand, and then the other, and I enclose you in the circle of my arms and stare up at you.

Lightning flashes, out at sea, illuminating the endless horizon of the sea for a split second.

Your hair is loose, hanging around your shoulders. I lean back in the chair as far as it will go, taking your weight as you lean over me. Your hair drapes on either side of my face, and the standing lamp in the corner shines on you, the light playing through the strands of your hair.

You straddle me, and though I just came, arousal stirs through me at the sultry, seductive, pleased, happy, sated expression on your face, and the beautiful glow of your creamy perfect skin and the softness of your curves against me, and the feel of you in my hands. I let my palms skate over your silken flesh, everywhere I can reach.

The chair allows me to lean backward almost horizontal, and I prop my feet up on the desk, and you're on top of me, all around me, above me, gazing down at me. The smile on your face is one of purest love.

There is a long moment of silence as you stare at me, letting your love shine on me.

You palm my cheek. Touch your lips to mine, ever

so gently, ever so softly, with an exquisite tenderness that steals my breath and makes my heart thump and freeze and then hammer and expand and swell and float on ether.

Both palms on my cheeks, then. Another soft, warm, slow kiss.

Your voice is barely above a whisper, but I hear each word as if it is being carved into my bones, etched into my soul:

"I love you with everything that I am, Christian St. Pierre."

13

Conakry, Guinea, Africa; November 21, 2016

My name is Christian.

My name is Christian St. Pierre.

It is nearly midnight as I sit on the veranda. Crickets chirp, and mosquitos buzz, and the noises of the night echo around me, providing a soundtrack for my thoughts. It is pitch black beyond the small pool of light shed by the dim orange bulb over my head. I hold the notebook in my lap, the pen in my hand. I have been writing for hours—my hand aches from it.

I felt that memory bubbling up inside me—I ached with it for weeks, felt it pressing on the insides of my skull, burgeoning against the walls of my soul, and now, finally, it has emerged.

Writing it and then reading it was like reliving it. I was there. I remember the way she smelled, like perfume and arousal. She'd brushed her hair out before she showed up at my office door—I know, because when she brushes her hair out she sprays something on it to give it luster and make it smell good. I know that smell. I know the scent of her perfume, too—it's light and crisp, with a hint of fruit and a touch of lavender. Her arousal is the sweeter perfume, the more intoxicating scent. I can—I can almost smell her on my fingers, can almost taste her on my tongue.

Christian.

I savor the name. It is mine—I feel this truth in my bones, in my gut.

But what does it mean for me to have my name back? There's no sudden rush of memory filling in the spaces. I have my name. I have my relationship with Ava.

I know we loved each other desperately, deeply.

But then...why am I here, alone? Where is she? I was shipwrecked; I remember that much. But did she die in that wreck? Or was I alone? If I was alone, why was I alone? Where was Ava? I must try to remember this.

At the same time, I fear to remember.

I fear the truth which lies in the darkness beyond the moment that heart monitor flatlined. My son, Henry, dying—that is the darkness, and what lies beyond it terrifies me. The man it might reveal me to be terrifies me. I almost don't want to know, but...I must. I must know.

I fear to leave this place, this hospital. Life will begin, once I depart. So far, being here has been a time-out. A reprieve from reality. But once I leave, I will have to reclaim myself, find myself, and accept who am and who I was, and there will be no slowing it, no stopping it. Life is slow, here. It just floats along, outside time. Life has not changed within the bounds of this coastal African hospital for many, many years.

I have convalesced. I am hale. I have my name, which is the key to the rest of me. I cannot, in good conscience, remain any longer.

I am out there somewhere, and I must find myself.

Ava is out there somewhere, too, and I must find her.

November 22, 2016

"You are sure?" Dr. James toys with his spectacles as he gazes at me steadily. "You do not want to perhaps stay a little longer?"

I shake my head. "I have to go."

"Why so soon? You only just remembered your name. There is no rush to leave. You are welcome to remain as long as you like."

"I know. And thank you." I sigh. "I can't thank you enough for all you have done for me, Dr. James. You, and all the nurses. But I have to find Ava."

A nurse appears then, as if summoned by magic, and Dr. James converses with her in Susu. She is one of the nurses who helped care of me ever since I first regained consciousness—her name is Martha. Once Dr. James finishes speaking to her, Martha gives me a rare smile, softening her features, momentarily—she is an older woman, hardened from long years of medical work on a continent forever racked by war and turmoil and death.

"You find her now." Martha gestures toward the sea, the waves crashing in the distance; it is Martha who accompanied me to the sea, that day. "She out there. You speak her name, all the time. In your sleep, you call to her. You will find her. I see this—I *see* this."

And then, with a brusque nod, Martha bustles away, head high, features schooled back into hardened stillness.

"The nurses, they have rumors and they tell stories, you know. They say Martha used to be a witch. A seer. Some say she still is. She live here, in this hospital, for many years. Before I come here, she is here." Dr. James smiles, as if to silently dismiss the idea. "She is a very good nurse, this is all I know for sure."

"She is very kind," I say.

"She knows many things." Dr. James, I think, is perhaps more superstitious than he'd like me to believe.

"You give credence to what she said?" I ask.

He shrugs. "Who knows? I am a doctor. A man of science." He waves to the east. "But yet, I grew up out there, far from science and medicine and universities. I have seen things which perhaps even science cannot explain. I am a doctor, but I also believe in life beyond our life."

"I don't know what that means."

Dr. James only smiles at me. "I think maybe you do."

I think of the dreams I've had, of Ava—the dream I had only last night, or this morning, early, in the gray hours of dawn, and I nod. "Maybe I do."

"Will you tell me?" Dr. James sees something in my expression, perhaps, or maybe he is just very perceptive.

"I had a dream." I close my eyes and tilt my head back, letting the sun beat on my face as the shreds of the dream float through me. "It's hard to remember it exactly. I was…I was on the shore. Here. Where Martha took me a few days ago. I was on the shore, wading in the sea. It was up to my knees, and the current was strong. The sea was very, very cold. A single gull was flying around overhead, cawing, floating on the currents. The sky was gray, and hard, and I knew it was going to rain. It was just me on the beach. Just me and the sea and nothing else. Like…like there never had been or ever would be anything else—that's the feeling I had. And the gull, crying and crying …god, I don't know how to put it. The sound it made was—echoing. But that's not the right word. Not echoing like off the walls or something, but echoing…through time, or across space. Like, if I was on the other side of the Atlantic, I would be able to hear the echo of that gull's voice. The sound just…*echoed*. I don't know else to put it."

"I think I understand," Dr. James says. "I have had a similar dream, once. The day my wife died in the riots, I was in Ghana, doing work for a UN mission. I was asleep, in a hospital, in a chair, after working for forty-six hours without stop. I dreamed of my wife, and then I dreamed of a lion. A big male lion, out in the savannah, sitting in the tall grass. Looking at me and shaking his head. And then he roared at me. Teeth bared, and he had blood on his teeth. That roar, it—*echoed*, just as you say."

I nod, glancing at him. "Exactly." I draw a breath, hold it, and let it out slowly. "In the dream, the sound… *shivered*, if you know what I mean. It made the air shake. I felt it in my bones, in my belly. And suddenly I was flying across the ocean. Maybe I was the gull, I don't know. I just know I followed the sound across the sea. It was like I was flying low, like in a movie, you know? Following the surface, so low I could see each wave. So close I could almost feel the waves spraying as they broke on each other. The gull was making that long, keening sound they do when they're riding a strong wind. I could hear it, even though I knew I was too far out to sea for a gull. But I could hear it. And then I saw her. I saw Ava. She was on a boat, I knew this somehow even though I'd never seen the boat before. I just saw her, curled up under a thin blanket, and she was shivering. I don't know how I got there, I was just suddenly there, in the room with her. And she was shivering, whimpering. And the gull cawed again, and she sat up suddenly, with a sharp gasp. And for a second, just a split second—I thought she could see me. For a moment, it felt as if I was really there. I almost said her name, but I didn't. I think she heard me anyway."

I had to swallow hard against the hot lump in my throat.

"She said my name. She whispered it, and I heard it." I pause. "I heard her say my name, and the moment I heard it, I woke up."

"Do you believe in dreams, Christian?" Dr. James asks.

I blink a moment, and then shrug. "Do I believe in dreams? I don't know. I know I have them. Sometimes they're more…visceral than others."

"When I dreamed of the lion, roaring at me with the blood on his teeth, I woke up, and the first thing I saw was the clock." He toys with the end of his stethoscope. "Later, I find out the very moment I had the dream, the very minute and hour I woke up from the lion's roar, this was the exact moment my wife was shot here in Conakry."

"So you believe the dream was real?"

A shrug. "All dreams are *real*, but does that mean all dreams are *true*? I do not know. Only that…perhaps dreams *can* be true. Perhaps…perhaps it is easier to believe dreams are *not* true, so we do not have to believe in something beyond what we can see and grasp and taste.

As a doctor, I know this of myself. But I also know we must believe in the things beyond ourselves. I am just a simple man trying to help whomever I can. I want to think I am just a small piece in a very great puzzle and that maybe, with our dreams, like your seagull and my lion, that we can sometimes catch the most fleeting glimpses of what is…*more*."

I rub my forehead with a knuckle. "I honestly don't know what I believe, Dr. James." I close my eyes again, as if speaking truth is easier if I cannot see. "It felt real. And…that's not the first time I've had a dream like that about Ava."

"You miss her. You wish to find her."

"So…so it could just be my mind creating these powerful dreams, because I miss her so much."

"Or, it could be something else. It could be that which is *more* trying to bring you back to her."

"I have to admit, it's a very tempting idea."

"What does it hurt, to believe?"

I shrug again. "If I don't find her, or it doesn't turn out right, or whatever…" I hesitate. "If I were to let myself believe and it goes wrong, if she's dead, or it turns out I was a terrible person, or something…I think my capacity to believe in anything would be crushed."

Dr. James tisks. "Bah. You are not so much of a coward as that. I know—I, who have lost two wives to death—*I* know we must continue to believe, even though this world is full of death and suffering. This world is full of *shit*—" he spits the world explosively, vehemently, "but it is also full of beautiful things. We cannot let shit win out against beauty. Beauty must win. Life must win. Love must win. Or why else do we even try? I know patients will die, so why do I try to save them? Because I believe in *life*, Christian."

I only nod.

Dr. James is quiet a while, and so am I, each of us lost in our thoughts. After a time, Dr. James points at me with the arm of his spectacles. "You go west, now?"

"Yeah, I guess so. That seems the best way to go to find Ava."

"The same fishermen who saved you from the sea, they too go west to find the fish. You go with them." He pats his knees twice, and stands up, with a gusty sigh. "I will see to it."

"Really? They'd take me all the way across the Atlantic?"

He shrugs one shoulder. "Your story is something of a fable to them, like a myth they have lived through. They have told this story to many people, and the fishermen around here, it is a small community, a close community of men who are all very superstitious."

"I wouldn't think local coastal fishermen would like to cross the ocean," I say.

"It is asking a great deal of them," Dr. James admits. And then his gaze fixes on me. "To go west once more, to be alive, to have your name? It is a second chance you have been given, Christian. It is a gift. Do not waste it."

I swallow hard. "I—I won't," I say.

And so, the next day, after I bid goodbye to the nurses, Dr. James drives me to the local port. I embrace him, knowing this man saved my life once, and now he is saving it again.

Dr. James claps my biceps in his hands. "I have done everything I can for you, Christian. You have a chance to regain your life. Or perhaps not to regain it, for it will not be as it was—I think you know this. It is a chance to build it into something new. What you make of your life, now, it is up to you. I say to you yesterday, this is a gift you have been given, and that you must not waste it. I say it again—do not waste this."

My eyes burn, and my throat is tight. "You—you've saved me, Dr. James. I can't—I can't thank you enough. I'll never be able to repay you for what you've done."

"One does not repay a gift, Christian."

"I just—" I scrub my face with both hands, and then embrace him once more, fiercely. "Thank you, Dr. James. Thank you."

When I let go, Dr. James backs away, clearing his throat gruffly. "You are welcome." He shoves a hand into his trouser pocket. "Maybe you send us a postcard here, when you find yourself settled, yes?"

"I will."

And then, with a wave, Dr. James turns and strides away across the docks back to his car. I have no possessions except a tattered old carpetbag with a few changes of clothing, donated to me by the hospital, my notebooks filled with my writing, some pens, and a card made by the nurses for me, with their signatures and phrases of goodbye and well-wishes in various languages. I carry this bag with me across the gangway from dock to the gently rolling deck of an aging but well-kept fishing vessel. I am greeted in French by the captain, an older man with a gold front tooth and what appears to be ritual scarring on his cheeks. The other crewmen all stand clustered together, staring at me with something like awe and perhaps a little superstitious dread. One man whispers something to the man beside him, and another man makes some sort of gesture with his hands, to ward off evil or to call down good fortune; they rescued me from the sea, and now I'm going back out into it. My rescue was miraculous, so I am either fool, a madman, or cursed.

I can't say they're wrong.

But yet, I must go.

I stand at the railing as we cast off and leave port, watching the sea churn, watching the coastline disappear, listening to the familiar clink and grind of a fishing vessel.

I'm coming, Ava.

From Christian's handwritten journal;
November 23, 2016

There is nothing but the Sea,
      The scudding of the wind,
      And the twisting melt of Time against my
skin.
    Nothing but the knowledge of our sin,
    And my guilt, oozing under my flesh like sludge.
    Nothing but your dark truth,
    coating the fine hairs on my arm like a mist.
    Fever dreams in the darkness, as I lay in the belly of
a beast:
    You, love, with your lips sewn shut,
    each stitch written in ink-black threads,

The wounds where needle threaded flesh raw and red and bleeding;

Me, staggering through venomous shadows,

alcohol seeping from my skin like leaking poison;

A grave, the marble headstone gleaming wet in a driving rain,

the mound of grass jeweled with raindrops—

Old, rotten flowers going gray, forgotten 'neath the stone—

five letters, scribed deep in the marble,

old pain and fresh agony howling and screaming from the name:

H E N R Y

I speak softly,

Whisper to the winds;

The Sea answers.

She shouts in storm syllables,

Howls in hurricane stanzas,

Writes truth in tempest,

Sings of half-remembered sorrows in shrieking gales.

You, love, with your lips sewn shut.

Me, lost in the wilderness, skin leaking poison.

The Sea spans the space between us.

The waves know you, and speak of you.

They sing of you, whisper of you.
But I don't understand all the words,
And I know I'm missing something,
Half-understood truths slipping past me,
And if only I could comprehend,
I would find you.

I smell your perfume on the wind.
I hear the soft sigh of your voice,
That dulcet sound you make as you come apart with
me.
I can almost taste your skin in the soak of the brine
on my lips.
If I stand at the prow and close my eyes, I can almost
feel you.

Darkness gathers around me;
I wear it like a cloak.
I wrap the shreds of shadows around my shoulders
like a tattered coat,
Because the light, the sun, the warmth,
They are too real, too bright, too unforgiving…
And I prefer to hide.
I am king of shadows, wading the shoals at full
moon,
storm clouds as my crown;
I play in the deeps,
cavort with the weird, translucent, eyeless creatures

that lurk there beside me.

If I emerge into the light, you will see my ugliness.
The Sea will go glassy,
It will become a mirror,
reflecting my flaws back to me.
I don't want to see them;
I don't want you to see them.

Must I give up my crown?
Must I shed my cloak?
Must I show you all my sins,
worn on my flesh like warts and boils and scabs?
Must I see them, myself?

You are beautiful,
You are perfect.
You are a carving of ivory,
a thing of unmarred porcelain—flawless and elegant.
I know this is a fiction,
but such are the games played by Memory,
Such are the vagaries of Time,
Those mischievous sisters of the trickster, The Sea.

You, love, with your lips sewn shut,
Me, lost in shadows, skin leaking alcohol, leaking
poison, leaking truth.

You, love, sighing in the silence.

You, love, reaching for me with a sleepy smile.

You, love, collapsed against a headstone, weeping.

You, love, your spine presented to me,

You, love, wasting away, silence wrapped around you like ice.

You, love, shrouded by the miles and the months.

Where are you, my love?

15

From Ava's handwritten journal;
November 23, 2016

I feel him.

Christian.

It feels as if there's a magnet sewn into my skin, pulling me toward him. I dream of him. I see him on a ship, a storm raging. He gazes into the maelstrom, and I would swear he sees me.

But this is not what devours all my waking moments, now.

It's not Christian, but my child, my Henry.

I see it all happening again in a flick-frame montage:

Giving birth, holding the messy bundle that is my newborn son—

Changing diapers, breast-feeding him, swaddling him, rocking him back to sleep at 3am—

Being exhausted and exhilarated by motherhood.

Then, suddenly, Henry howling in obvious and heart-wrenching agony I can do nothing to stop—

A doctor in a white lab coat, balding with a terrible comb-over, stethoscope over his shoulders, pens in his pocket, an earnest and compassionate expression expertly pasted onto his pudgy face, his mouth moving in slow motion, words distorted, only a few syllables clear: brain cancer…inoperable…palliative care—

A darkened room in the pediatric oncology wing, Henry in a crib, tangled cords and tubes and wires making him look more like a science experiment than a human baby, a monitor beeping slowly, an oxygen machine pumping even more slowly, the green accordion bag inflating and deflating in decreasing intervals, until the moment of flatline—

A tangled mess of blurry days and moments, signing papers, events swirling around me rather than to me, Christian always beside me, but like a thing of iron and marble, an automaton—

A bright sunny day, brilliant and cloudless and hot; a group of black-clad individuals with somber expressions, standing around a tiny casket, a miniature thing of polished black wood with bright silver accents; a minister speaking words, Christian tossing a handful of brown soil onto the casket landing with a loud clatter, Christian trying to get me to do the same. But I can't. I said good-bye when he entered the arms of the angels, and I cannot bear another goodbye to my son.

The montage ends there—

With my inability to say goodbye at the grave.

I see it again and again and again—Christian with that handful of rich dark loam, letting it trickle over the edge of his palm onto the casket, a ticking rumble as dirt hits wood, a hollow sound, and then he upends his palm suddenly and abruptly, opening his fist so the handful of dirt vanishes into the hole of the grave. I see Christian doing that, again and again.

I'm standing behind him. I have a thick wad of tissues in my hand, sodden with my tears. He turns, stretching out a hand to me.

"Come on, Ava," I hear him say. "One last goodbye."

"I can't." I hear myself say the words. "I can't. I already said goodbye to him. I can't do it again."

I see myself turning away, my heels digging into the grass. I see myself walking away from my son's grave.

I see this on repeat, a series of moments stitched together and looped.

And then there's AFTER.

After the burial, once we arrived home.

I left one of my shoes in the living room, on its side, just behind the couch. The other I left in the hallway our just outside our bedroom, upright, but the toe facing back toward the living room; I can still hear the shoe wobbling on the hardwood as I trudge listlessly to the bed, the shoe tipping side to side before going still. I remember lying there, under the blankets, in my funeral dress, staring at the photo of Henry and me. He's so happy in that photo. Grinning ear to ear, a gummy, happy grin, eager and innocent, a bit of drool on his chin. His hands are in the air, blurred, mid-wave.

I stared at that photograph for so long that it is burned into my brain. I can see each individual detail: I am wearing a red tank top, the strap just barely visible, and I have my favorite tiny diamond studs in my ears—the same earrings I'm wearing now, actually, which are the first gift Chris ever gave me, for my birthday a month and a half after we met. My fingernails are painted a pale purple, and my hair is pushed back over my ears, held in place by the silver arms of a pair of sunglasses—an old pair of Christian's aviators. Henry is wearing a tank top/ shorts romper, gray with red and white pinstripes down the sides and a koala embroidered on the chest. Henry has a red pacifier in his left hand, blurred into a pinkish smear.

I remember taking the selfie, and I also I remember that within seconds of snapping that selfie, he started fussing and crying, and shoved the binky into his mouth, his forehead wrinkled in pain. But in the moment of the photograph, he was so full of joy, so happy just to be taking a picture with Mommy. And I, in turn, was just as happy and joyful, in that moment.

After, as the fussiness took him, worry replaced joy. Panic replaced happiness.

But for that moment, I was blissfully joyful.

I remember lying there in bed for days—for weeks—staring at that photo, trying to remember what it was like to be that happy.

I wish I knew, even now.

I climbed into bed, and I stayed there. Christian would come in and sit on the bed, and murmur to me. Tell me he loved me. Try to get me to sit up. To eat something. To say something.

I couldn't.

I remember it all. I remember being utterly unable to so much as form a sound—my grief was just so HEAVY, an elephant sitting on my chest, crushing me, pinning me. I couldn't breathe. I'd lie there, and I'd be barely able to draw a breath. Because, if I drew too deep a breath, I'd start sobbing and I'd never stop. I'd drown in sorrow. So I just remained still. Wishing I could die, wanting to just fade away.

I felt each individual moment and sensation with crystal clarity. I felt the hunger pangs, the thirst. Headaches. Withdrawal from caffeine. Stiffness, soreness. Pressure on my bladder or bowels. I felt it all; I just felt the sorrow and the grief more acutely, and those utterly buried and dwarfed the rest. Nothing mattered except that Henry was dead.

It crushed me.

It shattered me.

I'd buried myself in that little box. Christian, with that handful of Florida dirt, had interred me in the ground along with Henry.

I remember too the desperation in Christian's voice. The way he would plead with me. Beg me. Bring tray after tray of food.

I remember the anger, so vividly. It was an inferno inside me, consuming me.

I stared at the photograph and thought back over each moment when I'd KNOWN deep down something was wrong with Henry and had chalked it up to fussiness or colic or something else. I blamed myself for not realizing. For not bringing him to the doctor sooner. If I'd found out sooner that he had a tumor, maybe they could have done something to save him. I felt anger at Christian for not insisting we get him checked, for thinking I was paranoid. Anger at Christian for not protecting our son. In the twisted snarl of grief and sorrow and anger inside me, I managed to blame Christian.

I lay in bed and I stared at the photo and I slept and I fought tears and I fed on the anger, and ignored the hollow hunger in my stomach. All I had within me was anger. I heard his words and felt nothing, only anger. Only rage. Only sorrow. Only grief. But it was all mixed up and twisted and wrong.

Who was I really angry at? Myself? Him? The world? God? Everything?

Rage was such a wildfire inside me, so full of fury and hate and sorrow, that I couldn't move. Couldn't breathe. There's no way to put what I was feeling into such a paltry, mortal, intangible thing as mere words. Things like <u>SORROW</u>, and <u>RAGE</u>, and <u>ANGER</u>, and <u>GRIEF</u>...they're just words. They don't—can't—encompass what it feels like to watch your helpless infant son suffer such awful torture, watch him sicken and die and know there's not a single goddamn thing you can do to even ease the pain. You can give him drugs, but only so much, because those'll kill him too.

You can only watch as he suffers. You can't suffer with him, you can't take it from him, and you can't die in his place—you would, in a heartbeat.

You would suffer all the evils this world has to offer if only he could be spared this hell.

But it doesn't work like that. And so, he dies.

Yeah, that'll make you angry. But how do you put that into words? How do you describe what you feel in the moment the monitor goes flatline and you know he's gone, your son, your baby is fucking GONE?

You don't.

You just...die inside.

I'd been scooped hollow—I remember reading that phrase somewhere, used to describe the grief at losing a loved one, and it is absolutely accurate. Everything that was me had been ripped away and scraped away, leaving nothing in its place.

That creature lying in that bed, staring at that photograph? It wasn't me, that wasn't Ava St. Pierre. It was...a THING. A void.

There was nothing inside me. That's why I was so unresponsive—I wasn't me anymore. I'd been tortured into madness.

But now?

Now I hear Christian's voice.

I hear the pain, the agony.

I hear the grief.

He'd suffered through everything I had.

Not only that, but he'd had to watch me starve myself. He'd lost his son and his wife at the same time. And he had suffered this alone.

I did that to him.

I'd twisted the knife in his heart, and then sprinkled salt on the wound.

I'd abandoned him when he needed me most.

No wonder he left me.

On board Le Coureur D'onde; off the coast of Africa; November 26, 2016

Being on board a ship feels like coming home. The bucking and tilting and rocking of the deck, the spray on my face, the sight of the sea everywhere around me...it is home. Brings me back to myself. The men crewing this vessel probably think I'm a little crazy, because I never want to leave the deck. I do the work of three men, hauling and coiling lines and mending nets and the million other jobs there are to do aboard a fishing vessel. I sleep little—I'm too excited about being in motion, finally, about being on a ship, and feeling memory return.

I'm finally beginning, in some small ways, to feel

like myself.

I have a name.

I know I am a writer.

There is a woman, Ava, who loves me.

But yet, there's still a dark undercurrent roiling inside me. Some knowledge I dread to unearth, a memory I'm not sure I want to regain.

So I work, and I sit in the galley with the crew learning new words and phrases in half a dozen languages, laughing at jokes told through gesture and facial expression and messy mixtures of languages. We drink pots of coffee and relieve each other on deck and eat huge piles of food, and work side by side through night and day.

It's cathartic, for me.

I don't write.

I try not to remember—or rather, I don't try to remember. I let the memories come as they will, and they do come.

I remember being at sea. I remember the snap of a sail, the wind slicing across the bow. Spray on my face. Joy in the journey. Nights at anchor, in the harbor of a tiny island somewhere remote, watching fish leap and the moon rise, watching bioluminescence wash ashore with a blue-green glow.

I remember shopping with Ava, simple grocery shopping, grabbing cans of soup and testing fruit for ripeness and putting boxes of cereal and bags of bread and cases of beer into the cart, all done in easy synchronization.

I remember Henry. Changing his diaper in the middle of the night. Playing with him on the floor of our condo. Pushing him in a stroller down a sidewalk, Ava at my side, smiling, bumping me with her shoulder, a coy smile on her lips.

Sitting at a computer for hours, fingers flying.

Signing a contract selling the film and merch rights to my book to a major production company.

Buying a new car with Ava—a Range Rover Sport Supercharged, a sleek white powerful beast, a symbol of our new success.

Ava, Ava, Ava in a million images, a thousand different emotions, hundreds of expressions on her beautiful face—laughing, crying, angry, drunk, sleepy, crawling across the bed with hunger for me in her eyes…

I remember it all.

But what is it still lurking underneath the surface, like a circling shark? It's the reason I was found in the ocean, shipwrecked, it's the reason I'm alone, the reason I'm crossing the ocean in search of her. What happened?

I don't want to know…God help me, I don't want to remember.

But I have to.

I feel it at my teeth, pounding at my heart, throbbing against my skull, and I know I have to excise it.

I retreat to the narrow cot I share in shifts with another man, prop my notebook on my thighs, and begin to write:

From Christian's handwritten journal;
November 26, 2016

The bottle is a silent judge, a sentinel reminding me of
my sins.

It is a tall bottle, square-sided instead of cylindrical.
A label across the front—Johnnie Walker Black Label. It
once contained 750ml of blended scotch—that scotch is
now almost all gone, coursing through my bloodstream.

Where am I? It's hard to tell; the world spins, twists.
Topples. Whirls. Blurs.

Blackness, but woven through with blips and washes
of silver; movement. What is it I am seeing?

Stars. Waves.

The sky and the sea.

Where am I? I am not moving—the world is. Am I
on a boat? I don't think so.

I hear a sound, a susurrus, a constant, soothing,
shushing noise: the crash of waves on a shore. The waves
are to my right, close.

Something cold licks against my right side, licking,
ceasing, licking, ceasing.

Above, stars. Not a lot of them. A few, here and
there. If I focus hard enough, I can see them. The brightest stars, brilliant silver specks.

Beneath me, grit. Cold. Bitter. Sand? It makes a firm
mattress beneath me, yet soft and shifting as well. Grit
under my cheek. In my ear. Crunching between my

molars. Coating my lips. Speckling and dancing in my nostrils as I gasp for breath. Fluttering under my eyelashes as I blink.

I am on a beach. On my stomach in the sand, stars above, the sea to my right. The tide is coming in, the cold seawater lapping at me.

I cannot move. My limbs are weak, full of jelly and lead. I try, however. Push my knees under me, dig my palms into the sand, until it covers them to my wrists. Make it to my hands and knees, but I'm off-kilter, and the world is spinning like a top, wobbling as in the moments before it loses momentum and topples over. Pause on my hands and knees for a moment, squinting—there, the condo building. Rows of orange-yellow squares, windows; light; home.

Ava is in one of those squares. Which one? Bottom row, third from the left. Ground floor. She'll be on the couch, and she'll be in little better shape than me—on her back, head propped on a throw pillow, a bottle of wine dangling listlessly from one hand, empty. Another bottle or two on the coffee table, also empty. The TV will be on, reruns of some reality show flickering, faces and voices and occasional glimpses of cars and city scenes.

I crawl a step. Two. Wobbly, like a newborn calf.

I lurch, and topple forward, face-planting in the sand. I roll to my back, groaning, and spit out crunchy flecks of grit. Above, six or seven of the brightest stars coruscate and glint and wink, and then spin and twist and multiply. I plant my hand and elbow in the sand and try to roll back to my stomach, but only make it halfway before slamming back down.

I lie there for who knows how long, counting the same few points of light—there is too much light pollution to truly see the stars, and as I lie there I half dream of being on a boat, out on the sea, the stars above countless in their millions.

My stomach clenches, mimicking the crashing roll of the surf.

I barely make it to my side before vomit slams against my teeth, and then I spew it into the sand, bitter and acidic and hot.

Vomiting clarifies my mind, somewhat.

But I don't want clarification. I want the blurred nothingness. I want to drown in dizziness.

Because with clarity comes memory.

The flatline beep.

A nurse in maroon scrubs solemnly silencing the monitor and removing wires and tubes. Ava sobbing, crumpled on the floor. My own tears, silent but sharper than razors. My inability to sob—I simply cannot. I want to, but cannot.

Ava, her mind gone, her eyes vacant. A thousand questions, decisions to make. Casket choices. Burial plots. Which minister will perform the service? Will there be a memorial?

Coming home from the hospital, finally, and seeing

his bedroom. The blue binky on the floor, next to a stuffed lamb. A board book, and one of those things with the colorful rings of ascending size, for stacking. The trash can with dirty diapers still in it. The changing table, a drawer still open, a half-empty package of Huggies protruding, a diaper half out of the ripped-open hole. His closet, open, with a sailor suit and his first Halloween costume—the Stay Puft Marshmallow Man—and sweaters and little blazers from Old Navy and The Children's Place. I had to close the door before I shattered into a million pieces.

I don't want these memories.

I still see Henry gasping. I still see the green accordion bag squeezing and expanding ever so slowly.

No, no, no. Please, no.

I don't want it anymore. I don't want to see it.

So I force myself to sit up, reach for the nearly empty bottle, and take another drink, glugging until the bottle is empty.

Throw it aside—the bottle clunks into the sand with a dull hollow thud; wind blows, whistling across the mouth of the bottle.

The sky and the sea move and rotate around me. The ground beneath me heaves.

Shadows weave themselves around me, cling to me, reach up and drag me down. The sand welcomes me. The shadows play around my eyes, play ring-around-the-rosy games. Darkness is a constricting ring. I can't stay awake.

I have enough sense to roll to one side, until sand presses cold and gritty against my cheekbone.

I welcome the darkness.

The darkness swallows me, subsuming memory and pain…

If only briefly, temporarily.

And then I see you. You're striding toward me. It's the pink-gray-orange of just before true dawn. I'm in the sand, facedown, head twisted to one side, my body angled partly toward the sea. I see you blurrily, multiples of you twisting and rotating. But it's you. You haven't left the condo in weeks; you're skeletally thin, frail, and delicate; you've just started eating again.

You haven't spoken to me in weeks.

My eyes want to close, and I see you through the haze of my eyelashes. Do you know I'm awake? I don't think so.

You plop into the sand beside me. I cannot move, don't even try; even breathing requires effort.

I see the outside of your thigh, your knees drawn up against your chest, arms around your legs. Your chin rests on your knees.

"I fucking hate you." Your voice is a whisper, raspy from disuse; are you speaking to me? I don't know. "He's dead…he's dead, and it's your fault, and I fucking hate you for it."

Are you talking to me? To yourself? To God? I haven't

moved, I'm barely breathing, and my eyes are nearly shut, so it's hard to believe you'd know I was awake.

I don't know anything, right then.

I believe you hate me, though. I believe you blame me. I blame myself.

You sit there for a while, and I drift in and out of consciousness. Eventually, you stand up, brush sand off your butt, and you walk away.

I watch you go and I barely recognize you, as I barely recognized the hoarse rasp of your voice.

Your words toll in my skull like a bell.

I FUCKING HATE YOU.

It's all I hear, again and again.

I see the grave, and his name etched into the stone. The dates of his birth and death, representing a tragically tiny fraction of life:

Henry Christopher Michael St. Pierre
Beloved son, gone too soon.
June 24, 2014—April 3, 2015

Your hatred of me was a palpable thing. It seethed in the air of our condo. Filled it like a cloud of poison. You never spoke it again, not after that moment on the beach—in which you may have been talking to yourself or to God.

I know I said similar things to myself, and to God.

I never said them or thought to you or about you,

though. I never hated you.

I still don't hate you.

Even as I write these words, on a boat in the middle of the Atlantic, in the middle of the night, I don't hate you.

If anything, I hate myself.

All this is awful to remember.

Your hatred.

The ice between us.

The silence which exuded from you was an arrow shot from a bow. It hit dead center, right in my heart. The silence struck me full force, and in many ways, killed me.

I died. Not just in the ocean, eight months ago, but before that.

I died the day I walked away from you.

I remember that, too:

I walked through the condo one last time. Paused at our bed, staring at it. I saw in my mind all the love we'd made in that bed. I wondered if I'd ever see you again. Wondered if I'd ever touch you again. Wondered if I'd ever peel away your clothes again and reveal that perfect creamy skin, your lovely curves, your perfect softness. I wondered, as I stared at our bed, if I'd ever have you in my hands again, if we'd ever move and breathe and whisper each other's names in the silence of a lazy morning.

That nearly broke me. Nearly cracked my resolve.

Maybe…maybe if I try again, I thought, maybe if

I try harder, I'll reach her, finally. Maybe, just maybe, she'll respond to me. Maybe she'll love me again.

I'd already written a goodbye note, already moved all my things to the boat; all that was left was to leave.

I hadn't really even needed to come back here.

But I did.

I came back to say goodbye.

Because I knew nothing would change. I knew I'd never get you back. I knew I couldn't take the hatred and the silence anymore.

So I left our bedroom, and our bed, and all the memories tangled up in those sheets.

Darcy, the puppy, was curled up at your feet, at the end of the couch. Bennet, the kitten, was prowling around, sniffing things, tail tip flicking. You were passed out. I knelt beside you; Darcy woke up and sniffed me, licked my hand as I reached for you.

I brushed a lock of your hair aside, hoping the touch would wake you. I had a brief fantasy, in that moment, that you would open your eyes and I'd see that love there again and you'd kiss me and we would make it through together.

But you didn't. You didn't even stir. I brushed the tendril of hair away, tucked it behind your ear. My throat clogged. My eyes burned, tears quavering at the corners, which I desperately fought to hold back.

"Ava." I whispered your name.

Hoping you'd wake up and would love me again.

"Ava." Once more, a little louder, no longer sotto voce.

It was a plea, from me to you—please wake up, please love me again.

Nothing.

Silence—as throughout the preceding three months…I received only silence from you.

I stood up—waited, barely breathing, for you to move, to stir, to look at me sleepily, like you used to, blueblueblueblue eyes soft and sweet with love and affection.

You didn't.

"Ava." I tried one last time, my voice breaking. "Please—" this last word was broken, barely an audible, intelligible word.

I choked.

The silence was thick and stifling, the silence was a fist around my throat, choking the life out of me.

No more—no more—no more. I couldn't take any more.

I backed away two steps, then three more, my eyes on you, asleep on the couch, too thin, an empty wine bottle on its side near to hand.

The silence was profound, and total. There wasn't even the ticking of a clock, only complete and utter silence.

Emptiness.

I stood there, holding the doorknob, watching you sleep, willing you to wake up and take it back, tell me you loved me.

Finally, no breath left in my lungs, unshed tears hot in my eyes, my hands shaking, I twisted the knob. Opened the door. Darcy lifted his head and watched me, curious, as I turned and walked out.

I left you, Ava.

I sailed away.

I knew you needed me, but I left anyway.

I was too weak. Too broken. Too dead inside. Too heavy with my own grief and failure.

I left you, Ava.

I left you.

God, I'm sorry.

I'm sorry.

Dakar, Senegal; December 1, 2016

Dominic is conversationally fluent in French; I guess it makes sense that someone who travels the world would know a smattering of languages. We arrived in Dakar around midday, which, according to Dominic, was something of a miracle, as it should have taken us much longer to get here, but the storm worked in our favor and pushed us east.

He's conversing with two men, using a complicated mixture of English, French, and gesticulation—one of the men is a translator who knows some English and French as well as the African dialect which is the only language the third man speaks.

A long, convoluted conversation is taking place, the

translator speaking alternately to Dominic and then to the tall, hard-eyed fisherman with skin the color of ebony. I'm not following any of the discussion but I've deduced that, somehow, the fisherman knows something about Christian. What exactly he knows I'm not sure. I've heard a few phrases here and there which I recognize, but nothing I can really follow.

After ten minutes of chatter and a fifty-dollar bill to the sailor and another to the translator, Dominic leads me away from the wharf to a small hole-in-the-wall café. Dominic orders us coffee thicker and blacker than actual sludge which is served in tiny cups, along with several dishes of spicy-smelling food.

"So." Dominic sips his coffee, and digs into the food. "We're in luck. We've got our first lead."

"You sound like a PI from a seventies cop show."

"I kinda feel like one," Dominic says.

"What did the guy say? Did he know Christian?"

Dominic holds out a palm and waggles it side to side. "Not directly. He's just in from Conakry, in Guinea, which is a few hundred miles south of here, and he heard a story being told by some other fisherman."

I dig into the food too, and sip the coffee with a lot of grimacing. "What was the gist of the story?"

"Several months ago, some fishermen were lost in a crazy out-of-season hurricane, and they hauled a white guy out of the drink. He had no ID, no memory, no nothing. He was half-dead, just floating in the ocean miles from anything."

"Oh my god, that could be Christian!" I exclaim.

"Exactly. So—according to the story our guy heard—these fishermen brought him to a hospital they knew of just outside Conakry, and they left the guy there and figured that was the end of it, right? Well, it doesn't end there.

"Fast forward to just a few days ago, and these same fishermen are getting ready to put out for a trip down the coast, trawling for whatever fish is in season over here. A doctor from the hospital where they'd taken the man comes aboard their boat and says the guy they fished out of the ocean is alive, has recovered his memory and is trying to get back to his life in the States, and he needs their help. Well, these are coastal fishermen, right? They don't do transatlantic crossings. Yet, somehow, the doctor convinces them to make the trip, with the same guy they'd plucked out of the sea a few months ago, half-dead and without a memory."

I feel a thrill of excitement. "So he's alive?"

Dominic makes a face and holds up his hands palms out. "Well, I don't want you to get too excited just yet. It COULD be him, but it may not be. I mean, there's a lot of white males out there, sailing the world, right? And it's entirely possible this is some other white guy who went missing at sea."

"But what are the odds?" I ask.

Dominic nods. "I know, I know. I have a feeling it's

him. I just…I want you to keep a level head, okay? We gotta take this one step at a time."

"So, what's the next step? Do we know where this hospital is? Where'd you say it was?"

"Conakry. Or, just outside it, actually. It'll take us a few days to get there, and then we just have to hope it was him, and that they know how to find him."

For the first time in weeks, in months, I have a glimmer of hope. Just knowing there is a possibility that the man they are talking about could be my Christian makes me feel about a hundred pounds lighter.

I just pray we aren't disappointed.

Conakry, Guinea, December 4, 2016

Three days later Dominic and I are standing on the hospital grounds and I'm showing a picture of Christian to a man named Dr. James.

"Yes, yes, this is Christian," he says in a thick African accent. The man speaking to me is on the far edge of middle age, portly, kind, and wearing gold wire-framed glasses. "Of course, he did not know his name until only a few days before he left us."

When it became clear the doctor speaks English fluently, and knew Christian, Dominic went back to the boat to give me some privacy.

"He was here?" I ask, scarcely believing it could be true.

Dr. James nods, handing back the photograph of Christian. "Yes, yes. For…oh, eight months. He was very near to death when he came here. He was most dehydrated, with breaks on his left arm and leg, a broken right wrist, many broken ribs, and a most severe concussion. It is a miracle he was alive, to be truthful. He was in the sea for a very long time, and I think only a very strong will and stubbornness kept him alive." Dr. James eyes me speculatively. "Or maybe it was you. You are Ava, yes?"

I nod. "Yes, I'm Ava. He…he spoke of me?"

Dr. James lets out a long breath. "Oh, my dear. When he did not know even himself, he spoke of you. The fishermen who rescued him said your name was all he would say, even when he was unconscious."

I choke, eyes burning. "Really?"

Dr. James nods. "Oh yes. To say that he loves you is…it would do the intensity of his love for you a great disservice."

"He had amnesia, I've been told?"

Another nod. "Temporary retrograde amnesia, if you would like the specific medical terminology. When last I spoke with him, he had recovered many of his memories, specifically of you, and your relationship with him. Many other memories he had of himself and his own past were still difficult for him to piece together, but he remembered his name and the shape of most things of his life, at least."

"How was he, emotionally?" I ask.

Dr. James hesitates. "It is hard to say with much certainty. He suffered a most extensive trauma. Not only the shipwreck, but also the events which preceded it. I think perhaps in some ways, his amnesia was brought on as much by the emotional trauma and his psyche's need to separate from it. It was as if he needed a rest from the emotional suffering. It was too much, perhaps, and his psyche attempted to repress his memories as a way of giving him a rest, so to speak."

"Where is he?" I ask. "Do you know?"

Dr. James waves a hand at the sea, audible in the distance. "Searching for you, I believe. He wanted to go back to the United States." A pause. "He left us around your American holiday of Thanksgiving."

I am about to cry, and trying valiantly not. "But I came all the way here looking for him!"

"The ship he is on is called *Le Coureur D'onde*. It departed some two weeks ago, heading eastward from the port of Conakry." Dr. James leans forward, takes my hands in his. "I am only a medical doctor, but may I offer you a small piece of advice?"

I nod, blinking back tears. "Please—yes, please."

"Tragedy comes to us in many ways, unpredictable and painful. We cannot avoid it, and we cannot pretend it did not happen." He removes his glasses by peeling them off sideways, with a twist of his head, and gestures with the arm of them. "You and he, you both suffered much. For your husband to remember, he had to write down what he remembered. It caused him great pain, and to understand some of what drove his pain, I must read some of these journals. So, I know of the loss of your son. This pain…there is nothing like it."

"No…no there is not."

"You must forgive." He smiles gently. "You must forgive first yourself, and then each other."

"Easier said than done, Doctor." I blink away more tears.

He nods. "Oh yes. That is quite true. But still, you must forgive or you will never heal."

"I don't know how." I can't blink these tears away anymore, they are too hot and too many, blurring my sight, running down my cheeks, and dripping off my chin. "I'm so angry. At him, at myself, at God, at life, at the Sea. I'm so angry at everything. I don't even know where to start."

Dr. James sighs, with another kind, gentle smile. "You begin where we must always begin—at the beginning. It is easy for me to make such pithy statements, of course, but where *is* the beginning; this is your next question, yes? The beginning is yourself. I do not know all that happened between you and Christian. I only read bits and piece of your husband's journals, to understand some of where he was in his mind and in his journey to remembering. But I do know from my own life that when I am most angry at myself, I find it much easier to let my anger at everyone else rise up and grow stronger and eclipse my anger at myself. But the root of it all, the real seed of it, is my anger at *me*. And so, in order to be able to forgive others, or God, or the World, or Life, or the Sea, or whatever else I am angry at, or have been wronged by or feel wronged by, I must first forgive myself. Even if I deserve the anger or the blame or the guilt, I cannot carry it forever. It is too heavy a burden for us to carry such things around on our backs all our lives. To live, to be truly free, we must put them down."

His gaze is dark and distant, staring beyond me into the past, perhaps, and I think he understands what he's talking about more deeply than I could ever imagine.

We converse a bit more, about Christian, about his time of recuperation here, and Dr. James's impressions of him.

The image that emerges of Christian is…it's of a man I'm not sure I would recognize, anymore. I might have, once. The Christian Dr. James describes is soft-spoken and quiet and gentle, introspective, humble. All the things Christian used to be, but that he lost along the way, to one degree or another.

He also describes a Christian obsessed with me, holding on to memories of me as the only lifeline keeping him from madness and despair. He describes a man who would sometimes drown in sorrow, especially as he began remembering what happened.

The Christian I remember, especially after Henry died, was hard and angry and distant. He tried, with me, but it felt as if he was trying out of obligation, or because he needed me. He also drank a lot and I cannot imagine that helped either; I know it didn't help my recovery or grief at all, only prolonged the hurt.

I think there was a chasm there, between reaching out to me and trying to help me because he loved me and wanted me to be okay, and doing so because he needed me for his own emotional well-being.

But then, I'm guilty of the same thing. I retreated into silence and apathy because I couldn't handle reality, I couldn't handle life. I withdrew utterly and completely.

Selfishly, I never even considered him in my grief, never thought of him or his needs or my love for him— he never even entered my mind. Once Henry died, the pain of his loss was all, totally consuming me, devouring everything I was.

He retreated into alcohol and the recesses of his own mind, and I, doing the same, had no idea where he was, emotionally, or what he was going through. We should have been there for each other, but we weren't.

We're both guilty of that.

He abandoned me, but I abandoned him too.

So…who's more at fault?

Does it matter?

I don't think it does.

All that matters, now, is finding him and—I don't

know. Forgive him? Then what?

I don't know. Find him first, figure the rest out afterward.

And so I find myself back on *The Glory*, standing at the bow of the boat, one hand on the railing, phone in the other. I call my sister, because I need her advice.

The handset rings, and after a few rings, Delta answers. "Hello? Ava, is that you?"

"Hi, Delta, yeah, it's me."

"Good to hear from you, honey. So, where are you calling from and what's the latest on your search?"

"Christian was alive as of two weeks ago. I'm calling from a place called Conakry, which is a port city in Guinea, an African coastal country. Christian was rescued by fishermen and brought to a hospital here. He had temporary retrograde amnesia, which just means he couldn't remember anything at first but eventually recovered most of his memories. When he finally remembered enough of who he was, he left and went looking for me."

"But...you're out there looking for *him*."

"Exactly."

"So now what? He's alive, but he's out there looking for you and you're out there doing the same thing?"

"I don't know what to do next, honestly." I have to hold back tears, which seem to be on the surface all the time now. "Do I go after him? He's got a two-week head start on me."

"I don't know much about boats and all that, obviously, but can't Dominic just hail them on the radio or whatever?"

"I don't know. I haven't talked to Dominic about any of this yet. I got back to the ship and I immediately called you. I'm just—I'm relieved and I'm frustrated and I'm confused all at once, and I—it's all too much, sometimes."

"You set out to find your husband, Ava. Well, you've almost done it, right? You know he's alive, you know he didn't just vanish, or die, or decide to not come back or whatever, so…this is all good news, right? I'm just saying, there's got to be a way of getting hold of the boat he's on. Like, you could take a helicopter or something. Like I said, I don't know how things work out there, but I feel like there has to be a better way of catching up to Chris besides chasing him all the way back across the Atlantic."

I let out a breath. "You're right. It's just frustrating to be so close yet so far. I mean, this doctor I talked to, he *knew* Christian. He treated him and took care of him for the last eight months. Helped him get his memories back."

Delta hesitates. "You know, I've heard that people who go through memory loss sometimes aren't ever quite the same as they were, even if they remember pretty much everything."

"Yeah, and from what this doctor told me, it seems like Christian is going to be…different."

"He's been through a lot. It'd be impossible for him not to be changed by everything, memory loss aside." She hesitated again. "For that matter, you've changed a lot too."

"I have? How?"

A long silence. I can hear the sound of people speaking in the background, and then Delta's answer. "You're more...internal, now. I don't know how else to put it. Inside your own head, if that makes any sense. More closed off. Quieter. A little more hard-edged."

"None of that is good," I say, with a deprecating laugh.

Delta didn't laugh with me. "Ava, honey. You lost your son, and then your husband left you, and then you went through a hurricane and almost died, and then you found out Christian had been lost at sea and was likely dead, and now you've spent more than a month at sea, which you hate...looking for the husband most people would assume is dead." A sigh, from Delta. "How are you supposed to go through all that and *not* come out the other side a little worse for wear? Everything you've been through is going to change you too, Ava. It *has* to. It's *going* to."

I feel one of those truths I've been hoarding deep inside trying to bubble up and out, and I let it. "I—I've had a lot of time to think, lately. Not a lot for me to do except cook and clean and think, you know? And...I—I've realized I don't really know who I am."

"Ava, come on—"

"No, for real. Like, my identity has always been so wrapped up in Christian and then Henry, and now I'm finally being forced to face the fact that I don't have either of them anymore, and I don't—I don't know who I am. What is it I do? I'm not blogging anymore, and I don't think I ever will again. I'm not writing anymore either, and again, I don't think I ever will. Not on a novel, at least. What would I write about? And my one novel wasn't worth shit, so why go through that again? So…if I'm not a wife, if I'm not a mother, and I'm not a writer, then who am I? What am I? What value do I add to this world?" I swallow hard, and my voice is more a whisper than anything else.

"I'm more closed off, hard-edged—that's what you said, and you're right. And yeah, that's just a natural effect of what I've been through. But…what do I do now? What do I do if I never find him? What if something else happens to him? What if we never find each other? Or what if we do, but there's nothing there between us anymore? I mean, we were horrible to each other, Delta. We both were just…*horrible*. We were husband and wife, and best friends—we should have been there for each other through the loss of Henry, but instead we both drank ourselves half to death and ignored each other. Or, at least, I ignored him, and then he left because he couldn't deal with my hatred anymore."

"Do you hate him?" Delta asks. "For real?"

I have to think about my answer. "I—I think...I think I was in so much pain I couldn't even process it, and the only thing I had was anger, and the only person around to be angry *at* was Christian. Do I hate him? No, I don't. I'm angry at him, but I'm just as angry at myself, so..." I shrug, even though Delta can't see me. "I don't know *what* I feel. It's all a big messy jumble of shit I can't process. I don't know what to do."

"Want to know what I think?"

I laugh. "Why do you think I called, Delta? You're my big sister. I'm hoping you have answers I don't."

She finally laughed with me. "Well, I don't claim to have the answers, just what I *think* you should do, in my opinion."

"Just tell me already!"

"Okay, so I think you should ask Dominic about the radio thing. There has to be a way of contacting the boat he's on and getting them to turn around so you guys can sort of meet in the middle. That's step one. Step two is, once you and Chris are back together—in the same physical space, I mean—you just...figure things out one day at a time. You won't know what he's like after everything that's happened until you see him, and that'll affect you both. Things are going to be different—you have to go into it knowing that much. You won't ever be able to go back to the way things were, right? You know that as well as I do. Too much has happened for that. But that doesn't mean you and Christian can't find a future together."

"I thought you didn't like him?"

"It doesn't matter whether I like him or not, Ava. I know he loves you, and I know you love him. So, unless you feel like you really truly don't love him anymore, or if he says he doesn't love you anymore, then there's *got* to be a way through this for you guys."

"A really huge part of me—pretty much all of me, in fact—doesn't even know what I'd do without him. Like I just—I can't picture my life without him. But I also can't picture our future. I see Henry. I remember the way I treated Chris, lying in bed for two months ignoring him, and what that must have been like for him, to be so alone with his own pain plus me being…whatever I was. I remember waking up one day and finding him gone, and then receiving that stupid fucking letter he sent me. And all the emails. That fucking story about the selkie, all that. What if we can't make it past all that?"

"Don't let *not* making it be an option, then."

"Is it that easy?"

She laughs. "Easy, no. Simple, yes."

"Helpful." I sigh. "Speaking of making it, how are you? We've been talking about me this whole time. What about you? How are things with Jonny, and the tour?"

A long sigh. "Oh, Ava. I'm happier than I've ever been in my whole life. Everything is just…magical. I'm playing music every day, my own music. I'm on the radio. I've got plans for another album, after this tour. And…I've got the most amazing man in the whole world who loves me and takes care of me."

"I'm happy for you, Delta. I really am."

"I am too," Delta says with a laugh. "I mean, shit, I've earned a little happiness, I think."

"How's Alex doing being on tour with you?"

"He's loving it. One of the guys on the crew used to be an elementary school teacher, so he's sort of acting like a tutor for Alex. We're doing an online homeschooling program. Jonny is teaching him Spanish, and now those two are jabbering away in Spanish all the time and I have no idea what they're ever talking about. Alex *loves* Jonny, like—he worships the ground Jonny walks on, which I understand. And Jonny is just amazing with him. Plus, Alex is surrounded by music all the time, and everyone on the tour is just amazing and they all treat him like actual gold. They let him help set up and tune the guitars, and every time I turn around someone else has him on their shoulders, or he's sitting on a speaker stack while someone sets up. It's not a traditional way to raise a kid, but it's working for us."

"Sounds like life is finally treating you right, huh?"

"Yeah, after damn near forty years of shit, right? But yeah, it's awesome."

"What are you guys doing for Christmas?" I ask.

"The tour is taking a break the week after next and we don't pick up again until the New Year, so we'll have time off. And, honestly, I don't know what we're going to do. The tour bus is our home, and we haven't really discussed where we'd call home base. We're kind of no-madic at the moment, I guess. We'll probably end up just staying on the bus and having our own little Christmas there. We have a little tree, and we have each other, and I think that's all we'll really need." A pause. "What about you?"

I choke. "Oh god, Delta, I have no idea. I guess it depends on what happens."

"You know you can always spend it with us, right? I mean, you're way over there in Africa, but I'm just saying so you know without a doubt that you've always got a place with us, if you ever need somewhere to just…be, I guess. I don't know. We're family, Ava. Don't forget that. I love you."

"I love you too. And thank you." I laugh, a little bit-terly. "If I wasn't so close to finding Christian, I would be there with you in a heartbeat because, let me tell you, Delta, I'm sick to fucking death of being on this god-damn boat."

At that moment, Dominic appeared beside me. "Good to know how you really feel about my baby," he said, patting the railing.

"Dominic, hey," I said, clearing my throat. "I just meant—"

"Relax, Ava, I'm kidding. It's no secret you don't ex-actly love life at sea." He jutted his chin at my cell phone. "That your sister?"

I nod. "Yeah, it is."

"Tell her to tell Jonny I said hey." He pats the railing again, this time with a closed fist. "You and I gotta talk when you're done there, Ava."

"Yeah, I'll only be another minute," I tell him, and then address Delta on the other end of the call. "That was Dominic—"

"I heard," she says. "I'll pass the greeting on to Jonny when I see him." There are voices on her end of the call, someone trying to get her attention. "Look, I gotta go anyway, they need me for sound check."

"Okay," I tell her. "Go be an important country music star."

She snorts. "Don't be a turd."

"I'm not a turd, you're a turd."

"How old are we? Three?" Delta sighs. "Ava, just know that you're in our thoughts. I don't know how this will shake out for you, but I know you'll be okay one way or another."

I sniffle. "I wish I had your confidence."

"I'm not gonna offer you any trite advice like following your heart or some bullshit like that. I'm just gonna tell you that I love you and I'm here for you, and I that I believe things are going to work out for you in the end. How I don't know, but you'll figure it out. You've always had your shit together, which is something I've always admired and been envious of."

I laugh at that. "I most certainly do not have my shit anything even remotely approaching together. Right now, I'm a hot mess, Delta. For real."

"You're allowed. Sometimes life just fucks us up, and we gotta let ourselves just be a mess for a while. You'll get your shit together and be back to being enviably fabulous in no time, okay? Believe in it."

"It's hard."

"Then fake it 'til you make it, right?"

I sigh. "I'll try."

"Okay, I really have to go." A muffled pause as she says something to someone on her end. "Go get your husband, Ava."

"Yeah. I love you, Delta. Break a leg, okay?"

"That's theater, but thanks for the sentiment." She makes a kissing noise. "Okay, hanging up now. Love you, bye."

On board Le Coureur D'onde; off the coast of Africa; December 4, 2016

A storm rages. It has been a nonstop barrage of storms for the past several days, each worse than the last. The fishermen, being superstitious, wonder if I am to blame. There is a story in the Bible like that. Jonah? Or Paul? A character who disobeyed God and fled, causing storms which threatened to sink the ship, and so the character threw himself overboard, or something like that. It is only a vague memory of a story I learned in Sunday school as a child.

After my pen disgorged those last, awful, incriminating memories, I wallowed in guilt and sorrow and anger and self-recrimination for days. Told myself I deserved what I'd gotten, that I didn't deserve Ava, didn't deserve life. I even stood at the railing early one morning while the storm raged, and thought about letting a wave take me over the side.

I was stopped by one of the crew. A large man, named Louis—pronounced the French way—with skin like the blackest ebony and a deep rumbling voice and broken English.

"You are much sad," he said in his cavernous voice and broken English, pulling me away from the railing and down to the galley; he poured me a mug of coffee and sat, blocking my exit from the booth.

I nodded. "Yeah. I did a lot of bad things—I abandoned my wife." The admission just pops out, unbidden. "I don't deserve—"

"You speak shit."

I stopped and stared at Louis. "What?"

He swallowed coffee, his huge hands dwarfing the mug. "We do not deserve, or not deserve. We do not take life, give life, end life. Only for God to do that."

"Yeah, well, I don't like God and I don't think he knows what he's doing."

Louis grinned. "I know this feeling. I lose my daughter. Much fighting, bad tribe, good tribe, all kill. My daughter, she is killed. My wife, she is rape. Much bad. I have anger. I fight. I kill."

"I would have too."

"Then I am shooted." He taps his chest. "Wife think

I am die. She leave. No more fighting, no more gun, no more sad. She leave. I am alone. I think of my hands. I kill with gun, I kill with machete. Much bad. I much angry. Think I do not deserve to live. I try to shoot me."

"You were only defending your people, avenging your daughter, your wife."

Louis shakes his head. "No. No. A priest come, speak with me. I see that I am wrong. It is not for me to take life—my life, other life. It is only for God."

I sigh. "Look, Louis, I see what you're saying, but—"

Louis's massive hand chops down, stopping me. "No. You hear." He gets up, refills our coffee mugs, sits back down. "You are sad. I was angry. It is same."

"God took my son from me. He was a baby, Louis. Not even two years old. He died, for no reason."

"No reason, or reason you are not see? Same. You are sad. Maybe angry. But are you weak?"

"I don't know. Maybe?"

"I see you. You think maybe the sea should take you. Jump over, or maybe only not fight for life, not hold on. You think it is better to be dead than to live so sad, with so much anger and guilt."

I nod, slowly. "Yeah, sort of."

"That is weak." He holds my gaze. "I was there when you come out of ocean. I pull you up. I carry you to my bed. We all watch you. Try to keep you alive until hospital. You fight for be alive, then. You strong. You fight for woman. For Ava."

I swallow hard. "I don't feel strong anymore, Louis."

"Strong is not feeling. Strong is *doing*."

I think about what he's saying, and it cuts through me. "Maybe you're right."

"I am right." He nods. "When I am sad, from lose daughter, lose wife, when I am angry at men, when I am angry at me for killing those men, I think, it is no good for me to be alive anymore. I am no good."

I nod. "That's how I feel."

"I cannot shoot myself. I try, and I cannot. The fighting, the sadness, the hate, it is too much. So, I run away. But always, it is there, because it is me—it is *in* me, so I cannot run away from it."

I nod. "I sailed thousands of miles, and never got anywhere."

"Yes, you see it. So then, I find this boat, these men. They do not speak me like I speak you, now. They make me work. Feed me. Give me drink. No questions. Only, never I am alone. Much time is passed, and one day, I know I am alive, and it is *good*."

"Just like that?"

He shakes his head. "No. Not so easy. Many days of hate for me, for God, for life, for everything. But you cannot be alive and find it good if you are dead. You must wait through the hurting. You must wait through the anger."

"I've *been* waiting."

"You must forgive."

"Why? How?"

"God forgive, so we forgive. Easy."

"I don't believe—"

Louis snorts dismissively. "You believe, you not believe, no matter. God is same. God believe. God forgive. You forgive. Strong is not feeling, strong is doing."

"Letting myself die is weakness, then, you mean."

"Yes. Weak is easy. Strong is hard. Hard is better."

I sigh, rub my face with both hands. "You sound like Dr. James."

This seems to please Louis greatly. "He good man. He fix me when I am shooted. He talk much to me. Listen much. Help much."

"Same for me."

Louis eyes me. "He do much hard work to fix you. Fix body, fix mind. You dead, you remember nothing, and Dr. James, he fix." A significant pause. "You let yourself die, then all his work is for nothing."

Guilt, then.

"And your woman, Ava?"

"I walked away from her. I abandoned her."

"She love you?"

"She used to."

"Baby die. She angry, she sad, she broken." He shrugs. "Like you. You forgive, she forgive, this is better. Not easy. I say this already. Easy is weak, easy is no good. Run away is easy, and where you go when you run away? Nowhere. So you do what is hard, what is strong. You find her and you forgive. You *live*." He taps my chest, my forehead. "You *live*. It is better."

I nod, but I'm thinking. I glance at him. "You're the one who pulled me out of the water?"

He nods. "Bad storm. I am on the deck. Big wave, much rain, much wind, I think we sink." He pauses, swirls coffee in his mug, and then looks at me. "God make my eyes see you. It is impossible. To see you in the water, with so bad storm, big waves, very dark? I never see you. But God, he say turn my head—look there. I turn my head, and I look. I see you. I throw you lifesaver, and you take it. You fight for be alive. I pull you in. You are hurt, you are die. You say this name: Ava. Ava. Ava. This all you say, even asleep, so much pain, almost die, but still you say this name—Ava, Ava, Ava, like so, much and much and much."

"You saved my life."

He shakes his head. "No. God save. I only help."

"Still…thank you."

His eyes are fierce, and knowing. "You make thanks to me? You *live*."

Something inside me catches fire, a flame that had gone out, guttered into darkness long since. His words spark, and the flame catches, burns inside me, warms me.

It is the fire of life.

I should have died.

In a way, I *did* die: I died when Henry died, I died

when I walked away from Ava, and I died when I went overboard all those months ago.

Louis saved me, Dr. James saved me. Ava saved me.

How could I be so thankless and weak as to make a mockery of what they all did for me by letting myself die? How could I do that?

It is weakness.

I groan, hold my head in my hands. "Thank you, Louis." I look up at him. "You're right. You're absolutely right."

He nods. "Now you live."

I reach out, and we clasp hands. "Now I live."

On board *Le Coureur D'onde; off the coast of Africa; December 6, 2016*

For two more days the storm continues to batter the boat, and it requires every man working double and triple shifts to keep us afloat. Exhaustion begins to take its toll. Men stumble down to the galley and suck down coffee and wolf down food, and stumble back up, eyes glazed, limbs weak and dragging.

There is no time to think, no time to feel. There is only time to react as best we can.

I am on deck, scrambling to keep nets from being ripped free, crates from coming loose, the crane from snapping. I am delirious with exhaustion, at the stage of sleep deprivation where I see moving shadows out of the corners of my eyes, and I hear things.

I have a loose cable in my hands, and I suddenly see a shadow to my left—a man, stumbling across the deck? Surely not, it must just be another hallucination.

I hear something, whispers bubbling just under the surface of awareness—*look, look, look; look in the water, look in the water, look in the water.*

It's not words, I don't hear words. It's…more of an idea. A knowing. A prompting.

The deck tilts wildly, and I slide downward, toward the railing and the sea beneath it. I slam against the railing, the wind knocked out of me. I gasp, groan, and then clutch at the railing as the deck tilts the other way and we twist and tilt downward again.

Look—look—look—

My eyes search the waves; for what, I don't know. A hallucination? A shadow?

But no, I definitely see something.

A dot of yellow in the crushing turbulence of the mountainous waves. A head. Arms flailing. I act on instinct, stumbling down the railing to where the life ring is, and I throw it, and I miss. I haul it back in, keeping my eyes on the head bobbing in the waves, remembering all too well how it felt to be lost in the sea just like that.

My next act is involuntary. I don't think, I just *do*—I hook the ring over my shoulder and leap into the icy, churning sea. I swim to the surface and haul at the water, eyes fixed on the bobbing glimpses of yellow slicker. A wave throws me head over feet, and I splash down, and the ring pulls me up and I gasp, coughing salt water, and then I feel something nudge my arm. I see the yellow slicker and black skin and wide scared eyes—it is Louis.

I wrap my arm under his armpit and around his chest, and kick toward the boat. I am able to loop the life ring over his head and under his arms, and I grab him with one hand and the rope with the other, and *pull*. Someone is on deck, I see glimpses of movement, of faces, hands, and I feel the line go taut as they haul on it for all they are worth, battling the rocking ship and the unrelenting walls of water.

"Breathe, Louis," I shout, gasping for breath myself.

He spits water, coughs, clinging desperately to the ring, and I cling to him and the rope.

The sea rises up under us, and the boat is suddenly beneath us and it's tilting and twisting, spinning. It crests a wave and I catch a glimpse of the screw and then the boat is slamming down the wave and Louis is jerked away from me, flying. My hands burn as the rope sears through my grip, and then I see Louis crash into the sea and then many pairs of hands are pulling him aboard.

I'm dunked underwater again, spinning, the storm and the water chew me up and spit me out. Sky and sea, salt and air. I feel something hard and plastic smack against me and I grab at it blindly—the life ring. I wriggle into it, and cling to it desperately. I hear voices shouting. I fumble for the line, and then feel it go taut as they haul me toward the boat.

Another giant wave rises up and becomes a mountain of angry brine, and I'm lifted with it like a child's toy. I glimpse the boat, and the rope, but I can see that the rope is pulled taut, and it is vibrating with tension.

I feel it, first—a release of tension. And then the wave shifts and changes course, colliding with another wave, and I lose sight of the boat, and the rope is trailing through the water. I have the ring, but it has snapped free from the boat.

Another wave curls over my head, and I'm dunked under and then all that exists is the fight to reach air, to keep my head above water, to pray and swim and hope for the impossible yet again.

I should pray to God, but only one name echoes inside me:

Ava.

Ava.

Ava.

Part 3

"Fishing vessel *Le Coureur D'onde*, come in, please. This is Captain Dominic Bathory, of the fishing vessel *The Glory of Gloucester*. Come in please." Dominic says this three times in English, and then repeats it in French.

"Oui? C'est Le Coureur D'onde. Qu'est-ce tu veux?"

Dominic responds in French. *"Je cherche un homme qui s'appel Christian St. Pierre."*

A pause. Then, in halting, broken English, a deep voice responds, a different person than first answered. "He here, in this boat. We find storm. Our man, Louis, he fall out of boat. Christian jump, he save Louis. Big wave take Christian away."

I hear what he's saying, but it doesn't register.

And then it hits me. No, no, no. Not again.

God, please.

I hear Dominic speaking, a mixture of French and English now. I hear numbers—coordinates? Dominic is scribbling on a paper, and then he's at a map with a pencil and compass, calling out instructions to Mack, who's at the helm. Mack is old and gray and leathery, exuding capability and silent calm. He spins the wheel and adjusts the throttle, nudging the lever forward so we go faster. I feel the engine grind louder under my feet, and we course down waves and up waves, recklessly fast. Dominic and the other man are still speaking, and their words seem to bounce off me.

All I can think is, *not again, not again, not again.*

I was so close.

Please, Christian.

Please, God.

Do I believe in God? I don't know. If I did, I'd be angry at him. For Henry, for this whole thing. But right now, I'm willing to beg a god I don't believe in to help me.

I feel big, strong hands on my shoulders, shaking me. "Ava? Ava!"

I blink at Dominic, tears streaming unheeded down my cheeks. "What." It's a listless statement, a question I don't have the wherewithal to articulate.

"We can find him. We're close to their position."

I only stare. "They had a two-week head start."

"I know, but they tried to skirt around this huge

storm, and then they got blown way off course by it. I don't think their captain is very experienced at navigating the open ocean. Point is, they're within a few miles of us, which is nothing in oceanic terms. It seems impossible that we could be so close to them with the head start they had, but it's true. I've triple and quadruple checked the coordinates against ours. We're so close we could almost see them, in clear weather. We can *find* him, Ava."

"How?"

"There's a freighter west of us, and south of *Le Coureur D'onde*, and they're starting to move in our direction, looking for Chris, creating a triangle around where he has to be. Between the three of us, we have a chance—a slim chance, but still a chance—of finding him."

I stare out the window at the storm, the lightning flashing, illuminating the shifting mountains of the waves and curtains of rain. "He's out there. He's gone again."

"Ava, you're not hearing me." Dominic holds my shoulders, his bearded face close to mine. "We're gonna find him."

"He's out there."

Something breaks inside me.

My gaze floats and flits around the room—to Mack at the helm, staring hard out the window, expertly guiding us down one wave and up another; to the stack of charts; to the instruments on the dash, lit up and blinking; to the radio, microphone dangling from the hook; and finally to the hooks hung with yellow rain slickers and orange life vests.

He's out there.

Christian is out there. Dominic is right—he's close. I can feel him.

Time stretches and stutters, words floating around me.

Mack is a stoic, stolid presence, and Dominic is a manic, bustling one.

Time hiccups and lurches.

How much times passes? I don't know.

He's out there; that's my only thought, as hours or minutes pass in jumps and taffy-slow stretches. The storm howls and rages.

He's out there. My husband, my Christian, he's out here again. I can feel him, as if a string is tied between my heart and his, binding us. If I could reach out, if I had the arm of a god, I could pluck him from the Sea.

He's out there; how can I stay in here, waiting, doing nothing? How can I sit by and wait for him to die, wait for him to sink beneath the waves?

He's out there, and I'm in here. I can't handle that reality any longer. I just can't. I have to find him. I have to be closer to him.

He's out there; it repeats inside me like a skipping CD.

Repeats until I cannot stand it any longer.

I stand up. Grab a slicker off the hook and put it on, along with a life vest. Dominic watches me for a moment, and then springs into action as I make for the door.

"What the fuck are you doing, Ava?" he snaps. "You can't go out there! There's nothing for you to do!"

I shove him, hard. "LET ME GO!" I hear myself scream it. "He's out there. I feel him. He's out there!"

I'm so broken. Shattered. I need him. I've traveled thousands of miles to find him, and now he's been taken from me again. Why? Why?

I'm outside before Dominic has time to recover. The wind blows me sideways, and I stagger. The rain is cold and beats against me like icy stinging fingers, like a million razors. It spatters against the rubber of the slicker with a ticking, spacking clatter. I can't see anything. I'm tumbling across the deck. I hit something hard with my shoulder, and instinctively grab onto it.

Christian—where are you?

I see him, in my mind or in reality, I don't know. I see him—he's twisting in the grip of a wave, tumbling, pummeled and crushed, swimming desperately.

I'm sorry, Christian. I'm sorry for everything.

The deck beneath me lurches. My stomach drops out, and I'm weightless.

I hear a shout, but it's lost in the howling shriek of the wind and the roar of the rain and the crash of waves.

A cold so piercing it feels hot as it smashes through me, envelops me. I can't breathe. Salt sours in my mouth.

I'm thrown like a bit of stick, and I taste air, and my lungs gulp at it.

Is this what it's like to die in the Sea? She has me. Your mistress, the Sea, she finally has me. She has us both.

Christian?

Christian…

Ava?

I hear her voice.

I feel her presence. It's a pull on my heart, a tug on my soul.

A tiny, quiet voice whispers to me, a voice hidden somewhere in the deepest recesses of my soul: *Swim, Christian. You're not meant to die like this. Choose life, Christian.*

And so, I swim. My hands pull at the waves. I seek air, and suck it into my lungs. I have no life jacket this time, only the ring around my chest. I'm tumbling under, unable to keep my head above the waves, swallowing too much water.

I'm cold. Or am I hot? Numbness—a sign that hypothermia is taking hold.

Lightning flashes—is it lightning? It is too bright, too steady for lightning. Sweeping evenly and rhythmically side to side across the waves, seeking and searching—what I see is a searchlight. Do I hear a rumble under the shout of the Sea?

I'm plunged under the waves and try not to breathe the brine. I fight for breath, and when I feel rain on my face, I cough and splutter and suck at the air.

Yes, it's a searchlight, and the rumble of a propeller churning, an engine grinding.

A wave throws me skyward and as I tumble I catch a glimpse of a massive shadow against the waves—a freighter. I recognize, even in a quick glimpse, the soaring superstructure and the endless deck and the high rounded bow.

I'm tumbling again in the twisting churn of the waves, surfacing, spluttering, then plunged under again, and the next time I surface, the freighter is towering above me, and the spotlight sweeps across me, returns, and I hear distant voices shouting.

Déjà vu.

Ava's face dances in my mind as my hands reach for the life preserver as it hits the water in front of me.

I see her face. Her black hair, loose around her cheeks and chin. Her blue eyes on mine.

One more glimpse of her—it's all I want.

Another part of my brain is telling me that what's happening right now, being found, is statistically impossible. Logistically impossible. The fact that I survived going overboard in the middle of the Atlantic once is in defiance of all the odds and realities of life at Sea: if you go overboard in the open ocean, on any ship, large or small, you will die, with almost total certainty.

I didn't die.

I survived.

I suffered hypothermia and broke a shitload of bones, and was dehydrated, and I lost my memories, but I survived that first time.

I knew, when I hit the water again, just minutes ago—or is it hours?—that I would die, this time.

Yet here are hands reaching for me. Pulling me in. Wrapping me in a crinkly, loud, awkward silver blanket made of what feels like tinfoil.

How?

Is that You, God? Are these Your hands, plucking me from the Sea?

I don't believe in You.

You stole my son from me.

You stole my wife from me.

You stole my joy, my happiness.

And now You save me from the clutch of Your merciless Sea, yet again?

What do You want from me?

Why pluck me from the jaws of death a second time?

In the hours of my drunken sorrow, after Henry's death, I cursed You. I railed against You. I told You I hated You. I didn't believe in You, but I needed someone to hate, so I cast my hate upon You.

And myself.

Thus the gallons of whiskey to numb the sorrow and

guilt and hatred, to dull the edge of shame, to blunt the razor of agony.

Thus the running away, like Jonah.

All of which I blame You for.

Even still.

Even now, as I cling to life yet again, I know You, and recognize the feel of Your hand meddling in my life.

Why?

Death's jaws are snapping at me, behind me, echoed in the roaring churn of the Sea all around me. And from this certain death, not once, but twice You have snatched me.

Why?

To what purpose?

What am I?

A whiskey-sodden wretch with a dead son and a wife who assuredly hates me, who is better off without me, who couldn't be bothered to even glance at me in our time of greatest sorrow.

I am nothing, no one, a fool with a ready pen and no substance; I am a soulless golem of cracked and drying clay, crumbling as the weight and sorrow and pressure of Life becomes too crushing.

Yet...

I hear Dr. James telling me to make the most of this gift of life.

Louis's voice, his words: *You LIVE. It is better.*

I hear the voice whispering to me from the waves:

Choose life.

I will live—I will live.

I choose life.

As I drift off to unconsciousness, I see you, Ava.

I see your hair framing your face, your eyes cerulean and bright, glowing with love. Gazing up at me. Your hands flutter up to my face, and you drag the back of your hand along my jaw. You laugh as I pretend to resist your advances, and your laughter is music. Your lips find mine and our breath tangles and skin brushes skin and then we're moving in synchronous beauty, and each touch is electric, each kiss a fiery burst, each thrust wondrous and silken.

I see you, Ava. I see you.

Then I see nothing, dizziness and unconsciousness and blackness subsuming me.

When I wake up again I see walls and exposed pipes, hear the clang of bells announcing the changing of the hour, soles squeaking on floors beyond a door. Fluorescent tubes buzz, hidden behind translucent plastic cases on the ceiling above me. There's an antiseptic smell. My eyes close again, exhaustion weighing me down.

A voice nearby, brittle and throaty with age. "Been at sea my whole life. Worked freighters and cruise ships, worked on destroyers and cruisers and even a carrier in the navy. Seen plenty of men go over in my time, and only a tiny handful ever even got found dead, much less rescued alive. Storm like this? You don't survive it. You just don't. Even finding a corpse is a laughable notion."

"He survived it." A much younger voice, then. "And so did she."

"My point exactly. People talk about the impossible odds of surviving going overboard, but a youngster like you wouldn't really understand. It's like winning the lottery—it ain't that the odds are against you, it's that the margin of possibility is skewed so far against you there ain't really any worth in thinkin' on it. So, these two, both going overboard in the same storm, and both getting picked up by us?" A disbelieving laugh. "That math don't work. It ain't possible. It just ain't. I don't believe in miracles, but…"

"But there they are, together in our sick bay."

A sigh, from the elder voice, almost annoyed. "Exactly."

I'm tired. So tired.

Thirsty. Dizzy. I still feel the twist and churn of the waves, even though I'm lying on something firm and soft—a gurney or medical bed.

I hear a groan—it's from me.

"Hey, now. Easy, bub. You been through a hell of a time." The older voice, his hand on my shoulder, gentling me.

Something tugs at me. Not physically, though it's like

a physical sensation; something pulls at my attention.

My head lolls on my neck, twisting to the side: I'm on a cot in the sick bay of a large ship, cabinets and counters, a blood pressure cuff, a hand washing station, a sharps container; another bed, near mine, not six feet away.

A thin form lies on that bed, chest rising and falling, wrapped in a silver blanket like my own, teeth chattering.

My heart lurches.

Stops.

Black hair, sodden and tangled. A familiar sweep of neck and line of jaw. A temple I've kissed countless times. Is she awake?

Is it really her?

I have to know.

I force myself into motion, ignoring the protests of the doctor. I kick and bat away the crinkly blanket. My feet touch the floor, and I try to rise, but my legs refuse to take my weight. I collapse to the floor, boneless, the exhaustion and hypothermia a brutal enemy.

I'm dreaming.

I have to be dreaming.

Why would she be out here? Why would they have pulled her from the Sea?

I'm dreaming.

I am dead, and this is my purgatory.

I crawl across the floor, ignoring the hands trying to help me, the voices speaking to me—they know my name, somehow. I ignore them and crawl to the other bed.

My hands latch onto the side of the bed and I pull myself up. I'm tired and weak and shaky and cold and chattering and shivering—am I naked? No, I'm clad in some kind of clothing, spare scrubs or pajamas or something, pilled and scratchy cotton. Why did I notice this? I don't know; my mind is going a million miles a minute, and yet as each moment crawls by, as I force myself upward.

Her teeth chatter, I can hear them clicking together. I see her whole body shivering. I'm at eye level with the left side of her face. There, just below her left earlobe where jaw meets neck, is a spray of freckles, six of them; I've lain awake at night tracing patterns in those freckles.

There is a tiny white scar on her jaw, on the underside near her chin, where a tree branch once whipped up and cut her; I have licked and kissed and nuzzled that scar, collapsed breathless in the moments after I have poured myself into her.

"Ava—" My voice is hoarse. "Ava?"

Her eyes are closed, her long lashes resting against her cheeks. At my voice, at her name on my lips, those eyelashes flutter.

I'm arrested by a memory—it hits me like a bullet, stops time, freezes me:

We are lying in bed together. Dawn is far away, still, and I'm not sure what has awoken me. I can see little but the shadows of our room, the shapes of dresser and door and the reflection of shadows in the bathroom mirror, and the dim ripple of the Sea out beyond the windows. I'm sleepy, my eyes wanting to slip closed again; I'm warm, comfortable, happy. I turn, and nuzzle against Ava. She murmurs sleepily, and twists to face away from me in her sleep, but her hand catches at mine and drapes it over her bare hip. She wiggles her butt against me, and then she's snuffling as sleep pulls her back under. Minutes pass, and I'm nearly asleep again. She shifts and twists back to face me. My eyes open and I gaze at her. A moment, then, when she's still asleep, her eyes closed, and then her eyelashes flutter and she blinks awake. The moment she sees me, a sleepy smile crosses her face, love filling her features.

I'm slammed back to the present.

She just blinks at me for a moment, unsure if she's awake or dreaming.

"Ava?" I whisper her name.

Her features twist through a barrage of emotions— hope, relief, puzzlement, fear, love, anger, joy.

"Ch—Christian?" Her voice is a raspy whisper.

"Ava." My voice breaks as I say her name for the fourth time.

The silver blanket crinkles, and her hand wriggles free. She reaches for me, fingers trembling. Her fingertips touch my face with delicate hesitancy: *Am I real?*— that's the question in her touch.

I make a mangled sound: laughter and sob, disbelief

and joy, love and wary hope.

"Is it really you?" Her voice is so soft, so quiet, and so broken that my heart is shattered by the fragility I hear in it.

"It's me."

20

He's real.

He's here.

I can't breathe, can't see, can't think, can't process. I'm cold. I'm thirsty. My brain is full of cotton.

He's in front of me, and I see his mouth moving, but I hear nothing.

His hair is long, hanging past his chin, lank and wet, sticking to his cheeks and neck. His face is obscured by a beard, wild and unkempt and thick, also wet. A long scar runs across his forehead, into his hair, a thick, ropy, pinkish line of puckered skin. He's thinner than he's ever been, but healthy looking despite that. His eyes search mine. His warm, familiar eyes sear into me, lush deep liquid brown, bleeding emotion.

I want to cry, but I can't; I want to reach for him, but I can't—I'm too weak, too tired, too cold. All I can do is stare at him, trying to process that it's really, really him. He's alive. He's here. He's real. My Christian, my husband, my best friend…I've finally found him.

What happened? I don't remember.

I'm so tired.

My eyes won't stay open. I don't want to fall asleep, though. I fight it. If I fall asleep, he'll be gone when I awake.

His hand is cold and clammy as he cups my cheek; I can finally hear his voice. "Sleep, Ava. Sleep, my love. I'm here. I won't go anywhere. I'll be right here when you wake up. I'll never leave your side again, I swear."

His hand on my hand. His cheek against mine.

Never leave my side again…

I have a momentary glimpse at the maelstrom of emotions swirling inside me, all the things I've been re-pressing and suppressing and ignoring and halfheartedly sorting through, all the emotions I've not known how to even begin to let myself feel. There's so much; too much. A glimpse at that storm of emotions inside me, just a glimpse, makes my heart twist and slam, and then I push it all aside. I'm too tired, too cold. I can't stay awake. I can't deal with any of that. Not yet.

I stare at Christian, squeeze his hand in mine, and then I feel my eyes sliding closed and I can't fight sleep anymore.

I wake up briefly, but fall back asleep again. I have no idea how much time has passed.

Next time I wake, I see that I have an IV in my arm.

When I wake up yet again, Christian is nearby on another bed, also with an IV in his arm, and he's asleep, facing me, mouth open, snoring lightly. I stare at him, taking in his features. He's changed so much. Thinner, harder. Long hair and beard where he was once clean-shaven and kept his hair neatly cut. The scar on his forehead belies some of what has happened to him since he left Florida all those months ago.

His eyes open and meet mine.

We just stare at each other, locking gazes for I don't know how long.

There's so much to say, but neither of us is ready to say any of it.

I'll never leave your side again, I swear.

My eyes struggle to stay open. I fall asleep with Christian's eyes on me.

"...Storm's finally blown itself out." I hear the rough twang of the doctor's voice. "Captain says the storm has put us behind schedule, and going out of our way to find you and Ava has put us even more behind, so we can't afford the time to detour out of our way to take you anywhere."

"So what are our options?" I hear Christian ask.

"There's a Coast Guard cutter about a hundred miles from our position. They're sending a helo to pick you two up, and they'll see you home."

"Okay. When will they be here?"

"Helo's on its way already, so shouldn't be too much longer."

I finally feel as if I can function again, though I'm groggy and my stomach aches with hunger and I have to pee. I work myself to a sitting position just in time to see the doctor—a grizzled, silver-haired, silver-bearded man with a heavy paunch and broad shoulders—turning to exit the room. Christian is sitting on his cot, opposite me. His hair, dry now, shows streaks of gray, and his beard is also shot with gray. I would know him anywhere, no matter what he looked like, but he is nearly unrecognizable.

"We're transferring to a Coast Guard cutter," he says.

I nod. "I heard."

Silence.

"Where will we go?" I ask.

He frowns at me, confused. "Home?"

I shake my head. "Our home is gone, Christian."

He slides off the bed and pads barefoot across the room to sit on the edge of my cot. I shift aside and he wiggles further on, and my feet press against his thigh.

"Gone?" he asks. "What do you mean, our home is gone?"

I duck my head, sighing. "The hurricane that wrecked your ship all those months ago? It hit Florida, too. Basically leveled half of Ft. Lauderdale. The stretch of beach where our condo was located was one of the hardest hit areas." I close my eyes, trying to shut out the memories. "I…it was bad, Chris. Really, really bad."

"Holy shit. Are you serious?"

I nod. "The condo is…gone. The whole building is gone. The buildings next to it are too. That entire stretch of beach and everything for miles around it were all just…ruined."

His brown eyes search me. "Were you…were you there, when it hit?"

I nod again, swallowing hard. "Yeah, I…I was."

He takes my hand in his—the touch of his skin is electric, making me tingle all over, making my heart thrum and hammer. Just my hand in his makes it hard for me to think, and I don't know whether to take my hand away or never let go.

"Were you hurt?"

"God, Chris—it was so terrible. I almost died. When I realized how bad the storm was I got in the tub with a bottle of water. I tried to get Darcy and Bennet in with me, but they were too scared and they wouldn't stay. Before I could even try to get them back, the roof collapsed, trapping me in the tub. I don't…I don't know what happened to Darcy and Bennet. I like to think they got out, that they got away okay, but I—I don't know." My voice breaks. "I was in there for a long time, for days, and the only reason I survived at all was because I had that bottle of water."

"Days?" His voice is shaky. "You were trapped for *days*?

I stare at the floor. "I ran out of water toward the end. I was so weak I couldn't even shout. I heard things nearby…voices, machines, and the rubble shifting around me. I was sure the building was going to shift and I'd be crushed, or that I'd just die of dehydration. But then I heard people close, like just a few feet away, clearing rubble. I was so weak and tired, but I knew my best chance for getting rescued was making noise, so I kicked and punched and shouted until my voice was hoarse and my hands and feet were bleeding. They heard me. I heard them shouting that they had found a survivor. Then I felt things moving as they started digging to get to me."

"Holy shit." Christian is stunned. "I can't believe you went through that."

"Jonny found me."

Christian just stares at me. "He…*what*? Jonny, my friend Jonny? *He* found you?"

I nod. "He was the one who pulled me out of the wreckage."

"He survived the shipwreck? How? And why was he there?"

"He got rescued, and came to deliver your box, like he promised he would, and to explain what had happened to you and him out on the ocean. When he realized the storm had wrecked the building we lived in—*I* lived in—he stayed to help."

Christian is floored, and I see tears in his eyes. "You almost died, and I wasn't there."

"You were gone—and Jonny had no idea if you were alive or dead. He assumed dead, but we...we wanted to hope you'd made it somehow."

"Where is he?" Christian asks. "How'd you get here?"

"That's a long story." I swallow hard. "A really, *really* long story."

At that moment, the doctor came through the door. "Your ride's here, kids."

"Thank you, Doc," Christian says, standing up and reaching out to shake his hand.

"Didn't really do much but put in an IV and make sure you got some rest. The boat captains are the real heroes." He glanced at us in turn. "You two beat all the odds, you know. Someone up there must be looking out for you in a big way."

Christian's laugh is wry. "This is the second time, for me. I was shipwrecked almost a year ago under similar circumstances."

The doctor stares at him in disbelief. "Son, if I were you, I'd get back to dry land and I'd stay there for good. A man's only got so much luck."

"I've been thinking the same thing." Christian looks at me as he says this, and I feel a thickness in the air between us—a chasm of unexpressed, unspoken, unanswered questions.

We're each given a hooded zip-up sweatshirt with the name of the freighter embroidered on the right breast, and a pair of flip-flops. Mine are several sizes too big, and I have to walk carefully to avoid tripping. The walk from the infirmary to the deck is a long, winding, confusing journey, and without the doctor to guide us I would have been lost immediately. We ascend several sets of stairs that are so steep they're nearly ladders, and then the doctor—whose name I still don't know—opens a door, revealing a flood of daylight. We step through and I smell the sea and hear the rush of the wind. A few steps out on the deck, and I'm immediately dizzied by the scope of the vessel we're on. The sea is far, far below, and the deck extends so far in both directions it seems endless. White-capped waves are tiny ripples in the distance. I hear helicopter rotors chopping at the air somewhere behind and above us. The doctor leads us along a walkway, and a metal railing is all that separates us from a fifty or sixty-foot drop to the water. Another ladder-like set of stairs, this one outside, leads up to the helicopter landing pad, the yellow "H" unmistakable. The helicopter is an enormous red and white hulk, its rotor a spinning blur. A door in the side is open, and a Coast Guard crewmember is hunched in the opening waving to us. The pilot is visible in the cockpit, wearing a headset. The wash from the rotors is monstrously powerful, and I have to lean forward and stagger into it to make headway toward the aircraft.

The doctor shakes our hands, wishes us luck, and then the crewman, wearing a helmet and headset, shows us to our seats, and helps us fasten our five-point harnesses. Once we're buckled in, he says something over the headset, and I hear something shift in the noise of the rotors—a thrum of power spooling up. And then I feel a lurch, and the side door is still open even as we ascend. The crewman slides the door closed, takes his seat and fastens his harness. I feel us tilt and twist, and then our nose dips and my stomach lurches as we are propelled forward.

Instinctively, I reach out and take Christian's hand, tangling our fingers and squeezing hard at the sudden rush of speed, so different from the sensation of being on a jetliner. This is raw, visceral, and frightening. I squeeze his hand, and feel his grip on mine in return.

It shouldn't feel awkward to hold my husband's hand, but it is.

Instead of dwelling on that, I look out the window, watch as the massive freighter disappears behind us, and then we're alone in the air and the ocean is a vast, flat, rippling expanse of blue, nothing but water in every direction. I begin to understand, then, what the doctor meant about the odds of being found. Even being out on the ocean on Dominic's boat, even seeing the charts and mentally comprehending the size of the ocean, it's not until now, until I'm several hundred feet in the air gazing out at an endless sea, that I truly begin to grasp the scope of it.

Being rescued as we were? It's like trying to find a specific grain of sand on the beach.

The journey to the Coast Guard cutter takes a lot longer than I thought it would.

Christian and I hold hands through the entire trip, but we don't talk. We have headsets but, with the pilot and crewman connected as well, there's nothing we're willing to say. Not yet.

We land on a USCG cutter, a massive, warlike ship bustling with activity. A serious young woman in a Coast Guard uniform guides us through the narrow hallways to a cabin with a single cot and a desk bolted to the wall. The room is little more than a cubicle, barely big enough for one person to stand up in.

"Short on space," the woman says, tersely. "You'll have to share. Tight, but it'll do for the night."

"It's fine, thank you," Christian says. "Do you know if we're staying with you guys all the way back to the States?"

She shakes her head. "No idea. Someone will be

along within the hour to take you in for a meeting with the captain."

"Thank you again." Christian smiles at her.

She nods curtly, and takes her leave.

And just like that, we're alone, sitting side by side on the bed.

It hits me then, truly, that it's been eight months since Christian went missing, and a year and a half since he left.

I haven't seen my husband in a year and a half.

The silence between us is so thick, so tense, and so awkward that it is physically painful.

"Ava, I—"

"I don't know if I'm ready to talk yet," I cut in.

He nods. "I know what you mean."

"There's just…so much."

I know we are both thinking the same thing: a lot has happened between us, and there is a lot to say.

"It's been almost seventeen months," Christian says. "Since I—since…"

"Since you left me?" I say, my voice tinged with bitterness.

"Yes." He says this with a pained, resigned sigh. "Since I left you."

I rub my face with both hands. "I'm sorry, I just—"

He interrupts me this time, which is good, because I have no idea what I was going to say. "When we do talk, it's not going to be easy. Or short."

"Right," I agree. "Which is why I'm not ready. And this…this isn't the place for it."

"No, it's not. So we'll wait until we're somewhere where we'll have time and privacy."

I nod. "Which raises the question…where are we going?"

Christian leans back against the wall, groaning. "Everything's gone, you said?"

I nod. "There was pretty much nothing left of the building." I have to stifle a sob. "Everything we owned. Our photos, our mementos, family keepsakes, everything. It's all gone."

It's his turn to rub his face with both hands. "Shit. I don't know, Ava. I don't know where to go."

"We don't have many options. Your mom's, or my parents, or we pick somewhere and start over."

"My mom's place is not an option," he says.

"Mom and Dad would take us in and give us a chance to figure things out." I hesitate. "But I just…I don't like that idea. It doesn't feel right. Not with everything that's happened…not with everything we have to figure out."

"I agree with you there."

I glance at him. "So…where do we go?"

He shrugs. "I have no idea. Anywhere pop into your mind?"

I laugh. "Not even remotely."

"I mean, we could look at this as an opportunity to start over, right?" He lifts a hand in a vague gesture. "A fresh start, a new page, all that. Anywhere we want, you know?"

Silence.

"You told the doctor you'd been thinking about getting to land and not going back out to sea…" I start, hesitating, and then continue. "So what if we picked somewhere not on a coast. Not by the ocean."

"I was thinking the same thing, but part of me just… even if I never go to sea again, would I go crazy not being near the water? The ocean has been a major part of my life for so long, you know?"

"But wouldn't that make it easier to start over? Being away from it would make it easier to let that part of your life go, I'd think."

He shrugs. "Yeah, maybe."

More silence.

He glances at me. "Let's start by narrowing a few things down. Are we interested in a major city, living in a suburb, or being out in the country?"

I blink at him, and then hear myself asking the question that's been burning inside me. "You're assuming we're going to be together. That there's still an *us*."

I see panic blaze onto his face. "I was assuming that, yeah." He doesn't shy away from letting me see everything he's feeling, the fear, the panic, the pain. "You don't want that?"

"I didn't say that." I don't hide my own welter of emotions—confusion, pain, fear, and uncertainty. "We have so much to deal with, and neither one of us knows how things are going to unfold."

He stares at me for a long time, clearly deep in thought. And then, hesitantly, he speaks, turning his eyes away, looking down at the bed. "I…I know that we…we made a mess of things, Ava. Things are fucked up, and there's no getting around that. But unless you don't want me, unless you don't want there to be an us, then I hope we *can* assume there's an us, that there's a future for us. That we'll figure it out, somehow—*together*."

"Chris, I sailed away from everything I knew—or what was left of it, at least—on a small fishing trawler with a bunch of men I didn't know in order to look for you." Our eyes meet again, and I see…so much, in his gaze. "I *had* to look for you because I couldn't imagine what my life would look like, what it would feel like, without you. Without knowing if you were even alive. And now that we're back together, I still don't know what life is going to look like, or what's going to happen, but I—you're alive, Christian. You're *here*. And I don't think I'm even *capable* of walking away from you. Not after all this. So… yeah. I want to try and figure it out."

He lets out a sob, wipes his eyes with the heels of his palms. "God…I'm such a fucking mess." He glances at me, his eyes red. "You hate sailing."

"I don't mean sailing as in a sailboat like yours, like *The Hemingway*. I mean sailing in the more generic sense." I laugh. "But yes, I do hate sailing, in every sense of the word. And let me tell you, this experience has only made that worse."

"I have so many questions."

"Me too."

Christian laughs. "We're still no closer to figuring out where we're going to go or what we're going to do."

I sigh. "I know." I eye him. "Do we have to figure it out now, though?"

"I guess not."

More silence, tense and strange and strained and unfamiliar.

There's so much to say that it's impossible to say anything.

I t takes us almost week to reach the States. We transfer via helicopter from that Coast Guard cutter to another one, closer to shore, and then later via helicopter once again to shore. We set down at a Coast Guard station in South Carolina. After thanking the pilot and the crew, we're met by a junior officer.

The past few days have been fraught with tension and strained silence. We slept uncomfortably in the same hard, narrow cot, barely big enough for one person, much less two, but it's all we had, so we made it work. It forced us to a level of physical proximity we were in no way ready for. We could barely manage a basic conversation about inane, simple things, because even a discussion of the simplest thing was weighted with the burden of all the things still left unspoken between us.

Now, here we are. Back in the States, together…with no home, no car, no clothes, no possessions.

Ava had a few belongings back on Dominic's fishing boat—Ava explained who Dominic is, how he rescued Jonny and then helped Ava find me; I owe that man a beer, if nothing else—Ava used the cutter's radio to contact Dominic and let him know she was alive, that she'd found me, and that we were heading back Stateside. Dominic agreed to ship her belongings to her, once we figured out where we were going. She also used a phone to get a hold of Delta and let her know she was alive, and that we were together.

It's a long, complicated process, reestablishing identities as functional members of society. We are at the mercy of the federal government, leaving us in a weird sort of limbo. The Coast Guard passes us off to some other official, I'm not entirely certain which department she's with, only that she's a frighteningly efficient and brusque middle-aged woman with bottle blonde hair named Judy. Judy takes us through the complicated maze of paperwork and the days of waiting it takes to obtain birth certificates, driver's licenses, social security cards, and bank account access. Our previous address no longer physically existing makes it that much more complicated.

While we wait for birth certificates and everything to arrive, we live in a cheap motel with a tiny kitchenette, and Judy provides us with a prepaid Visa card for expenses. It's a strange sort of purgatory. We are uncomfortable with each other, steeped in tension and awkwardness and a cold distance, but we still aren't ready to talk about everything that happened. We need to: it's a stress on our minds, and a burden on our hearts.

But we have no life yet—we are merely existing, subsisting from day to day.

So we wait.

We prepare simple meals and watch movies on cable.

We avoid talking.

We don't touch.

We sleep in the same bed, but on opposite sides, a huge gap between us.

It is painful, awkward, and difficult.

Finally, after more than two weeks, we have enough identification to enable us to resume something like normal life…if only we knew where to go, or what to do.

Fortunately, money is not an issue, once we regain access to our bank accounts.

When Judy finally announces that we're officially on our own again and drives away, Ava and I sit side by side on the bed in the cheap motel in which we've lived for the last month, tension brewing between us.

After a long silence, Ava speaks. "I have an idea."

I glance at her. "I'm listening."

"We buy an RV, and we just…drive. We explore the country. Eventually, we'll find somewhere we want to stay, and we just stay there."

"And while we're driving, we talk," I say.

She nods. "Takes the stress off of having to figure out where to go, what to do."

"It's a good idea." I want to touch her, but I don't want it to be awkward. I don't mean sexual touch, I just mean hold her hand. "Let's do it."

She offers a small, hesitant smile. "Yeah?"

I nod, smiling back. "Yeah. It's perfect."

My heart hammering, I reach down and take her hand in mine and thread our fingers together.

Ava shudders, a shaky sigh escaping her. "Why is it so strange just to hold hands?"

"I don't know, but it is."

A tear escapes from the corner of her eye. "I hate this awkwardness, Chris. I hate it so much."

"Me too."

She gazes at me, and I see a million thoughts rippling across her features, none of which I can truly read. "It's too much, Chris. Everything, it's just…it's too much. I have so much to say to you, so many questions to ask."

"I know." I stare at our joined hands. "I do too. But… where do we even start?"

"I spoke to Dr. James, in the hospital where you recuperated. I mentioned that same thing, that I don't even know where to start." She looks down at our joined hands, pointedly, and then back to me. "He said I had to begin at the beginning."

I laugh. "Sounds like something he'd say."

She stands up. Paces away. Her hair is long, bound in a ponytail. She tugs it free of the ponytail, runs her hands through it; her hands are shaking.

She stops, on the other side of the room from me, her back to the bathroom. She's staring at me, breathing hard.

"I hate you for leaving me—how about we start there?"

She says this quietly, but the words drop like bombs.

"I hate myself for leaving," I whisper back. "And I hate you for the way you withdrew. You left me too, Ava. You were there physically, but you might as well have been a thousand miles away."

Tears trickle down to her chin. "I just…I couldn't—" she shakes her head. "I didn't do it to hurt you."

"It did, though."

Her eyes lock on mine, crying freely. "I know."

"I was grieving too, and I went through it alone."

She doesn't look away, and the agony in her gaze mirrors my own. "I *know*."

Tears threaten at the corners of my own eyes. "I needed you, and you weren't there. You ignored me. You pretended like I didn't exist." Anger is building, wrapped in and around the pain like vines.

Ava wipes at her eyes with both hands. She walks slowly toward me, sits on the edge of the bed, a foot of space between us, but it may as well be a mile. She sits upright, legs pressed together, hands folded on her lap. Her spine is straight, her loose hair, kinked from the ponytail, is draped over one shoulder. Her chin is tucked against her chest, and she breathes slowly, deeply, and carefully.

"It's Christmas Eve, Chris." She whispers it, her voice as fragile as a skin of ice over a barely frozen pond.

"It is?" I had no idea—time, dates, holidays, none of it has meant anything up until this moment.

She nods, gaze still averted. "December 24. Tomorrow is Christmas Day." She glances at me cautiously. "Do you...do you remember last Christmas?"

I have to think carefully. "Um. We were in... Jamestown? St. Helena. I called you."

She nods. "That was...a really difficult conversation."

"It's a little fuzzy," I admit.

"It was almost as awkward as this is." She smiles, but it's a bitter curve of lips devoid of humor or warmth. "You had that woman on board with you. Martha?"

"Marta." I try the name, search for meaning or memory embedded in the syllables. "Martinique."

A fragment of memory assaults me:

A fumbling kiss, whiskey-stained lips. A sense of wrongness, the unfamiliar weight of breasts in my hands that are not Ava's, a kiss that lasts too long...

"Does she figure into your memories?" Ava's voice is thin, brittle, and sharp.

I lean forward, wipe my face with one hand. "Somewhat," I answer, at length.

"You slept with her."

I shake my head. "No. Nearly, but no."

She nods. "Ah, I remember now, there was a letter." She glances at the ceiling, recalling. "You said you still loved me, and that you stopped going any further with her because she wasn't me."

I nod. "It was just...wrong. It felt wrong, in the same way it would feel *wrong* to put a shoe on the wrong foot. But it felt wrong morally, too. I was absolutely hammered at the time, and I was lonely, and upset, and melancholy, and I don't even know what else. But it just wasn't right. You and I were separated, and there didn't seem to be any hope of us getting back together again, not after... everything. But I knew I still loved you and that what was happening with Marta wasn't right."

Ava doesn't respond for a minute or so. "Did you get my packet of letters?"

It takes effort to recall, but eventually, I do. "Yes. You had a similar situation, did you not?"

She nods, not looking at me. "Yeah." Now she glances at me. "Even though I get mad and jealous about Marta, I know, intellectually, that I don't have any room to feel that way."

Silence.

Silence.

Silence.

Desperate to ease the tension, I twist in place, facing her. "It's Christmas, and we're here, together. That's worth celebrating isn't it?"

A hesitant smile. "I guess so."

"So, we go somewhere and have a nice dinner. Spend Christmas together, and then we go buy an RV, and we start driving. No pressure. We work through things bit by bit."

"That sounds doable."

I stand up, and she follows suit. We're facing each other, space between us, and I feel every single inch of that space like the stab of a knife. This tension, this pain, this coldness…it's too much. I hate it.

I gaze at Ava, let my emotions well up and boil over. "When I was in that hospital in Africa, I couldn't remember anything about myself. I couldn't remember my name. I couldn't remember my childhood, or how I got there, or what happened, nothing. All I had were images of you. Not even real, full memories, just…*you*. Your face. A sense that you were…important to me, but that doesn't state it quite strongly enough. You were *all* I had. You were *everything*. I filled notebook after notebook, writing about you. Trying to remember more about you. More about us."

"God, Chris…" she blinks back tears yet again. "That must have been horrible, and so frightening."

I nod. "Yes, it was. That's why I was there so long. Even after my broken bones healed, I had massive gaps in my memory. I knew your name—I knew that you were my lover, wife, girlfriend—that you were my everything.

And that's *all* I knew. I started writing about us, about you, and gradually my memories started to come back. It took a long time, and it was…painful."

"Why painful?"

"Because I remembered…" I have to stop, clear my throat, and blink hard against tears blurring my eyes. "I remembered Henry. I remembered him dying. I—I remembered how we dealt with it, or more accurately, how we didn't. I remembered drinking myself into a stupor every day for months. I became my dad, which is the one thing I swore to myself the day I left home that I'd never become. I became him."

"No, you didn't, Chris." She steps closer, gazing up at me, love cautiously bleeding through the pain and doubt and fear and distance. "You *didn't*."

"My father was a violent, drunken pig. He was a worthless piece of shit, and he made my life utter hell every single day until I left home at seventeen." I can't stop the tears from falling. "And I became him anyway."

"You never became like him, Christian. Never." She takes another step closer. "You drank to numb the pain. You drank because…because I was—because of how I basically abandoned you, on top of losing your son. You were alone, and you were hurting, and you drank because it was the only thing you knew how to do to cope." She touches my face, gingerly, hesitantly. "You never hurt me, Chris. Not once."

"I have this memory of waking up on the beach

outside our condo in a pool of my own vomit, still drunk, and starting to drink some more, just to escape everything."

"I remember." She breathes carefully. "I went outside once, to get a breath of air. I found you passed out in the sand."

"You sat down beside me and you told me you fucking hated me." I choke on the words. "I was awake enough to hear that."

You shake your head and step closer yet, reaching up with one shaking hand, but drop it before touching me. "No, no. No, Chris. I was talking to God. To life. To whoever took Henry from me. I wasn't talking to you."

I find it hard to form words past the lump in my throat. "If this is going to get better, we have to be honest…with ourselves and each other."

Ava nods twice, head bobbing, wobbly. "You're right. I was, in part, talking to you. Not *just* you, though. At that point, I did blame you, and I did hate you. But only because there was no one else to blame and it just hurt so bad. You never became your father, Christian, I swear. You *never* hurt me. You *never* had a negative word for me. Even when I was…whatever you want to call it— unresponsive. In bed, not eating, ignoring you, wishing I could just die…you tried *so hard* to reach me."

Her eyes drop to her hands.

"You made me food three times a day, every day, for weeks, for months. Even when your own pain had to have been so deep, you *tried*. And I just—I couldn't…I couldn't make myself snap out of it. Nothing mattered. I didn't want to live. I wanted to die, but my body wouldn't let me." She looks up at me now, her blue eyes wet. "I haven't forgotten how you tried to take care of me. You told me you loved me so many times. You tried—" her voice breaks, and she sits back down again, shoulders shaking as she weeps.

"I gave up." I sit beside her. Close, this time. Not quite touching, but almost. "I gave up."

"What else could you have done?"

"Stopped drinking and kept trying?"

"Then why didn't you?" She doesn't mean it as an accusation, but genuinely asking.

I shake my head and shrug. "It hurt too bad. Everything hurt. I was going crazy. I didn't know what to do. I'd lost Henry, and it felt like I'd lost you, too."

"You did. I wasn't…I wasn't myself. I wasn't there. I was empty. Less than a shell of a person."

She's struggling to stay composed, and only partly succeeding.

"Alcohol wasn't letting me escape enough, I guess," she says. "I think, deep down, I knew if I kept going the way I was, I'd end up drinking myself to death, and so I left instead."

Her tear-silvered eyes search mine. "I was devastated when you left. When I woke up and discovered you were gone, it broke me more than I already was."

I can't breathe. I can't stop the tears, this time. I'm not a crier—I don't even know the last time I cried. But this? I can't stop this.

"I'm sorry," I whisper, tasting salt on my lips. "I'm *so* sorry."

Ava shakes her head, reaches up and wipes at my cheek with a thumb. "Christian…don't. God, please don't." She hiccups, a sob escaping. "I've never seen you cry."

I can't speak. I can only shake my head and endure the hot burn in my throat, the silent fall of salty tears on my cheeks, down my chin.

Ava stares up at me, and there's a moment of shattered, explosive tension, and then she slams into me. She buries her face against my chest, and her arms circle my middle, and then I'm clutching her against me and she's racked with sobs and my tears wet her hair.

"I'm so sorry, Ava, I'm so sorry. You needed me, and I wasn't there. I wasn't there for you."

She's speaking over me. "No, it was me—it was me. I wasn't there for you either."

No more words are needed, then. She lets go, unleashes everything she's pent up for so long. And so do I. We weep until we can weep no more.

I would say it's cathartic, but that's nowhere near powerful enough a word. It's a flash flood of emotion crashing through us both, and the walls of her heart and mine—they're blasted away by this.

I feel them fall, like the walls of Jericho.

A memory, an old one, from when I was three or so, drifts into my mind. I'm sitting cross-legged on a thread-bare carpet, surrounded by other kids. An older woman with gray hair has a felt board and she tells a story in singsong lilt about the walls of Jericho and the Israelites marching around it, and she has felt shapes to represent Jericho and the Israelites, and we each have a part to sing, echoing her…

The memory vanishes as quickly as it came. I'm not sure why I remembered it, or what it's supposed to mean, but I feel like Jericho now, after the walls have crashed down.

The silence is different now, broken now by sniffles as the moment of shattering ends.

Ava pulls away, just a few inches, just enough that she can look up at me with reddened, damp eyes. She's the same as I am now—vulnerable, and needy.

There's nothing to say, not in that moment.

We are broken together. The shards of our hearts and lives and souls lay mingled together, and all the miles, the months of distance and separation, the pain we inflicted on each other, our guilt, our sorrow, our shame—it's all there. It's there in her eyes as they search mine. It's there in her tears, in the way her hands are clawed into fists in the cotton of my T-shirt.

She needs me.

I need her.

We need each other.

I've written of this moment a thousand times. Remembered it. Thought of it. Dreamed of it.

Imagined it.

Fantasized about it.

But now that it's here, I'm scared of it.

What if it's not the same? What if she rejects me? What if we don't fit like we used to? What if it's too late? What if there's too much pain and guilt to overcome?

She looks at me and understands what I'm thinking. Her eyes flit back and forth, examining me. Her palm drifts up, touches my cheek. She lifts her chin, and her lips part.

My hand buries in her hair, tangles in her soft black locks, and I pull her to me.

I kiss her.

Ava's lips are warm and soft, pliable and hesitant. Her response is slow in coming. At first, our mouths just meet, and my breath is snatched away by the power of this moment, how it feels to finally have her lips on mine, to feel this with her. Softer, wetter, and warmer than I remember.

The feel of her mouth evokes a million potent memories, flashing through me all at once: kissing her in the kitchen, sun golden-yellow on us; kissing in our bed, rolling together, naked; pausing in a supermarket aisle to palm her backside and steal a kiss, her laughter against my lips.

Another moment of hesitation, our lips only touching, and then Ava comes alive.

She pushes up against me, and her fist in my shirt tightens, and one hand slides up over my shoulder and her fingers trail against my scalp, and then she's got a handful of my hair and she's pulling at me, bringing me down to her, as if to bring our bodies closer together, to erase the last vestige of distance between us.

The kiss shifts and heat explodes, and the world tilts as we slide down horizontal.

Ava is beneath me, and her hands are on my face, one feathering into my beard, pulling my mouth back to hers.

"Please," she murmurs. "Please don't stop kissing me."

I would promise to never stop, I would promise to kiss her forever, but I have no words, and to speak would be to stop kissing her, so I don't answer. I lose myself in her lips instead, in the frenzy of needing her, and feeling her need for me.

"More," she whispers. "I need more of you, Christian. *Now.*"

Her eyes are so blue, so soft, so fiery, that I'm left stunned breathless at the intensity, the cerulean fire of them.

"Ava…" All I can do is whisper her name; it's all I can manage.

It's enough, though. She hears everything I'm saying

when I whisper her name, thus:

"*Ava…*"

I kiss her again, and this time the kiss detonates into something else. Something more. We're both vulnerable, totally bared to each other, all our demons and guilt and pain exposed. Nothing left hidden. There's so much left to say, but in this moment, what we need to say to each other cannot be expressed in mortal language.

And so we commune, soul to soul, in the physical language of love.

I t begins with a tangle of breaths.

Christian's lips on mine, my hands roaming his shoulders.

My name on his lips.

We shed clothing as if peeling away layers, as if stripping away the miles and the sorrow. The months spent apart, the ache of missing each other, the acid of hating each other with all the power that only deepest love can engender, the tragedy we share, it all falls away, thrown aside with his jeans, my shirt, his socks, my bra, his underwear, my skirt, until we're naked together, skin to skin once more.

When was the last time?

I don't remember.

Before Henry's death.

So long. Too long.

I'm starved for this. For *him*.

His kiss is intoxicating, and I drown myself in the bliss of it, sweeter and stronger than any wine. I drink my fill of him, sipping at his mouth, nipping, gasping, raking my nails on his chest, luxuriating in the familiar heat of his skin, the shift of his muscles, the way his voice sounds as he groans in pleasure when his hands find my breasts, when our hipbones meet.

There is desperation, but no rush.

This is not the mad and furious assault of frenzied hormones. No, this is something else. Something deeper. This need between us burns hotter than the sun itself. I can't breathe for the need. But rather than claim the union as fast as possible, we draw it out. We indulge in the need, drown in desire. He kisses my lips, and then my breastbone, and then the valley between my breasts. His fingers trace my curves, and I clutch at his strength, caress the throbbing evidence of his desire. We roll in the blankets, tangle in the sheets. I kiss his shoulder, and he lifts my thigh to his hip. His breath is in my ear, and his lips move, and I know the syllables he chants like a song, like a prayer—my name.

Ava.

Ava.

Ava.

He fills me, and my voice breaks at the perfection of our joined bodies. It is more than I remember—more of everything. His movement is tender at first, punctuated with kisses, and then his teeth pincer my lower lip and my fingers knot in his hair, and my toes are curling and my thighs quaking, and I'm breathing his name the same as he is mine, because it's all the prayer of love we need.

Fire breathes between us.

My cheeks are wet, and his lips kiss away the tears, but he knows these tears are not of sorrow or shame or guilt or pain, but of joy, a deeper, sweeter joy than any I've ever known, a desperate relief. I'm laughing, as well, crying and gasping, all at once, as I cling to him and move with him, meet his wild, powerful thrusts with my own.

He rolls, and I'm above him.

"Christian…" It's my turn to chant his name. "Christian…"

I lean over him, and my hair drapes around his face. His hands slide up the backs of my thighs to my buttocks and then roam the curve and hollow of my spine.

For a moment, we are motionless, thus, eyes locked on each other.

The curtains are parted, letting in a sliver of sunlight that bathes us in a golden glow.

"I saw this moment," Christian murmurs. "You, above me, just like this. The sun, your skin…and that look on your face." His hands explore me, touch me, caress me everywhere, and his touch sets me alight, sends a flurry of emotions exploding through me—chief among them is love.

"Yes, *that* look," he says, his voice quiet but intense.

"Which look?"

"That look of love on your face right now." His thumb grazes my cheekbone. "I saw this moment a thousand times. I thought it was a memory, but it was this. This moment."

I begin to move, rolling my hips. My hands are planted on his chest, my weight on my forearms. I let love expand through me, burgeon, billow, and explode through my eyes. Let love rule my movements, let love morph into desperation as heat builds into a nova in my belly, in my soul.

His hands frame my hips and guide me to climax, and his eyes never leave mine.

My name is on his lips, his every breath as he comes apart beneath me, shattering with a shout, clinging to me, and then I'm falling with him.

I bury my face in the side of his neck and let myself weep with the searing beauty of this, finally reunited with my husband, my lover, my Christian.

"I love you—I love you—" his voice breaks again. "I love you, Ava. I love you so much."

I can't speak, can barely summon breath, but when I can, I speak through a scintillating million kisses, scattered across his skin wherever my lips can reach. "I love you, I love you—Christian...*god*, I love you—" this, whispered and chanted until we devolve into laughter and kisses, rolling across the bed together.

We end up, hours later, tangled in each other's arms. My head on his chest, my thigh across his, his hand on my hip.

He kisses my temple, and I twist my head to meet his eyes.

"Merry Christmas, Ava," he murmurs.

"Merry Christmas, Christian."

And, for the first time in nearly two years, I fall asleep in my husband's arms, sated, and truly loved.

23

It's not that simple, unfortunately.

We're not instantly fixed by utterances of love and forgiveness.

Everything Ava and I did, everything we endured, it all leaves scars. Issues take time to work through.

We buy an RV big enough for the two of us to live in comfortably, and we drive away from South Carolina. We follow the coast north, away from Florida, away from everything.

There are arguments. Explosive moments of anger as we dig deeper into everything that happened. We talk through our feelings of abandonment, and how we each toyed with infidelity. We talk through mutual feelings of guilt.

We listen to audiobooks on grief therapy, and

podcasts on conflict resolution. We read aloud to each other from books on forgiveness, and healing, and the nature of a healthy marriage.

In many ways, we have to create our relationship anew; we are both much changed as a result of the past year and a half, and I, especially, am far different from the man Ava met and married, different from the man I became as a result of wealth and success, and different again from the man who allowed grief to consume and cripple him. Ava, too, is different. Quieter, more given to long periods of introspection. Her passion lives more under the surface, now. She was always fiery and eager and quick to please, but now she's...needier. She needs my reassurance more frequently, my attention, my affection.

As I do hers.

She has this look she gives me, sometimes. She'll be sitting in the passenger seat of the RV as I drive, her legs tucked underneath her, a book open and upside down on her thigh, and she'll look up at me. Her blue-blueblue eyes will flit side to side, searching me, and she'll bite the corner of her lower lip, and her brows will furrow, and her breathing will nearly stop.

And I know what she needs.

I will reach out with one hand, and take hers. I thread our fingers together. "I love you, Ava. Always and forever, no matter what."

She'll smile in relief, always seeming a little

surprised that I know exactly what she needs to hear.

There are many moments when we falter, when we give in to doubt or worry. When old pain rears up. When living out of an RV is exhausting and stressful rather than fun and adventurous.

Times when we both just want somewhere to call home.

We drive north into Massachusetts, spend New Year's Day in Boston, in a dive bar drinking cheap champagne, laughing and kissing as the ball drops. We head into Maine, and then back down into New York, Pennsylvania, and Ohio, stopping for a day or two here and there when we feel like it, when we need a break from the RV. Our journey leads us into Michigan, as far as Mackinac Island, where we stay at the Grand Hotel for three amazing nights. We take the ferry over to Wisconsin. Cross westward through Minnesota and Montana and Idaho and all the way to the Washington coast.

We ease into a rhythm, together. We grow comfortable with each other once more, and conversations no longer wander into territory fraught with pain and re-membered wounds.

By early March, we are in northern California, and we are ready to stop traveling. We rent a cottage in a little village nestled on the golden California coast. We cannot see or hear the sea from our home, but a short drive will take us to the cliffs, to the crash of the surf and the caw of the gulls.

I send a large monetary donation to the hospital in Conakry, care of Dr. James, with a photograph of Ava and I together in front of a mammoth redwood tree, from a hiking trip we took through the Redwood National Forest. The money we send is a huge donation, several hundred thousands of dollars, but it's a drop in the bucket compared to what I owe Dr. James and the staff at that hospital. To Louis, I don't send money, but French-language Bible, with a note scrawled on the opening page:

I'll never forget your words, my friend—I've chosen life.
Thank you.
—*Christian St. Pierre.*

I owe him more than a Bible and a note, but it's a start. A recognition of what he did for me, in saving me from the waves not just once, but twice, and then saving me again by showing me the importance of choosing life. Weeks later, I receive a package from Louis in return: my notebooks, left behind on the boat when I went overboard. I am overjoyed to have them back, as they represent my journey back to self.

Ava sits on our porch for a week straight, reading through every single notebook from cover to cover, often weeping, or stopping to kiss me.

There is a somewhat larger town thirty minutes from our village; I take a part-time job at a community college there, teaching creative writing. Ava works in a coffee shop and bookstore, shelving books and making lattes and chatting with the locals, who soon accept us both as their own.

We never discuss it outright, but somehow, at some point, it becomes clear to both of us that we are here to stay.

I don't write, and neither does Ava; not yet. We're not ready.

I'm not. I will write again, eventually. But, for now, we have this.

We are happy. Content. We've found peace.

But yet…something is missing.

It's obvious in certain quiet moments at home, in the way Ava will search my face as if she has a question on the tip of her tongue, but she never says anything. It's in the moments when I wake up in the middle of the night, and Ava is awake, staring at the ceiling, chewing on her lip, lost in thought.

It's in the way, when I'm driving to teach class, that my heart yearns for something indefinable.

What is it?

I even try writing as a means of exploring it, of trying to finesse the notion into fullness, but the words won't come out, and the feeling remains vague and under the surface.

And then something happens which highlights what it is we're missing.

It's a Tuesday night. I arrive home a little after nine p.m., after teaching a three-hour class.

I'm tired, and out of sorts, though I can't put my finger on it. I've been out of sorts all day, and found it difficult to focus on teaching. I was looking forward as I drove home to opening a bottle of wine with Ava, sipping it as we stream a show on Netflix.

But, as I set my backpack on the kitchen island and dump my wallet, phone, and keys, I notice the house is too quiet. Silent. Empty.

"Ava?" I call out.

No answer.

Our home is a small two-bedroom cottage with one bathroom, a small kitchen, and a cozy den. There are only so many places she could be, and after a brief search, it's obvious she's not in the house.

Her purse, her phone, and her keys are here—we only have one car, as we live within walking or biking distance from the café where Ava works, but she wouldn't leave the house without her keys, much less her phone or purse.

I call the café, but at 9:15 at night it's been closed for hours, and there is no answer.

The door to the second bedroom—which we've set up as an office where I grade papers—is ajar. Our shared iMac is there on the desk, the screen asleep, silver key-board pushed up underneath it, out of the way. A stack of short stories waiting to be graded sit neatly aligned at the corner of the desk.

Something niggles at me—but what? Ava wouldn't come in here, except maybe to check for an email from Delta. I sit at the computer and pull up our email—we have both our email accounts on this one computer, so it's a matter of clicking on her inbox to see if she got anything that would have prompted this absence.

There's an email thread between Delta and Ava, from earlier in the day.

DELTA to AVA:

Hey, babe. Thinking of you, today. Hope you're doing okay. We're on the road today, so if you need me, I'm here.

AVA to DELTA:

Thanks, hon. It's hard. It's always hard, and it will always be hard. It's just extra tough today.

DELTA to AVA:

Why so? Are you guys doing anything together to commemorate the day, or whatever?

Commemorate the day? What are they talking about? It's connected to the niggling, out of sorts feeling I've had all day. Like I'm missing something. Forgetting something. Avoiding something.

AVA to DELTA:

It's like he's forgotten. I don't know. Things are good between us, but it's a new sort of good, you know? Like, I'm scared to bring it up. Today of all days, I need him, but he's working. I thought he'd take the day off at least. I thought we'd go somewhere and talk about it. I don't know. I don't want to push him, though.

DELTA to AVA:

I wish I knew what to say. Maybe it's just how he's dealing with it. I love you. Our tour ends next month, and Jonny, Alex and I are coming to visit you guys, if that's okay. Not the best time to bring it up, maybe, but I just want to put it on your radar.

AVA to DELTA:

I can't wait to see you. It's been too long! We heard your latest single on the radio the other day, and I about lost my mind. I'm so proud of you!

DELTA to AVA:

Thank you, Ava. It's been surreal, this whole thing. Selling out shows, adding dates. I got invited to headline a festival in Raleigh in the fall.

In other news, Jonny proposed last night.

AVA to DELTA:

WHAT?! And you're just now telling me? You accepted, right? OHMYGOD, you're marrying him?

DELTA to AVA:

Well of course I accepted, crazy head. Duh! I love that man more than anything in the whole world. We'll talk more about it when I get there, though. We can plan my wedding together. I'm sorry, I kind of hijacked this thread. I didn't mean to make it about me. Today is about you.

AVA to DELTA:

It's about us, Christian and me. It's about…everything. Which is why it's so hard today, because he's gone and I'm alone again, which right now just feels more significant than usual. I'll be okay. I'm also worried about something else, but I'm not quite ready to share that with anyone yet. I'm just…

I don't know.

I'm a lot of things.

DELTA to AVA:

Well, I know I'm no expert, but if you care about my opinion, I'd say that you should talk to him when he gets home. Be honest.

I'll email you tomorrow, OK? And call me anytime if you need me. I love you.

AVA to DELTA:

Love you too. Talk to you tomorrow.

And that's when my eyes land on the time and date on the top right corner of the screen: *Tues Apr 3 9:22 p.m.*

April 3.

April 3.

Fuck.

I lean back in the chair, scrubbing at my face.

It's April 3.

Henry died on this day, two years ago.

And I forgot.

Well, no, I didn't forget. I suppressed the knowledge. Coerced myself into forgetting.

I know where Ava is, though.

24

Moonlight on stained glass sheds a soft glow in the small church.

Rows of wooden pews march away behind me, hymnals and bibles and tiny pencils in the shelves. There's a cross on the wall, with elaborately painted stained glass windows on either side. A pulpit stage right, a piano stage left. Arrangements of flowers line the steps leading up to the stage.

It is utterly silent.

It's late, but the pastor of this church, who had been about to leave, let me in, turned on a few lights, and then retreated to his study to give me privacy, after inquiring whether he could pray for me.

I said I didn't know, that I needed somewhere to sit and just be.

So, here I sit, in the front row. I stare at the cross on the wall, and let myself remember Henry.

I let myself cry for him.

I haven't been on the pew for very long when I hear the church door creak open—it's Chris. I feel him.

His steps are slow and measured as he walks down the center aisle and sits beside me.

I don't look at him right away, and he doesn't speak. For long minutes, we just sit together in the sacred silence of the church, lost in our memories.

When I glance at Christian, finally, I notice he has something in his hands. A piece of paper. I glance at it, and then at Christian, quizzically. He hands it to me, and I take it, look at it.

It's a photograph of Henry and me, on printer paper. Grainy, but it's the image that counts, in this case. In it, Henry is a few weeks old. I'm sitting on our couch in Ft. Lauderdale, and Henry is in my arms, propped up in a sitting position on my lap. He has his fist in his mouth, and he's grinning. My smile is genuine and bright, but tired. It's just a quick snapshot, but it makes me weep.

"It was in my email," he says, by way of explanation. "I sent it to you, remember? I took it, and you asked me to send it to you so you could put it up on Instagram or something. You meant text it to you, but I emailed it, for some reason."

"I thought you forgot." I say it through sniffles.

He sighs, head hanging between. "I did, sort of. I don't know how to explain it. I could never forget, not really. But I just…I don't know. I'm sorry. I should have been there for you, today."

I slide closer to him, lean against him; rest my head on his shoulder. "I miss him, Chris," I say, gazing at the photograph. "I miss being a mom."

"I know. Me too." It's all he says, but it encompasses a lot—his understanding of what I mean, and his own similar pain.

"I don't know why I'm here," I say. "Why did I come to a church? I don't know. It just…it was the only place I could think of."

"An unconscious instinct for comfort, maybe."

"Yeah, maybe."

He sighs. "I read your emails with Delta, because I couldn't figure out where you were. And then, when I realized, I knew exactly where you'd be. I knew you'd be here."

I fight tears. "I just…I miss him so damn bad, Chris. It hurts. It just…it still hurts."

He wraps an arm around me. "I know, honey. I know."

"And I just get angry," I say. "I get angry at God for taking him."

"Me too."

A long silence, and then Chris reaches into his pocket again, and pulls out something else. A small black box. He opens it, revealing three rings nestled together on the black velvet.

He plucks up one of the rings, shows it to me. "I've had these for a few days, and was waiting for the right time to give them to you. This feels like it."

The ring is simple, a princess cut diamond solitaire on a thin titanium band. Around the inside an inscription is engraved: *Ava—you are my everything.*

I sniffle with happiness and relief as I slide the ring onto my finger, admiring the way the dim lights reflect on the diamond, soaking up the joy of having a ring on my finger again.

"God, Chris. I don't—I don't know what to say, besides thank you."

"New rings, for a new life, right?" He lifts out the other two rings, matching titanium wedding bands, simple and beautiful. Slides the smaller onto my finger to stack against the diamond.

"With this ring, I thee wed," he whispers.

I take the larger band from him and slide it onto his ring finger. "With this ring, I thee wed," I echo.

He touches his forehead to mine. "I love you, Ava."

"I love you too, Chris." I glance at our hands, at our fingers tangled together. "I have something for you, too, actually."

I sit up, shifting away from him a little. Dig in the back pocket of my jeans and pull something out. Hold it in my hands. Stare down at it, marveling at the confused mix of emotions the object causes.

Christian glances at me, at the object in my hands. "What's that?"

"The other reason I'm here," I say. "I'm not sure what I believe, totally, but if there is a God, he sure has a strange sense of timing."

I hand Christian the object. It is long and slender and white, with a blue cap. Christian takes it, and stares at it.

Then he glances at me, his expression carefully neutral. "Ava…"

There is a small rectangular box in the middle of the object, within which, in gray digital lettering, is a single word: PREGNANT.

"Are you…are you for real?" Christian's eyes pierce mine, searching.

I see emotion begin to bleed through his careful wall of hesitancy.

I nod. "That's the third test I've taken today." I breathe out shakily. "I haven't had a period since we were on the RV, which means I'm about four to six weeks along."

He stands up, the test still in one hand, and paces away. Stops, facing the cross, and a hand passes through his hair—he cut it when he started at the college, but left the beard, albeit neatly trimmed; it's a mature, handsome, rugged look on him, and I love it.

I watch him process what I've just revealed to him.

Abruptly, startling me, he spins, takes a lurching step, and falls to his knees in front of me. Puts his body between my thighs and takes my face in his hands.

"You're...*pregnant?*" He whispers the word hesitantly, as if to speak it out loud might change it.

I nod, smiling through my tears. "I'm pregnant."

Joy floods his features, and he takes me by the hands, pulls me to my feet. He takes me in his arms with sudden, fierce strength, and spins me around so my feet leave the ground. I squeal in surprised laughter, which severs the moment. Christian sets me back down, more carefully.

"Sorry, sorry. I just..." His eyes roam my body, as if he could see some sign already.

I shake my head, laughing. "Don't be." I stroke his beard, nuzzling against him. "I wasn't sure if you'd... how you'd feel." I'm hesitant, admitting it. In the face of his joy, now, the doubts I felt earlier now feel foolish.

He hugs me, intense but gentle, as if I'm fragile, rather than merely six weeks pregnant. "I'm glad. I'm happy. I'm excited. I'm—I don't know. A million things I don't know how to express, right now."

"Me too." I cling to him. "I'm a little scared, too, though."

"I know," he whispers. "I know. I am too. But it's going to be okay. Okay?"

I nod, and I believe him.

I feel it.

I know it.

His palm covers my belly. "I love you."

I laugh, gazing up at him. "Are you talking to me, or my uterus?"

He lets out a breath, a great, shuddering sigh. "Both, my love."

Epilogue

December 24, 2017

Brighid St. Pierre was born on December 16, 2017.

Ava named her after the character in my short story, "The Selkie and the Sea".

Brighid is, in every way, a joy. A blessing. A wonder. A miracle.

Today is Christmas Eve. It is midnight, and Brighid is asleep in my arms.

We are in church, the same church Ava came to eight months ago seeking peace. This time, the chapel is lit by a hundred candles held in a hundred hands. But for the glow of the candles, there is no other light. On stage, a young man with reddish-blond hair plays "Silent Night" on the piano, and a hundred voices are raised all around us, singing the words.

Brighid sleeps through it all, her tiny mouth open, a pink hat on her head, one little fist clenched around my finger. I rock her, bouncing side to side as I sing. Ava's arm is wrapped around my waist; she insisted on coming, despite having just had a baby a week ago.

She is strong, and she is beautiful, and she is mine.

Brighid, and Ava—I mean both of them.

Ava is on my right; to my left is Jonny, and beside him is Delta, their hands tangled together, and on the far side of Delta is Alex, young and earnest and wide-eyed. The European leg of Delta's tour ended a week ago, and she came home and announced that she was taking time off to record a new album after more than a year of nonstop touring.

Jonny and Delta are engaged, with a wedding scheduled for April…and, if the way Delta has been cooing at and coddling and hogging time with Brighid is any indication, I think there will be another addition to our family next year.

We finish "Silent Night" and after a brief silence, the young pianist begins playing "Away In a Manger", and the congregation joins in, and Brighid wakes up, squalling briefly. Ava takes her, whispers to her, and then Brighid sees the light of the candles and her crying stops, and she looks around in wonder, babbling baby noises as if she too is singing.

This—this moment, candlelit, voices raised to sing a

hymn, surrounded by family and friends, my wife beside me, my daughter in my arms…

It's everything.

THE END

A poem, written on a sheet of paper ripped out of a spiral notebook, in a masculine hand, and a feminine; it is undated, and the ink is smudged— black ink for the masculine hand, and blue for the feminine; the page is framed in a shadow box

You rescued me, my love
It was the memory of me, not the truth of me
I drowned, I died, I lost myself in the salt of the sea
I died with you, I drowned with you, I lost myself, same as you
Sometimes I think the days spent wallowing in memory,
Seeking you—those days scraped away the old flesh of me,
Scooped hollow the last of who I was,
Carved out of me the selfish creature I used to be
Love, love, love—I was hollowed out, too, you know,
Left breathless, sightless, soulless
Who taught you to breathe again?
Who taught you to see again?
Who returned your soul to you?
Who filled you again? Was it me?
No, it wasn't you, it couldn't be you;
That was the lesson all along:
I needed to be me without you before I could be me with you

Me without you, you without me, us without him—
It's a tangled web of need and sorrow
Not tangled, only interwoven; not a web, but a tapestry
If we are a tapestry, then you are my warp, and my weft
And you are the thread, and the image in the yarn,
and she is the frame of the loom, and the shuttle weaving it all together
I dreamed of you, my love, when I was a shell of a thing,
without memory or awareness or anything at inside me but fragments of you
I felt those dreams, I tasted them,
I followed them across the Sea;
I followed the skein of your dreams, the flavor of them
What did you see, what did you feel, what did you taste?
You, all that is you—the scent of you,
the scrape of your stubble across my skin,
the press of your lips on mine, your breath on my flesh
I dreamed of your eyes, the love in them, the shudder in your voice
I dreamed of moments in the sun,
Hours under the moon, and your whisper as you love me
It was never a whisper, my love, but a shout—
a barbaric yawp, in the words of Whitman
It was more than that, so much more
It was a song, sung in the shadows, in the silver of

the moon,

in the instants between quavering breaths

We are a poem, my love

Then you are my stanza, and my refrain

The lyrics imprinted on my soul

The flavor of words as they sparkle on your tongue,

as they flow from your pen,

gyrating in your mind

they are like the high from a drug

The way a song or a poem or a photograph or a play or a film

tolls within you, somehow, the way it strikes a chord,
resounding familiar,

echoing in some secret portion of your soul

Are we speaking of Love, or of OUR love?

Of Love, with the capital L, and of OUR love,

And of the love that moves this world,

The seed of prose and the source of poetry and the structure of who we are,

At the core of us

I still dream of you, even when you slumber beside me

I don't "slumber"—I sleep, gracefully, and delicately

Even so, I dream of you; and I wake,

And there you are, real and perfect,

With love glowing from within you as if you are lit inside by a sun

That glow, that love—it is the fire you light inside me,

When you look at me as you do,

hungry, wild, possessive, and tender

The memory of you, rather than the truth of you, you said?

My love, they are the same—the truth of you and the memory of you,

to me, then, it was all I had,

and all I needed to find you in this wide world

And you rescued me, as much as I did you,

the truth of you and the memory of you

Put the pen down, my love, and drown with me

Drown IN you

Be my breath

Be my sight

Always, my love

Always

Visit me at my website: **www.jasindawilder.com**
Email me: **jasindawilder@gmail.com**

If you enjoyed this book, you can help others enjoy it as well by recommending it to friends and family, or by mentioning it in reading and discussion groups and online forums. You can also review it on the site from which you purchased it. But, whether you recommend it to anyone else or not, thank you *so much* for taking the time to read my book! Your support means the world to me!

My other titles:

The Preacher's Son:
Unbound
Unleashed
Unbroken

Biker Billionaire:
Wild Ride

Big Girls Do It:
Better (#1), Wetter (#2), Wilder (#3), On Top (#4)
Married (#5)
On Christmas (#5.5)
Pregnant (#6)
Boxed Set

Rock Stars Do It:

Harder

Dirty

Forever

Boxed Set

From the world of *Big Girls* and *Rock Stars*:

Big Love Abroad

Delilah's Diary:

A Sexy Journey

La Vita Sexy

A Sexy Surrender

The Falling Series:

Falling Into You

Falling Into Us

Falling Under

Falling Away

Falling for Colton

The Ever Trilogy:

Forever & Always

After Forever

Saving Forever

Standalone titles:

Yours

Non-Fiction titles:

You Can Do It

You Can Do It: Strength

Jack Wilder Titles:

The Missionary

To be informed of new releases and special offers,
sign up for
Jasinda's email newsletter.

Made in the USA
Columbia, SC
28 January 2018